W9-BNR-760

# Tales Under
# A Full Moon

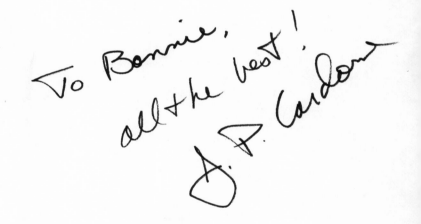

# Tales Under A Full Moon

## A COLLECTION OF SHORT STORIES

# J. P. Cardone

Copyright © 2006 by J. P. Cardone.

Second Edition 2008.

Library of Congress Control Number:        2006906237
ISBN:                Hardcover            978-1-4257-2388-0
                     Softcover            978-1-4257-2387-3

All rights reserved. No part of this book may be reproduced or transmitted in any form or by any means, electronic or mechanical, including photocopying, recording, or by any information storage and retrieval system, without permission in writing from the copyright owner.

This is a work of fiction. Names, characters, places and incidents either are the product of the author's imagination or are used fictitiously, and any resemblance to any actual persons, living or dead, events, or locales is entirely coincidental.

This book was printed in the United States of America.

**To order additional copies of this book, contact:**
Xlibris Corporation
1-888-795-4274
www.Xlibris.com
Orders@Xlibris.com
29174

# Contents

In loving memory of my mother

Eleanor Cardone

1924–2004

This book is dedicated to my children

Jenna and Christopher

who inspire me by their determination and drive.

# ACKNOWLEDGEMENTS

Special thanks to my wife Kathy who suffered through the early drafts of these stories and who listened to me brainstorm ideas while offering me both ongoing support and encouragement. And thanks to my friend Terri, an exceptional nurse who was kind enough to help me fill in the medical terminology used in these stories. A special thank you to my long-time friend Nick, a retired deputy sheriff who not only encouraged me to write while we paddled along in our kayaks, but who also reviewed for accuracy the police procedures I incorporated in some of these stories. To my friend Walter, an English teacher of note, a thank you for his help in the copyediting of this book. No one appreciates the value of a talented copyeditor more than I do. Thanks to Dennis, who made the final copyediting of this second edition better yet. And thanks to all my other friends who helped me along the way when I needed a push or who listened when I needed a sounding board. A special thank you once again, to my friend Rosa who showed both her artistry and her patience in helping me with this book's cover art.

# INTRODUCTION

The experience of writing a short story is quite different from any other type of writing I have attempted; certainly more difficult than a journal article or a magazine piece, and in many ways, different than the challenges of a novel. A short story requires the writer to both grab the attention of the reader and to develop the plot quickly. While the story line is short, it also needs to be particularly interesting and appeal to many types of readers. I had fun with these stories and I tried to use different voices and different storytelling techniques. Some are in the third person with dialogue and in others, I used one of the characters to tell the story. For example, in "Thirteen Apple Blossom Lane" the story is told only by the memory of a thirteen-year-old girl. In "A Change of Heart", I opened the first two pages using only dialogue, an interesting approach to story telling. In "Jeepers, Creatures", the story begins through the eyes of an angora cat. And in "Crazy is as Crazy Does", the calm, collected voice of someone who has more than a few screws loose explains why that may have happened using only one voice—no dialogue and no narration. Of all the stories in this collection, this might be my own personal favorite, or maybe it's "Jeepers, Creatures", because it's so close to home. But then again, "Little Secrets" is so downright honest. I mean, how do you decide a favorite anything anyway?

Many people have asked me where did I get the ideas for these seven stories. I always answered with the simple fact that most of these stories came out of a conversation or an experience with someone, a family member or a friend. For example, my brother, Eugene, required the medical procedure outlined in, "A Change of Heart", and thinking about what could have happened formed the basis of that story. Then there was a friend who had a romantic adventure with a girl online and he inspired me with his explanations to write, "One Web, or Another." I had a great deal of fun bringing to life, in an imaginary way, many of my childhood friends on the pages of "Jeepers, Creatures." Or, should I say at least what I could remember of Johnny Jam, Jippy, and the others in our gang, along with the alleyways of the apartment buildings where we grew up. Then, there is the Internet and the idea that if you *Google it*, who knows what monster might turn up? Yet, after explaining all that I always added, " . . . Besides it seems I have a vivid imagination."

Perhaps that's not enough of an answer though because after thinking about that question, my answer does seem to fall a little short of the mark. For me, there were influences everywhere and some I would like to mention. Of course, back in my junior high school days, there were the readings of the great Edgar Allan Poe. His stories including, "The Tell-tale Heart", "The Murders in the Rue Morgue", and "The Purloined Letter" still send shivers down my spine to this day. Then there is my most favorite writer of all, J.R.R. Tolkein, who created, *The Lord of the Rings, The Hobbit,* and *The Silmarillion.* Tolkein's works are all exceptional masterpieces of imagination. I often asked myself, how could one person imagine so much over so many pages? There is Frank Herbert who brought us the *Dune Trilogy*. What a marvelous work of imagination in science fiction! And lastly, perhaps the most prolific writer of all time, Steven King the master of the modern horror story. In his non-fiction book entitled, *Danse Macabre*, a modern day review of everything horror, he taught me among other things, that almost always, the monster behind the door is scarier than the monster in front of you.

Of course, I grew up watching every episode of *The Twilight Zone* and *The Outer Limits* (even if they were in black & white). These scripts, written for television, showed very clever imaginations with every twist that was uncovered. And there were many early television shows that displayed never-ending creativity and kept me laughing and thinking. Included in this group would be Jackie Gleason's, "The Honeymooner's"; "The Abbott and Costello Show"; and of course, "Amos n' Andy" which has been banned from reruns since 1966 due to its negative stereotyping of blacks. All of these TV shows had great casts, but also great writers whose imaginations never hit empty.

Yet, with all these influences in fiction writing, something must be said for the simple fact that sometimes, reality can appear to be stranger than fiction. Don't you agree? Just pick up a newspaper on any given day and there will be a news report of an incident or event that will have you shaking your head in disbelief. Yes, you don't have to look very far if you want your imagination stimulated and I guess over the long haul that's what happened to me. So, enjoy these stories that I think, without a doubt, clearly fall under a full moon—when people act strangely and weird things happen.

# THIRTEEN APPLE
# BLOSSOM LANE

*You give but little when you give of your possessions.*
*It is when you give of yourself that you truly give.*

Kahlil Gibran

I remember when it all started like it was yesterday, except it wasn't yesterday; it was the summer of 1982. I was thirteen years old then, going on thirty, as my mother would say and my brother Christopher who was eight would be turning nine in a few months. Christopher was on the small side for his age and that was something he heard about at every meal. My mother had driven the car, loaded with our personal things she wouldn't trust to the moving company, the twenty or so miles non-stop. We could barely move in that back seat with all the little bags and boxes she had piled up. Even Puffy, our miniature white poodle, couldn't lie down on the seat. I had that dog on my lap almost the whole trip. My little brother, Christopher, never let go of that raggedy, old, stuffed rabbit of his either. Even though he was eight, he got away with holding onto that thing. My mom would say, "Oh Sara sweetheart, what's the harm?" He called that dirty old thing, Bunny, I called it Stupid.

This new town was a lot different from Queens. Everyone we knew who heard the name Sea Cliff asked, "Where's that?" and my mother would roll out the same answer, "Oh, that's that quaint little town up on the North Shore of Long Island. Very nice there." Like that explanation helped anyone we knew figure out where we were heading. The truth is, I didn't want to move, and my brother didn't want to move, and I'm not sure that my mom wanted to move either. She would say, "Sara, we will have a great new start in Sea Cliff. We'll have our own house, new schools for you and your brother, and a safe neighborhood, how can we go wrong?" Except, I don't think her heart was in it, I mean how could it have been?

So, we pulled up on this narrow street called Apple Blossom Lane and my mother said, "Oh dear God, there it is, number thirteen." As the car rolled to a slow stop we all looked up and saw it together for the first time. It was a large three-story house with a high-pitched blackish gray slate roof. I remember looking at it and rolling my eyes in my head because I don't like old things very much and this house was very, very old. It had slate blue, painted, clapboard siding on the front that was chipped all over and old, cruddy, white shingles on the sides. There was some kind of dirty green mold on most of the lower part of the house. A couple of the shutters were missing from their places next to the front windows and another one must have lost a nail because it was hanging crooked.

One of the things that caught my eye was this strange little room on the very top of the house past the roofline. It was round with windows in every direction. Later on I learned that it was called a widow's watch because when these old houses were built, the married women would sit in those rooms and watch the harbor for their sailor husbands to return from the sea. It was a sort of watchtower. Of course, in those days, many of the sailors who left on those tall ships never did return. Truthfully, it gave me the willies looking up at that strange, little room. There were a lot of shrubs and trees on the hilly property and there was an old, run-down fence around one side. Most of the evergreens were overgrown and untrimmed on a lawn that appeared to have been uncut since the beginning of the summer. And it was already the middle of July.

I guess I made some sort of weird groan because that marked the very first of the incidents. As my throat made that sound, both Christopher and my mom looked at me and that's when I saw the light reflect off one of the upper windows on the widow's watch and some shadow of a person moving. I said, "What's that up there Mom?" But, when my mom turned back around to look whatever I saw was gone and I was the fool. Except, I think Puffy saw what I saw because he was growling and more than a little restless. Of course, Puffy could only be my silent witness.

"What Sara?" my mom remarked in her typical annoyed voice and my brother looked at me with those crybaby eyes, looking puzzled as usual. I guess my mom collected herself because she broke the uneasy silence first, "Okay, it's time. Let's pull into the driveway and start unloading, the moving men will be here soon." So, she put the car into drive and as she made the wide turn, I looked up to check out that window again. I wasn't sure what I had seen and I didn't think much about it. Well, at least not right away.

The long cement driveway had more cracks in it than one could imagine and bits of grass and ugly weeds growing all over. As we parked the car over that old driveway and opened the doors, I had this weird feeling that we were being watched. I looked around at the neighboring houses, but all I could see was a man painting on a ladder up the block. We walked up to the porch and noticed some of the boards that made up the floor had rotted away in some places and there were some missing planks. My mom fiddled with the key in the lock while she muttered some interesting truck driver words. We had been told, more than once, to ignore those kinds of words whenever we heard them. As my mom pushed open the door for the first time, the squeak was loud enough to make everyone flinch. The effect resulted in my brother's whimper, "Ma, do we have to live here?" That was ignored too.

Inside was amazing. We walked into a great room and compared to the size of our Queens apartment, this was huge. It was a bright, sunshine yellow with many large windows facing the main road. As a result, there was a lot of sunlight in that room. My mom asked me in an excited voice, "Can you see it Sara? Can you see our couch over there by the windows and the old rocker here next to the fireplace?"

I looked this way and that way and said, "Sure Mom, sure I can see it." I said sure, even though I didn't want the couch by the windows and the old rocker by the fireplace. I mean, who wanted an old rocker anyway?

My mom took Christopher's little hand in hers and feeling his resistance to the whole idea, practically dragged him along the floor while she suggested, "Your room is right down the hall and one flight up."

All he managed was, "Mommy . . ." which was more like a plea than anything else.

I followed them out of the room and just as we arrived at the foot of the old wooden stairs, we all jumped out of our skin as the moving truck sounded its air horn to signal their arrival. "They're heeeeere," my mother said turning slowly mimicking her favorite horror movie, *The Poltergeist*. Christopher and I ran out that door like we needed some fresh air and found our way over to a broken wooden box to sit and watch the men work. They were big men—one black man, one white guy, and a third fellow who looked Mexican. The black man was the biggest and when I saw what he lifted on his own, I figured he was the strongest too. The white man was the fattest, with a large, round belly that stuck out of his soiled tee shirt. Whenever he bent down to pick something up, his backside crack showed up at the top of his jeans. Christopher and I laughed and elbowed each other at that sight every time. They loaded the furniture onto these large wagons and hand trucks and paraded them into the house single file. When the white man slid the couch off the truck while the Mexican guy guided it onto the dolly, Christopher yelled over, "That goes by the large windows in the first room." No one looked our way, but I couldn't help stare at my little brother wondering what came over him.

Five hours later that big, long truck was empty. The men were sipping cold lemonade and wiping their foreheads with wrinkled handkerchiefs they had pulled from their back pockets. My mother went over to talk with them and I could hear her thanking the men for their hard work and for being so careful with the furniture. She paid them whatever it was my mom had owed them, plus a little extra, which I saw each man put into his pocket as smiles grew on their faces. They climbed into the cabin of the truck and there was a puff of black smoke as the engine started. When the truck moved forward, we all jumped again as the air horn belted out a few honks. "Whew, am I glad that's over." my mom said as she waved us inside.

I asked her in a pleading voice, "Mom, do we have to put all that stuff away now?"

"You know Sara, there's really no rush, we have the whole weekend and then some. How about we take a break? We can ride into town and get something to eat. How's that sound?"

My brother spun around and went, "Yippee."

I was just glad that we didn't have to unpack those boxes right away. The truth was I didn't want to unpack them at all.

What we saw along Main Street confirmed what I felt about this town. There were the typical historic types of shops, each older looking than the next. First, we saw a dusty antique shop; then, the old fashioned bakery; after that, the barber shop with its old style chairs; followed by the hardware store, with the old wooden floor; and a worn out looking cabinetmaker's shop with a ton of furniture stuffed into the front window display. My eyes opened wide when I spotted this firehouse with huge wooden doors and an old-fashioned fire truck sitting in front. When I saw that old thing I thought, who would try to fight a fire with that? Later on, I read in a book from the library, that Sea Cliff is an old harbor town on the northern part of Long Island. It wasn't a whaling port or anything cool like that, but it had a long history because people had settled there as long ago as the 1800s.

Down one of the side streets, we found a store that had just about every knickknack in it. We spent some time checking everything out including a strange cheese grater that Christopher picked up. On the corner was the main market where we stopped to pick up some milk and eggs. My mother liked the fresh loaves of bread and selected a round loaf along with four rather huge ears of yellow corn. The man in the store was friendly and told us his wife baked the bread herself and the corn was from one of the local farms. My mom placed an order for groceries and the man said he would have the delivery boy bring everything around in a few hours. While he was talking about the town with our mom, we were busy looking at the penny candies in the display case. Christopher and I couldn't care less about that town stuff, but our mom seemed to enjoy the idea that we were finally in the country and away from city life.

Mom decided to take a drive around the neighborhood to show us the harbor the man at the market had told us about and to learn more about our new hometown. Sea Cliff is a very hilly place and the funny thing is, the streets don't ever go straight; not like they do where we lived in Queens. In Queens the streets run pretty much parallel to each other like square blocks. Here, the streets cut across themselves in all different angles and directions; sometimes at the corners and sometimes right in the middle of one street, another street angled off. I wondered how anyone could find their way around? The streets were also very narrow and as we headed for the harbor, we were driving mostly downhill. I could see most of the houses were a lot like ours, big and old. I thought it was funny how the houses were built in this new town. It was as if they had decided to build these houses facing all different ways instead of straight. Sort of like when you drop pick-up sticks, they end up going where they want to go. Some of the houses had old, wooden fronts and others were painted, some had large porches and some were built right on the hill. I just shook my head a lot wishing we never had to leave Queens at all.

The next thing I knew, my mom turned onto this street called Shore Road and just down a ways we found a beach. Christopher liked that idea and asked, "Mom, can we get our bathing suits and check it out? This is so cool, we have a beach right in our own neighborhood." My mom had to ditch that idea, "It's a little late now, but we'll come back another day Christopher, I promise." As we drove by, Christopher climbed up on the backseat and stared out the rear window watching it get smaller and smaller like he had never seen a beach before.

"Oh, brother," I said, and my mom laughed.

We headed back to the house before the sun completely hid behind the earth and there in the sky was a deep crimson glow across the western horizon. We paused for a moment as my mom stared out at the horizon. That's when she said, "Wow, look at that, that is one beautiful sunset." She paused, appreciating the sight before us. Then, she started the saying, "Red sun at night . . ."

" . . . Sailor's delight," My brother added, as if he knew anything about what sailors liked. When we turned onto Apple Blossom Lane, I immediately glanced up at that window in the little room and was happy to see nothing there. We walked up the steps to the front door and were all surprised to find it open a crack. I backed away while my mother's jaw dropped and then little Christopher did something no one would expect. He just stepped right up and pushed the door open.

My mom took a couple of steps inside and said loudly, "Hello? Is there anyone here?" Not a sound was heard and no one answered back. My mother asked us cautiously, "I closed that door and locked it, right?"

I told her, "Yup, you did. I saw you."

"Then, how did it get opened?" She asked matter of factly, while at the same time realizing we were getting pretty scared. "Maybe, I just thought I locked it? Sure, that's it." She said, giving me a little look, so I wouldn't make more of it than that. But, inside my brain I was thinking, I knew she closed the door and I saw her put the key in the lock and wiggle it till it turned. Someone else opened that lock and left the door ajar while we were gone, but who?

Inside, everything was in order and as we took a good look around nothing appeared missing. All the boxes were right where we left them stacked in the different rooms. My brother wanted some help unpacking his boxes. I figured I'd give him a hand and at the same time I just thought it would be good to have a little company, any company. Honestly, I was spooked and that line, "they're heeeeere" just kept bouncing around inside my head. The way I was starting to feel, I didn't need to be thinking about any dead people buried around this house. So, I made a deal with him. "Christopher" I said, "You put that old rabbit down anywhere you want and I'll help you unpack." His eyes went from me to the rabbit and back to me at least four times until he finally remarked, "Okay Sis, it's a deal." I figured he must have really wanted help to put it down or he was as spooked as I was; maybe even more. I yelled to him, "You're it!" and tagged his shoulder. Then as we started to chase each other around the furniture in the front rooms, we spotted someone standing outside the front door and that froze us in our places. We heard this squeaky voice trying to yell. "Hello, grocery boy. Hello? Anybody home?" As our mom walked in to the room, we ran upstairs giggling and let our mom take care of the grocery delivery.

Before we knew it, our mother's voice found us as she yelled up, "Christopher it's time for bed and Sara, you put on your pajamas." We knew from experience she wasn't kidding. When she said it was time, we knew it really was time. So, Christopher grabbed his PJs and headed over to the upstairs bathroom to brush his teeth. I went to my room and closed the door. It was a tiring day all around. I was happy that my mom made the beds and I had clean sheets. I lay down on my bed and stared up at the ceiling, it was really high. After a while, I started to wonder how many ceilings are there in this house anyway? So, I closed my eyes and tried to remember what I saw when we first pulled up. Umm, there was the first floor, and then there was the floor above, and then there was the small dormer, and then finally the little window in the circular room. That meant four floors; three more ceilings above. Then, I remembered something else. I smiled as I said out loud, "and don't forget the ceiling on the basement." Wow, I thought as the realization hit me, counting the widow's watch ceiling, this house has five ceilings. I opened my eyes and looking at the ceiling above me, I wondered if all the ceilings were as high as this one? That's got to be what, ten, twelve feet? "Hey?" I asked myself, which window did I see that shadow in? Was it the dormer, the attic, or the window in the widow's watch? Come on Sara use your brain girl. I smiled because that's what my mother always said to me. And as the picture of the outside of the house came into focus in my mind I saw the reflection and thought, oh yeah, it was the window in the widow's watch, the small room above the dormer.

At breakfast the next day, mom made French toast the way we all liked it, with a lot of ground cinnamon mixed into the milk and egg batter. After it was cooked to a golden brown, we'd sprinkle some powdered sugar on top and add plenty of Log Cabin syrup letting it drip over the edges. I ate mine up like I'd been sent to bed without supper. I always loved that French toast. As I sat there at the table, putting the last of the cut up pieces into my mouth, my mom asked,

"Sara honey, Christopher can't find Bunny this morning, have you seen it around?"

"The last time I saw that stupid rabbit, I think Christopher was putting it on top of his toy chest while we unpacked his clothing boxes last night," I said innocently, in-between bites, picturing the scene in my mind.

"Sara", my mom started with her best don't fool around now voice, "I really would appreciate it if you would just tell me where you hid it this time?"

"Mom," I said putting the fork down on the plate. "I didn't take Bunny. I know I used to fool around and hide that thing on him, but not this time. I was laughing a little when I started to say, "Maybe he put it down somewhere and . . ."

"Sara," she stopped me, "this is not funny. He's really upset, and right now we don't need anything more to upset us."

"Honest Ma," I said trying to convince her. "I didn't touch his rabbit. I'm sure he just forgot where he put it." Then she got angry with me.

"Well, how about you just stay inside your room today until we find it?"

"What? Are you grounding me? I said I didn't take it."

"Sara, if you didn't take it, who did?" she asked, as she pulled up a chair. She looked at me with a frightened expression on her face as if to say—*please say it was you honey, please.*

"Mom, how would I know?" As I ran up the stairs with some tears in my eyes, I yelled down to her just to be spiteful, "Maybe it's the same stupid person who opened the front door last night?"

I slammed my bedroom door shut and cried my eyes out for the next hour. I must have fallen asleep because the next thing I remember, I heard my brother playing with his toy soldiers in his room. This game was his favorite thing whenever it rained keeping him from playing outside. You didn't ever need an official weather report to tell you what was going on weather wise when he was playing with those little plastic soldiers. I could hear Christopher giving commands and mimicking the soldiers responding.

"Take charge of the patrol and don't bring back any prisoners."

"Sir! Yes, sir."

"On the double now corporal, move it out. I said move it!"

That's about when I heard it, a box dropping onto the floor above us, which was followed by sounds of smaller metal objects spilling out of the box. I know my little brother heard it too, because Christopher stopped giving commands and stayed quiet like me. Then suddenly, there was a commotion out in the hall as Puffy ran around with his little high-pitched yelps. And mom yelled up from the bottom of the stairs.

"What's going on up there you two?"

I went out to the hall and yelled back over Puffy's yelps, "Nothing's going on up here, except we heard a box or something fall above us." I looked over at Christopher's doorway and he was half sticking out with a fearful look and worried eyes. As I nodded his way to confirm what I was telling our mom, he nodded back, with a little extra nervous punctuation.

"Sara," my mom started, "how would a box fall all by itself in the attic?" And then she added, "Why don't you collect your brother and come down here, I think we all need to have a little talk. Oh, and get Puffy to quiet down, pleeeease."

"Okay Mom, okay." I said okay, but I didn't want to hear another lecture. After all, I had nothing to do with the box, or whatever it was that fell, or with Christopher's missing rabbit, or the open front door, or with the reflection in the window. Why would I, or anyone, want to be lectured? Really!

So, I bent over to scoop up Puffy who must have suspected something because he got real quiet, and I grabbed for my brother's hand to lead him downstairs. My mother was waiting for us in the main room across from the couch sitting in what was, at one time, my Father's favorite chair to relax in. Seeing my mom sitting there with her legs and arms crossed reminded me of my dad, and how much I missed him. It was eight years since that dreadful day. I was going on five at the time and I'll never forget that particular day even if I live to be a hundred years old. I'll always see those two soldiers at the door and my mom listening carefully to what they were telling her and my mom crying. And to this day, my brother and I wanted to know why? Why did *our* dad have to die? Why couldn't it have been someone else's dad?

"Listen you two," she started. "All of this stuff has to stop and I mean now!" Christopher and I looked at each other with the same questioning faces. What did the words, . . . *all this stuff has to stop* mean anyway? Like we had something to do with any of the things that happened. We had an interesting conversation about this.

Christopher started it off when he asked, "Mommy, can we move back to our apartment?"

"Move back?" mom said, asking a question, but really making a statement. "Christopher, we've only been here for two days. There's no reason to be going anywhere."

"But Mom," I started. "We don't like living in this house very much. And these things that have been happening, well, we don't like them very much either. It's scary and nothing like this happened where we lived in Queens."

Christopher added, "Maybe, this ugly, old house is haunted and there are some ghosts scaring us?"

"Now Christopher," mom explained, "we don't have any ghosts living here and no, this house is not haunted."

"Mom, how do you know there are no ghosts?" As I asked that question, Christopher slid a little closer to me and I knew he wanted that question answered too.

"There are no such things as ghosts and I'm sure there are perfectly good reasons for these things that are happening. I left the front door open by accident and Christopher just put Bunny down somewhere and something could have fallen in the attic. I mean there's always a lot of stuff in attics, especially old attics."

Then I asked, "Mom, what about what I saw when we first pulled up?"

"I'm sure that was just the sun reflecting off of a passing car or a bird making a shadow. We don't have anything to be jumpy about."

As if we didn't have enough strange things going on, all of a sudden, there was a bright flash of lightening that lingered in the big windows and as we all looked at the glow, the thunder rocked the sky rumbling along in deep, cavernous sounds. We all let out a scream and jumped as if we were in some scary movie. Christopher mimicked my mom, "they're heeeeere." And we all laughed out loud together more to release the tension than to indicate how funny it was.

Now, it's not like my mom is really mean or anything like that. It's just that she tends to stick to her guns that's all. So, even though we were laughing at that moment, my mom called my name, "Sara," and pointed upstairs while looking over at me and I knew that meant I was still stuck in my room for the rest of the afternoon even after the powwow. So, I slipped away with a gloomy feeling as the rain and thunder of a summer storm rattled and pounded this old house on Apple Blossom Lane. I shut my door, lay down on my bed and let my eyes close while I heard the wind howl and the rain splatter on my bedroom window. I forced myself to think of something pleasant and an image of my dad popped into my mind. I could see my mom using our camera to take some home movies of my dad dragging me along the snow-covered road in our American Flyer sled. I wore a fuzzy pink snowsuit and my dad had his wool aviator styled hat with the big flaps pulled down over his ears. He always looked so funny wearing that hat. Every year after, at holiday time we would watch those old movies while we sang, "It's lovely weather for a sleigh ride together with you. Giddy yap, Giddy yap, Giddy yap, let's go." Then we would yell, "Yahoo." And everyone always laughed till our bellies hurt. We even watched them after my dad died. I must have seen those old movies about a million times. Those were my warmest memories of the times before my dad died. And still, to this day after all those many years, no one ever answered the question, why? Why did *my* Dad have to die?

Some weeks after those soldiers came to our door and made my mom cry, there was a funeral for my dad and lots of tears and sobbing. During one of those nights, my mom sat me down and told me the story about how he died, how he was carrying a buddy over his shoulder with one arm and shooting his rifle with the other while the ground exploded around them. My Dad carried that special friend to safety before he collapsed. His back bleeding badly from the red-hot mortar fragments lodged in his skin. He died right there, right then and there in what they said was safety.

I don't know if you remember much about the Vietnam War, it happened a real long time ago. And I think back then, my dad had very bad timing when he was shipped there. It was during the time when the war was ending, and more soldiers were being sent home than being sent there and my dad was one of the unlucky ones. At the time, many of the soldiers had their orders changed to go someplace else, but my dad got to go anyway. Years later I had read that the real war ended in January 1973 because there was a ceasefire signed. But actually, it was many months after the ceasefire when all the combat soldiers in fact left and my dad was part of the last combat soldiers over there. They were only supposed to be guarding the base near a City called Saigon, when the North Vietnamese got too close and there was a big battle. We learned that his friend had only been wounded by rifle fire and later we heard he recovered in the hospital. We never met him and we didn't know his full name. We heard he was called Mooch because over in Vietnam, he got into the habit of mooching for things like cigarettes, food, and candy. The story was when he returned to the States, along with many other messed-up Vietnam veterans, he dropped out of sight. A long while later I learned that what made loosing my dad so hard for my mom was the fact that my brother was born the same year that my father was killed. You see, just a few months before he died, they had met for a little vacation during something called R and R on a beautiful island in Hawaii. She said it made Christopher special; I mean who would argue with that.

I guess I had fallen asleep again thinking about those very sad things because the next thing I remember, I smelled some fried chicken as my eyes spotted a dinner plate on my dresser. I felt so hurt; I mean sure my mom was great to make me a plate for dinner, but she was wrong to accuse me of kidnapping my brother's rabbit and making me stay in my room. I took a closer look at that plate and thought, yummy, double dipped batter, southern fried chicken. It was Grandma's old country recipe and it was always a delicious treat for us. The mashed potatoes were piled up with a reservoir of gravy floating inside. And the corn on the cob my mom picked out at the market was still steaming with a pad of butter melting on top. I pulled a chair over and dipped my fork into the potatoes. Umm, I thought, as I started to fill my empty stomach.

Later that night, my mom came up to my room and talked with me. She asked for more help with making our situation better. She explained that this house was our new home and all it needed was time. And she tried once more to explain all those strange things that had happened since we arrived. I didn't believe her explanation, not before and not now. But I did promise her to try to like this new house more.

"Sara, I baked a nice chocolate cake with that dark fudge icing you and your brother like. Let's all go down to the kitchen and have some cake and milk, it'll be fun."

"Sure Mom, if you say so."

We went over to Christopher's room to tell him about the chocolate cake and as we neared his door we heard him having a conversation inside. At first, I thought he was just playing soldiers again, but then, I realized that the other voice didn't really sound very much like Christopher's voice at all. Mom even looked taken aback—we hesitated outside his door. I whispered,

"Mom, do you think he's playing with his toy soldiers? I heard him before playing and he used a bunch of different voices."

"I don't know Sara, let's see for ourselves."

Mom knocked, waited a couple of seconds and then walked right in, and there was Christopher, lying stomach down on the floor with his legs crossed up in the air. He had placed his dark green army blanket in front of him creating a hilly battlefield. There were a bunch of his small tanks lined up on one side and a couple dozen soldiers lying around. In his left hand was one toy soldier and in the right, was another soldier. He was barking orders and wiggling those little toys around paying no attention to us. I looked over at my mom.

She stood there with her mouth open while her eyes searched the room and a puzzled look appeared on her face. Then my mom surprised me when she asked,

"Christopher, who were you talking to?" I quickly looked over at my brother waiting to hear his response.

"Oh, hi Mom, hi Sis. That was my friend."

"Your friend?" mom asked.

Christopher replied, as if nothing was new, "Yeah, I met him last night and he visits now. He likes to watch me play with the soldiers."

"Christopher, what friend?" I asked.

"He's just somebody I met. He helped me last night when I was scared. Now, I don't feel so afraid."

"What's his name?" My mom wanted to know.

Christopher said simply, "Tommy."

My mom took a deep breath, exhaled and said, "We're going to have some chocolate cake, want some?"

"With the fudge icing?" Christopher asked.

"Yes, with the fudge."

Christopher didn't hesitate, "You bet mom."

Mom asked, "If you want, ask Tommy if he would like some too."

"Oh, I don't think he would want to sit with us Mom. He's shy."

We went downstairs to the kitchen and mom served us the cake while I poured milk for Christopher and me. Hearing her ask about this new friend made me feel even more uneasy. I just sat there quietly licking the icing off the fork with each little piece of cake I carved off. I should tell you that my mom is a very good cook. She really likes to cook too; just about the first things she unpacked were her kitchen things. I like almost everything she makes. Even little Christopher isn't very finicky about the food our mom cooks up for us even though he's funny about other things. Like he hates any juice with pulp in it. If you pour him a glass of orange juice, it better not have any pulp in it or you'll never hear the end of it. Imagine that, no pulp, like fruit was made to have only clear liquid inside. I mean really. And this so-called imaginary friend he conjured up just adds to his strangeness. Mom was asking all sorts of questions about him. Like, how tall his friend Tommy is? How old he is? The kind of clothes he wore? What he weighs? Things like that and the spooky thing was Christopher answered all those questions without much hesitation.

"Tommy? Oh, he's about six feet tall"

"He told me he was forty-three"

"Old army clothes, just like my toy soldiers"

"He's kind of skinny mom, with a long dark beard"

I was wondering how he made up all that stuff so fast, like the part about the beard. I thought the whole thing was weird. My mom didn't eat any cake, she hardly ever does. Did I tell you about my mom? No, I don't think I did. I won't give you details about what my mom looks like, except that she looks just like Goldie Hawn, but instead of short blond hair, she has long, dark brown hair. And instead of Goldie, her first name is Denise and her married name is Fisher. My mom is the best dance instructor around, well around Queens anyway, I don't know about Sea Cliff. And she watches what she eats all the time. She watches what we eat too most of the time, this delicious cake was just a treat. Actually, I think my mom was being clever and using the chocolate cake with its fudge icing and that southern fried chicken as distractions. It was working too, because during the rest of the evening nothing worth mentioning happened.

And the next day was quiet too. The landscape company showed up to mow and clean up the outside. I watched them from my bedroom window amazed at the speed in which they worked. They looked like a movie in fast motion. I laughed at them setting up the sprinklers; a couple of the men were spraying each other with the water as they fiddled with the nozzles. Before I knew it they were loading their equipment on the truck and driving off to their next job. We all went about opening the boxes the moving men stacked in our rooms and putting away our clothing and the other junk. Oh, my mom called it junk. "How did we ever get to collect all this junk?" She said it about a thousand times.

For a while I was busy putting some of my favorite books up on the shelves of my bookcase. There were some old Nancy Drew Mysteries and *The Hobbit*. I giggled when I picked up *Charlotte's Web*, and another old favorite, *Puff the Magic Dragon*. I let out an "oooohh" in amazement as I spotted, *Where The Wild Things Are*. I picked it up and thumbed through the pages instantly recalling how that little story scared the daylight out of me whenever mom used to read it at bedtime. I placed it with the others and thought; I know where the wild things are. They live right here at Thirteen Apple Blossom Lane.

I left my room and was planning to go downstairs when I overheard my mom talking on the phone. I sat down on the top step as she was explaining how Christopher was talking to an imaginary friend again like he did once before. At one point, I heard her say, "So Doctor Allen, I don't have to worry about Christopher? This imaginary friend thing is just a phase that goes along with moving into the new house? I see, okay, thank you for your time. Yes, I'll let you know how he is doing." And then I heard a clunk as she hung up the phone. I knew who Dr. Allen was. He's the psychologist I went to see a few years after my father was killed in the *safety* area. Dr. Allen kept asking me questions about how I felt about this and how I felt about that. Sometimes, I just wanted to jump up and ask him, "How do you think I feel, you stupid idiot?" but I never did.

Later that afternoon we all went for a walk. I watched my mom lock the door and holding the doorknob shake it to make sure it was locked. We found this small park a few blocks away by an old school building. Christopher played on the swings while I sat on the bench thinking what it would be like if we got back to that house and found the door open again. Then, I heard Christopher ask our mom about the war medals that our dad was awarded in the army. He wanted to know if he ever received a special one called the Bronze Star? Our mom explained that he was awarded the Bronze Star for heroism, when he saved his friend Mooch during the war in Vietnam. "How did you learn about that medal?" My mom wanted to know. When I heard that question, I decided to walk over to them so I could hear the answer too. Christopher just explained, "Tommy was telling me about the medals, he mentioned the Bronze Star, that's all." I shook my head in disbelief and watched my mom hug Christopher tenderly. I was getting pretty tired of hearing about this Tommy guy.

We started walking back when Christopher asked, "What's for dinner tonight Ma?" She turned and walking backwards bent over to tell him, "How about some nice gizzard bone soup with old rotten carrots and spoiled potatoes?" She said that with a teasing voice, but I just looked over and said, "Really Mom" annoyed as can be. Christopher looked at me and stuck out his tongue. And of course, I stuck mine out at him and our mom ended up laughing. She took our hands and made us skip. Then she started us off with, "We're off to see the Wizard, the wonderful Wizard of Oz." We must have been some sight skipping and singing because there was an older woman across the street talking to someone pointing at us as we skipped away down the street.

Then we came to our house and we stopped the skipping and singing and we stopped the laughing and just stood there. I know we were all looking at the same thing, that door on the porch. Mom went up the steps and my brother and I held our breath as she went to turn the knob. But, it didn't turn and the door was still locked. And our mom looked back at us as if to say, *see I told you so.* She put the key in the lock and opened the door and at that point, something in my head told me, you can breathe now Sara, go ahead and breathe. I guess I must have heard that, because I gasped for air just as I rushed up the porch steps into the house.

I decided to help my mom get dinner started while my brother sat at the kitchen table watching me peel the carrots. And that's about when the next incident happened, at least that's when we learned of it. You see, my mom wasn't really making gizzard soup, she was figuring on heating up the leftover southern fried chicken and making some vegetables to go along. Except, when she grabbed the bowl of chicken from the refrigerator and placed it on the table and lifted off the lid she let out an "Uh, oh." It wasn't just an "Uh, oh" . . . it was more like an "Uh, oh." And hearing those words froze us. We all looked inside the bowl as she counted the three pieces and asked us,

"Where did the other three pieces go? When I put the lid on last night there were six pieces."

Christopher answered first, "I didn't take any Mom."

And I added, "I didn't have any either."

"Oh? And I suppose I should march Puffy in here and give that little dog the third degree, eh?"

"Mom," I said, "stop kidding around, where did those chicken pieces go? Are you sure there were six pieces left over?"

Christopher really looked frightened as my mom and I went on and on about the missing fried chicken. He started biting his nails again and that's something he really had worked hard at giving up. I knew then how nervous he really was. As mom noticed what I noticed, she started to hesitate. She looked over at me, and then back at Christopher, and then she sat down and placed her head between her hands and began sobbing. Christopher and I looked at each other recognizing that our mom, the pillar of strength for us, had lost it. A sight I hadn't seen since the news about our dad.

Then, suddenly, we all looked at each other with wide open eyes and fixed our gaze upstairs as music started to play. It was a love song and one that our mom played often whenever she wanted to remember our father. It was called, "Unchained Melody" by some Right Brothers or somebody or other. As we heard the words, " . . . *and time goes by so slowly,*" Christopher ducked underneath the kitchen table and I hid behind my mom thinking, I can't wait to hear her explanation for the music. Mom took a few steps to the staircase trying to stretch her neck upward as if she would be able to see the cause of the music. She took one step up and then another. Slowly she climbed a third, and then another, and another, looking around to make sure no one was waiting to hit her over the head or something. With each step, the music grew louder, and we grew more scared. I was right behind my mom and Christopher was right behind me. Finally, we reached the upstairs landing and mom paused. She pointed toward her bedroom and we nervously followed behind. She looked inside while holding a hand up to us signaling we should stop. But, I couldn't stand the waiting, so I peeked inside just in time to see her switch off the music playing from a cassette on her alarm clock radio. The silence was deafening. Mom turned around and seeing us standing at the doorway remarked, "It was just my clock radio, I guess I forgot that I had set it to remind me to make a call to the real estate agent." Now truthfully, I don't know if my mom really had set the alarm or if the clock just went off on its own or if someone turned it on just to scare us even more. But, I liked the idea that our mom had set the clock better than any other reason so I just went along with it.

"Oh boy," I said trying to be funny wiping my forehead for effect. "I thought it was one of those ghosts. Am I glad we got that one cleared up." I started to walk out of the room and as I passed by Christopher I made a funny face to make him laugh, except he didn't laugh. We all went downstairs again and my mom put her arm around me and gave me a little hug. I think that hug was her way to say thank you for not making the music-playing incident a bigger deal than it already was. Have you ever felt good about doing a good-deed? Well, that's how I felt right about then. Even though inside my head I still wanted to know how that music started playing? It was a question that kept on repeating itself. And the more I thought about it, I didn't really think any of the reasons my mom had mentioned were good reasons, nope, not a one.

My mom picked up the telephone and told me to go play with Christopher upstairs. But who wanted to go up those stairs again? I got the idea that she wanted to be alone when she called whomever it was she wanted to phone. So, I looked over at Christopher and asked, "Hey, you want to play Candyland?" He answered back, "You bet." We raced each other up the stairs to his room and while my brother went inside to look for the board game, I lingered at the doorway. I wasn't going to miss this phone call. When I heard her ask for Dorothy, I knew she was calling the real estate office that helped with the transfer of ownership. It was a name I heard her say many times before. I found out when you get a new house the real estate agent becomes a best friend and you spend a lot of time talking to your new friend. Oh, I should tell you something important. This house was actually a part of our family, well sort of. It had belonged to my Great Aunt Yvonne. Now, my Great Aunt was the black sheep of the family. And there's a story there too, but I'll tell you about that later. My mom was asking Dorothy if she had ever heard about this house being haunted, and I can imagine what the reaction was on the other end. My Mother asked if anyone ever died here. Then she started to explain most of the weird things that were going on. It sounded like my mom was starting to believe there was a ghost or two living here after all. Dorothy must have explained that the house had no history of any ghosts because my mom kept asking, "Are you sure?" and "Really, nobody was ever murdered here?" I guess my mom got the answers to her questions because she said goodbye right after that.

My brother yelled louder than he needed to, "Hey Sis, are we gonna play or not?" So, I went into Christopher's room and sat on the floor where he had set up the Candyland game board.

"What color do you want to be?"

"I'm gonna be green." I told him. So, we sat together there on the floor for a couple of hours moving the green guy and the blue guy around and around the board. The only break we took was a pee break for me while my brother went downstairs to get some cookies. When he came back up Christopher told me,

"Hey Sis, mom wants to talk with you."

"About what?"

"Something about a lunch bag, I think?"

"A lunch bag, what's that about?"

"I don't know Sara, but mom's crying again."

So, I went downstairs to see what was going on and my mom was pacing back and forth in the kitchen wiping her nose with a tissue. I sat down at the table quietly. I knew I was in big trouble when she started,

"Really Sara, what were you thinking?

"Mom, what's up? You're scaring me."

"I would like to know one thing, no, two things. First, what have I done to make you start lying to me?

"Lie?"

"Yes, young lady, lie? And I would also like to know, when did you become so mean?"

I must have looked bewildered, because right after she wiped her eyes and blew her nose she continued in a very upset voice like she had been crying a long time. "I went up to your room to dust and empty the trash container and that's when I found this." She was pointing to a small lunch-size bag on the table. "Go ahead Sara, look inside." I was feeling nervous about opening that little brown lunch bag and looking inside. Maybe it was someone's brains, I thought. I mean, my mom was acting awfully weird and I couldn't imagine what would make her like this.

"Do I have to?" I asked, hoping she would just smile and say *no, you don't have to open that bag.* But she didn't.

Instead, she frowned and said in an upset voice, "Let me Sara, let me open that bag and show you what I found in your room, in your trash container." She reached over, and opened the bag and turned it upside down and out they came sliding down and onto the table.

I stood up, gasped and said, "Oh my god, how did those chicken bones get into my room?"

"That's exactly what I want to know too . . . how indeed?" She said sternly, "And you better stop lying right now young lady, if you know what's good for you."

I sat down, looked at the chicken bones and at the bag and my trash container and wondered about all this while my mom blew her nose again and wiped her eyes. It seemed to me that if Christopher didn't do it and my mom didn't do it and I knew for sure that I didn't do it, then, it had to be someone else. And if someone else took the chicken pieces out of the refrigerator, ate them and took the bones and stuck them in that brown lunch bag and left the whole thing sitting in my trash container, then that meant we were all very much in danger. This wasn't a case of maybe mom did or didn't lock the door or a reflection of a bird in a window or if a box fell all by itself in the attic, this was a case of someone coming into our house and doing this. So, I just looked at my mom and in my most serious voice told her what we needed to do.

"Mom, I think it's time to call the police." Hearing that made her stop crying. She looked at the evidence on the table and understood what I had realized a few moments before. She picked up the portable phone on the table and dialed 9-1-1. After a couple of rings, she started speaking nervously to the person on the other end.

She said, "I'd like to report that there has been an intruder in our house.

No, there is no one in the house now.

No, there doesn't seem to be anything missing.

No, there's no one hurt.

No, there's nothing broken or messed up.

No, there are no broken windows and no doors have been forced in.

What makes me think there was an intruder? Ahhh, ahhh, well, aahhh—I don't know, just that there have been strange things going on.

Yes, I know that 9-1-1 is for emergencies.

I'm sorry, it seemed like an emergency to me.

Okay, I'll call the precinct. I'm sorry."

Then, she ended the call and went to the closet for the phone book. At this point, Christopher came down and asked, "Mom, what's going on?" Mom didn't answer; she kept thumbing her way through the pages for the Nassau County Police phone numbers. He saw the lunch bag on the table and the chicken bones and said, "Tommy said he was sorry." Mom picked up the phone and started dialing the police when Christopher added, "He thought it would be funny. And didn't realize how upset everyone would be."

Mom said, "Not now Christopher, please, let's talk about it later."

I brought him over to the hallway and asked, "Did he say he was sorry for anything else?"

"No Sis, just for taking the chicken and leaving the bones in your room—that's all."

"Christopher, mom's right. This is not the time to be telling us what your imaginary friend told you."

"He's not imaginary Sara, he's my real friend."

"Yeah right, and I am really a princess. Go upstairs and tell Timmy it's . . ."

"Tommy, his name is Tommy."

"Okay, Tommy. Tell Tommy it's okay and thank him for telling us."

I turned away and noticed that my mom was looking in the phone book again. "What did they say Mom?"

"Well Sara, they said they don't have the manpower to be chasing down strange things happening in a house and that maybe the local police in Sea Cliff would take it up."

"Will you call them, Mom?

"Yes, I think I better."

My mom opened up the phone book again and started looking for the phone number for the Sea Cliff Police Department. I didn't even know this town had its own Police Department. Well, this might be a good time to tell you more about our Great Aunt Yvonne. First of all, a great aunt is not like a regular aunt. A great Aunt means she is a sister to one of the grandparents. In our family, Great Aunt Yvonne was my father's mother's sister. You see why that's so confusing? Oh, and secondly, she was also my dad's Godmother. Aunt Yvonne was never married and she lived a real long time. I had heard she was born in this house a very long time ago. When she died, she left a lot of what she had to my dad in her will, including this house.

She wasn't liked very much by my other aunts and uncles, and I think she felt the same way about them too. Sometimes in families, things are said that makes a lot of anger among relatives and I think that was the case for my Great Aunt too. Except, I was told, my Aunt Yvonne had very special feelings for my dad. I learned she adored him more than anything else in the world. I heard more than once, that everyone was jealous because when he was young, she bought lots of nice gifts for my dad and nothing for them. My parents never took me for a visit because even though she lived a long time, she didn't like young children to visit. My Aunt lived alone for so long it seems she just grew to dislike company. I never understood that, of course my brother wasn't even born at the time.

When my Aunt Yvonne died, she left this house to my dad. Except, these two men who lived somewhere down south claimed the house was theirs, because they were blood relatives, or something like that. So, it took a long time for the courts to hear everything and to examine the evidence. In the end, the other men lost the case and my dad got it all. This happened while he was in the Army and my mom was the one who had to take care of everything. Then when my dad died, it went back to the courts because the judge had to make a final decision on who owned the house and property. It was a little more than a year ago when the lawyer came to visit and he told my mom that the whole thing was over and we had the deed to the property. At the time, my mom couldn't decide to sell the house or not. At first, she thought it best to put the house up for sale with the real estate agent I mentioned before. After a while, when the house didn't sell right away, my mom had second thoughts about it. Eventually, she changed her mind and decided to take the house in Sea Cliff. After all that, we moved here from Queens like I told you in the beginning.

My mom ended up calling the Sea Cliff police and someone was very helpful there. He listened for a while and then he said he would send over one of the officers in the morning to take a statement and to investigate. My mom was satisfied with that and started to make us dinner. As she was taking the ingredients from the cupboard, and the bowls from the closet, she said, "That's strange? I thought I put it right here next to the flour? Umm . . ."

"What Ma?" I said not really wanting to hear there was yet another thing to upset us.

"I thought I put a twenty-dollar bill and a ten right here between the flour and the sugar canisters. You know, a little cash in case? And now, the twenty is missing. Did either of you take it?" She asked that question and yet, there was something in her voice, in the way she asked it that told me, she didn't ever want to hear the answer.

"Nope, not me" Christopher responded like this was becoming an everyday thing. I said, "No, I didn't take any money, Mom."

My mom was looking at the cupboard and added, "I guess I just miscounted then. Oh, well."

It was just one more little incident to make you wonder and scare the dickens out of you. And just as I said it I thought, where did I learn that word, dickens?

Since the chicken was gone, our mom decided to cook us some pancakes. Christopher asked if she would make them shape pancakes and mom said shape pancakes they would be. Have you ever had shape pancakes? My mom was very good at it. She could make almost any shape we asked her to make. One time, I asked for spider pancakes and my mom made these delicious long legged pancakes. She spilled the batter in the frying pan into long thin shapes and made oval ones for the bodies. When she put them on the plate she attached a bunch of the leg shapes to the bodies and boy, did they look like big spiders. Christopher asked for snowman pancakes and my mom made them up too making three different circles.

Having the pancakes was a good idea because that took our minds off the house where the *wild things* lived.

It was about 10 o'clock the next morning when the doorbell rang and Puffy yelped as usual to let us know he was still around. I opened the door and in walked Officer Hughes. He was very tall and thin. He wore his sandy colored hair very short in a crew cut fashion along with a thin mustache. As I watched him enter our house, I was thinking that he looked very young to be a police officer. He was extremely polite and asked all of us questions about every incident that happened from the very first, the reflection in the window of the widow's watch. He wanted to know if anything else besides the twenty-dollar bill was missing and mom said no. He took a lot of notes as my mom explained the details. Then after that, he asked if he could take a look around including my room where the chicken bones were found. He also checked the front door and the back door for lock tampering. Officer Hughes told my mom that there were no signs of a break-in and since nothing of value was missing, there wasn't much he could do. He did say he would come around in the patrol car a few times every day and that we should let the station know if any other incidents occurred. My mom thanked him for his time and walked him to the door.

"So, that's that," mom started, "now, the police are on our side and everything will go back to normal." When I heard that I thought, yeah right, whatever normal is?

Christopher asked, "Mommy, does that mean we don't have ghosts here? Tommy said he didn't think there were any ghosts here either."

Mom asked him, "How would Tommy know if this house has ghosts?"

"He's been living in the house for awhile, at least that's what he said."

I had about enough of this imaginary friend of his and said, "Tommy salami, its all baloney" and then I left the room in a huff and sat on the big couch by the windows.

Well, over the next few days nothing much happened. There were no more signs of the ghosts or the wild things or any incidents to bother us. Things just went along pretty much normal like my mom had said. And every once in a while, when the timing was right, Officer Hughes drove slowly by our house in his patrol car and Christopher and I waved hi to him. Almost all the boxes were unpacked by now and everything was put away. Our house was starting to look like a home. We were all smiling and getting along just fine. That is until no one could find the portable phone. Mom thought she had put it down on the kitchen table and when she wanted to make a call it was gone. After the peace and quiet we had been enjoying, none of us wanted to think things would be starting again. So, we all looked for it. We searched everywhere including the cabinets and drawers in the kitchen, under the tables in the living room, even the closets in the upstairs rooms. We met up in the living room and had another powwow. Christopher asked the question we all wanted to know.

"Mom, what does it mean that we can't find the phone?"

"It doesn't mean anything Christopher," she said trying her best not to worry us anymore than we already were. "I must have set it down somewhere and I have just forgotten where."

"Mom," I said, "Why don't we use the intercom thing on the phone base and listen for the ring it makes? Two of us can go room to room while one of us keeps pressing the intercom button.

"That's a great idea Sara."

"Can I be the one who pushes the button?" Christopher asked that with a little worry in his voice, like he didn't want to be the one searching around in the rooms.

"Sure you can Christopher. Sara and I will split up. We'll start downstairs, I'll do the kitchen and Sara honey, how about the living room? And I'll tell you what, we can make a game out of it. Kids against the mom—if the kids find the phone we'll go to the movie of their choice."

"And if the mom wins?" I added.

"Well, if the mom finds the phone, how about the kids have to clean their rooms?"

Christopher jumped on that one. "That's no fun."

And I added, "Phooey!"

"All right," mom decided, "how about if I win, I get to choose where we go to have dinner?" So, that's how the game was decided and we went ahead and started looking.

Christopher would press the intercom button on the telephone control box and yell out, "Do you hear it now?" And there would be an echo of "No's" from my mom and me as the rooms were searched. There was no beep in the kitchen, none in the living room, none in the dining room, the downstairs bathroom, the den, or the pantry entranceway by the kitchen door. We went down to the basement together and kept hearing Christopher yelling,

"Do you hear it now?"

And we would yell back, "No!" This went on for a while until we searched every room downstairs and in the basement. My mother wondered if the battery in the phone was dead. But, since we didn't really know, we kept the search going. It came time to go upstairs and I have to tell you that the more we searched for that portable phone, the more I started to worry. Who would take the phone? I thought. Who and why? And then, the time came when I had to go up those stairs and search the upstairs bedrooms again.

It was harder for Christopher to hear us from upstairs and harder for us too. The yelling got louder and we moved a little slower until every room and every closet was searched while

Christopher pressed the intercom button over and over. We were about to give up when I was in the back of the upstairs hallway and I heard a slight little beep when Christopher yelled, "Do you hear it now?"

I wasn't really sure that I heard the intercom or not. So, I yelled down, "Press it again Christopher." And I heard it a second time; a slight beep, beep sound. "Mom, come here—listen to this. Press it again," I yelled. As my mom and I stood really quiet and listened she said, "I think that is the phone beep Sara—but, where is it coming from?"

"It almost sounds like it's coming from behind the wall." I explained.

"You think so? I think the beeps are coming from the ceiling."

"The ceiling? Mom, how could that be?"

"I know, I know, I wasn't anywhere near the ceiling, but still, that's where the beep is coming from. I'm sure of it."

"The attic is up there, right Mom?"

"Yes, but Sara, I wasn't up in the attic with the phone."

"How do we get up in the attic anyway, Mom?"

"We don't Sara, you stay here. There's a pull down ladder in the corner closet."

I stood there and watched my mom go into the closet and lift the staircase and yank it down from the ceiling. She climbed up half way, stuck her head in, and said, "I need a flashlight Sara, can you get me the flashlight? And ask Christopher to press the intercom button a few more times." I went to the cupboard and got the flashlight. On my way back, I explained to Christopher that mom was looking in the attic and she wanted him to press the intercom button a few more times. When I got back upstairs, my mom told me, "It's definitely the sound of the intercom on the portable phone, but I can't see it. I think I have to climb up into the attic." I handed my mom the flashlight and watched more of her disappear into the attic. She yelled down, "I still don't see it, ask Christopher to press the intercom one more time."

I stuck my head over the railing and shouted, "One more time, Christopher." As he pressed the button, I heard the phone go beep, beep.

My mom heard it too because she said, "Oh yeah, it's up here. I can hear it as clear as day."

She took a few more steps up the ladder until she completely disappeared into the attic. I felt weird not being able to see her, so, I followed along up the steps until my head was in the attic too. My mom was standing a little bent over, shining the light around. We both saw an enclosure, a framed out room with a small door set to the left side. There were wood boards leading right up to the door placed across the ceiling joists. My mom said, "I think the beep is coming from behind that door Sara. And if you ask me, this is a good time to call Officer Hughes." I backed my way down the stairs and my mom did the same. Then, she closed the folding stairway back up into the ceiling and we both went to the kitchen.

"Did you find the phone?" Christopher wanted to know.

"Yes and no, we heard it, but couldn't see the phone." Mom told him.

"What does that mean Mom?" He asked nervously.

"It means I'm calling Officer Hughes to ask him for help searching up there."

"Tommy knows his way around up there. I bet he could help if I ask him."

"How does he know Christopher?"

"Because that's where he lives, Sis."

"Wait Christopher," I asked him slowly, "You mean he lives in our house?"

"He's lived here for a couple of years now and knows the house better than anyone."

"Christopher," our mom asked, sounding frustrated. "Why don't you have your friend come into the kitchen with us right now. We could use his help after all."

"It doesn't work like that Mom. I don't know where he is."

"But Christopher," I asked, "You just said he lives in our house."

"Yeah, but he comes and visits me—I don't get him."

"Never mind," our mom decided, "I'll just call Officer Hughes—he did say I should call if anything else happens."

The next morning, Officer Hughes drove up our driveway in his police car once again and rang our doorbell. He was polite as usual and asked my mom a bunch of questions. Then he asked her to show him where the stairs to the attic were. And we all followed him to the upstairs corner closet. Officer Hughes pulled down the stairs and climbed up into the attic. I could hear his feet on the boards above as he took some steps. All of a sudden, the noise stopped and there was nothing. No sounds at all and unexpectedly, there was this big racket coming from the attic. This was followed by, "Hey you, stop! It's the police, stop right there fella." We heard awful noises from up there like a fight was going on. Boxes were falling and crashing down on top of each other. I could only imagine what was happening up there to Officer Hughes. Then, there was silence.

We were all pretty shaken up by what just took place and my mom signaled us to move away from the closet. I figured the *wild things* might have eaten Officer Hughes because it was so quiet up there and Christopher looked so scared. We all moved downstairs quietly as if we could fool them and escape. Then, the strangest thing of all happened. Christopher was looking out the front living room window pointing and he yelled, "Hey, that's my friend Tommy." And he bolted out the front door before we could stop him. So, my mom ran after him and I ran after him too. Except, I had no idea why I was running. What was my rush anyway? Well, as soon as I got out the front door I couldn't believe my eyes. Officer Hughes, who was bleeding from a big cut on his lip, was putting this tall handcuffed man with a beard dressed in army fatigues into the back seat of his police car. At the same time, he was trying his best to hold off Christopher; who was yelling something about his friend Tommy. What a sight! Then my mom picked up the screaming Christopher in her arms and pulled him away from the car as Officer Hughes radioed in for assistance. About this time, the neighbors were gathering around and everyone was talking and asking questions. The entire scene was right out of a movie. What a commotion!

It didn't take long for some other police cars to show up with their sirens blaring and lights flashing. Watching all this I wondered, what in the world did our mom get us into anyway? I could see Officer Hughes explaining to another police officer with all these stripes on his arm what had happened and he was pointing over to our house, to us and to that strange man in the back of his police car.

Shortly after, Officer Hughes came over to us and asked my mom, "Did you know there was another room in the attic?"

"No, I never went up into the attic except to poke my head in to look for the portable phone. I saw a wall and a door, but a room, that's amazing."

Officer Hughes continued, "We figure this guy must have been sort of living up in the attic. There wasn't much of a home up there, but he had furniture, some clothing and shelves of food."

"Wait," my mom interrupted, "you mean to tell me that over the last week, while we moved in and were living in that house, he was living there too—in the attic?

"Yes, ma'am." Officer Hughes explained, "After we struggled, I chased him down the back staircase behind the room that leads into the pantry at the back door. That's where I nailed him and put the cuffs on him. It seems there's a maze of hidden walkways behind some of the walls that lead into the different rooms. He could pretty much come and go as he pleased."

My mom asked, "Is there anyone else with him up there?"

"No, ma'am, there doesn't appear to be anyone else with him. But, before they leave, the officers will be going through the house just the same"

I stood there in awe as my mom asked, "Who is he?"

"We don't know yet, we arrested him for trespassing and resisting arrest and we'll have plenty of opportunity to question him. We'll contact you and go over the details as soon as we know them."

We watched Officer Hughes drive away with Christopher's *imaginary friend* handcuffed in the back seat. Most of the police cars were gone at this point and the people that had gathered were heading back to their homes. The remaining police officers were talking with my mom and explained that there was no one else in the house. They asked us not to go up into the attic because there would be a further investigation and we shouldn't disturb anything. When I heard that, I was thinking, no one has to worry about me going up there.

So, we went back into the house and sat together for a while. Our mom asked us how we were doing and if we felt funny. We both shook our heads "no" in response. A few minutes later mom asked, "Christopher, about your friend Tommy . . ."

He interrupted her with an angry tone. "I told you he was real. I told you both. He's my friend and now he is locked up with the police like some dirty crook."

Mom answered, "I'm sorry Christopher, but we just didn't understand that he was a real person." He looked over at me, but I didn't dare say a word even though I wanted to call him stupid for not making me understand for real.

Now, you might think that was the end of a pretty weird story, but wait until you hear the rest. I couldn't believe it and I'm sure you won't believe it either. In a couple of days, we talked with the police again and learned everything. It turned out that Christopher's imaginary friend wasn't really an intruder or a squatter at all. He was invited to live there. That's right, he was. His full name was Thomas R. Burke and he was an ex-soldier who, after returning from Vietnam, had nowhere to live and nowhere to go. His nickname was Mooch and he was the soldier that my dad had carried out of the battle to *safety*, the place where my dad died. Mooch had explained to the police that our dad and him were best buddies over in Vietnam. Over time, my dad had learned that Mooch was an orphan and joined the Army because he had nothing much going for him in the States. And my dad felt really bad about Mooch not having a place to live. He had told him that when they get out of the war he could move in with his family.

Mooch knew everything about my mom and about me, but he didn't know about Christopher at all which is why they became friends. It seems when you're a soldier fighting a war, you get really close to other soldiers and you end up talking a lot about your family and your entire life before the fighting. Mooch also knew all about the house my dad had inherited here in Sea Cliff. Dad had told him that the house was huge and there would be plenty of room for him, buddies forever they had said. After my father was killed, when Mooch got back from Vietnam, he wandered about for a while. That is, until he just figured he would go look up that house, and when he did, he found it empty. He recalled his buddy's promise and decided to move in and keep an eye on the place. When we moved in that sort of upset the apple cart, as the saying goes.

When the police searched the attic, they found some duffle bags full of stuff. Inside one of the bags they found an old banged up cigar box of snapshots from over in Vietnam. They asked my mom to look through all those pictures and she cried because my dad was in a lot of them. She talked with

Mooch too about how it was for them over in Vietnam. After that conversation, she told the police who this man Mooch really was and that they should drop the charges against him. Since there was no reason to keep him locked up, they released him. Mom asked Mooch to come over to the house and have supper with us and she told him, "You know Mooch, you don't have to be Christopher's imaginary friend anymore."

So, I took a deep breath and said, "And that's how the story ends." I closed the covers of the book and smiled so deeply recalling those long ago memories. Then they chimed in, "That was great Mom, can you read it again? Please, Mom!"

And I looked at my children and laughed. "You always want me to read it again. And we will, another day."

# A

# CHANGE

# *of*

# HEART

*When one door of happiness closes, another opens, but*
*often we look so long at the closed door that we do not*
*see the one that has opened for us.*

Helen Keller

" **A**ll right Mr. Simms, we're ready to start. How are you feeling?"

"I'm okay, a little nervous, but okay."

"Now, you don't have to worry, the doctor has done this many times before."

"Yes, well, it's my first time."

"I'm just going to release the brakes now and I'll take you to the procedure room. It's just down the hall. Let's bring that arm inside the railing now, we don't want to bump it do we?"

"Does this take long?"

"Long? No, not long at all. Before you know it, you'll be all finished and back home resting. Right through those doors now . . . and over to the table. Okay Mr. Simms, step up on the stool and lie down on the table, go easy, that's it, very good. I'll just place this strap around you, sort of a seat belt. Okay, you're all set. The anesthesiologist will be with you shortly and Dr. Tanner will be right along. Don't go anywhere now."

"Hi, Mr. Simms. I'm Doctor Pallen, the anesthesiologist. Let me ask you a few questions. "Have you had anything to eat or drink since midnight?"

"No, nothing."

"Good, and do you have any allergies?"

"No, no allergies."

"Have you ever had anesthesia before?

"Ah, once before, when I had a tooth surgically removed."

"Any problems with that?"

"No, it was fine."

"Very well, I'm going to start by putting some leads on your chest; these will be a little cold. You all right so far?

"Yes, I'm fine. Just a little nervous."

"Nervous is okay, just remember, you're in good hands and we'll keep an eye out for you. And now, I'm putting this little device on your index finger, it's a pulse oximeter. It sends a signal to the monitor over there so we can measure your heart rate and the oxygen saturation of your blood. This is the blood pressure cuff; you'll feel some pressure on your arm as it pumps up. Is that too tight?"

"No, it's okay."

"Good, and now, I'll start the I.V. for fluids. And as soon as Dr. Tanner comes in we'll start right up. How's that sound Mr. Simms?"

"I guess."

"And how are you feeling this morning Mr. Simms?"

"Hi Dr. Tanner, I think I'm all right? Just feeling a little strange."

"Don't you worry now, I went over everything, right?"

"Yes, you did, but you know?"

"Yes, yes, we know. All right, Dr. Pallen, let's put our patient to sleep now."

"Take a deep breath Mr. Simms and count back for me from one hundred."

"One hundred, ninety-nine, ninety-eight, . . . ."

Before he got to ninety-five, Paul Simms was asleep and ready to be shocked. It was a procedure to restart his heart, to correct an irregular heartbeat. It sounded simple enough. First, they put you to sleep and then they take these small wired-pads and attach them to your chest and run what they say is a small current through your body. The jolt restarts your heart, and when you wake up—Voila! You have a different heartbeat, problem gone.

A couple of weeks before, Dr. Tanner had explained to Paul and his wife Linda that it was just a routine procedure called electrical cardioversion. Dr. Tanner informed them that he performs close to one hundred of these cardioversion procedures a year and that there is about a ninety-five percent chance it will work. He explained that there is a one point five percent mortality rate. When Paul asked about his chances of dying during the procedure, Dr. Tanner had told him, "You're as healthy as an ox, just a little irregular heartbeat. I don't see any problem."

Paul thought it all sounded creepy and on the way home from the consultation he had asked Linda, "What if they can't restart my heart? What if when they shock me, my heart decides to call it quits?"

"Dr Tanner explained all that Paul."

"I know, I know, I heard him, but still . . . ." Paul sat back and recalled when everything first started.

It was about two months ago when he had felt that first tug. He had parked his car in the town parking lot and was walking over to the corner bar, a place called Mugs. He was meeting his brother Jonathan for a couple of beers and a little TV hockey when it happened. The tug was a sensation inside his chest, not a serious pain like a heart attack, but a tingling that made him feel like something was not right. Then, it happened again the next day, while walking up the stairs to his bedroom after a long day at the office. A few days after that, he had felt it when taking the dog out for a morning walk. Each time the sensations grew and each time that it happened, he found his imagination running to the worst-case scenario. He could picture the cemetery stone with his name across it and right underneath the years of his life were the words. *Here lies Paul Simms, beloved husband and father.* At times like these, Linda would just encourage him to see the doctor. "Why worry about it Paul? Just go." In the end he told her, "You're right sweetheart, I'll make the call."

So, he went. First, there was the appointment with the family doctor for a check-up and physical.

"How often do you feel those sensations Paul?" Dr. Gilford asked him.

"Not too often."

"And when did they start?"

"Just a few weeks ago?"

"How about when you are running, any problems with your heart or with your breathing? Anything bothering you"

"No, I've eased off the running doc, but no, there is nothing bothering me."

"Well, let me take a listen to your lungs first, any coughing going on?"

"No, not really,"

"Umm, okay take a slow deep breath in . . . and hold it. Okay, let it out slowly. And again. Good. What about your job Paul, anything there bothering you? How's the business these days, good?"

"Just the usual difficulties. Except I did have a problem with one of the clients and I had to let one of the junior accountants go. That was hard for me to do."

"Umm, I see. Let me listen to your heart, just breathe normal."

Dr. Gilford slipped the stethoscope back on, he bent down and placed it gently on Paul's chest. He focused on what he was hearing letting go all his other thoughts. He could almost feel Paul's heart beating. Then, he heard something in-between the beats, about every fourth heart beat. He moved the stethoscope to another spot on Paul's chest and listened again. And then, a third time. As he did this, Paul could feel his own breathing change. This simple process was making him feel very uncomfortable. After all, at the age of thirty-eight, Paul had never really been sick. Sure, there were the colds and an occasional flu bug. But, except for a physical every few years he never had a reason to see the doctor. He kept his weight down, exercised on a regular basis, and ate a well-balanced mostly healthy diet. Paul had developed a lifestyle of calm relaxed living through the study of Yoga and Tai-Chi. However, with this more than careful examination of his heartbeat he was sensing something was going on.

"Umm, so let me tell you Paul, I do hear something I don't like. There appears to be an irregular rhythm to your heart. I've never heard this before in any of your other examinations. I think we should get it checked out with some tests."

Paul heard that and started to feel even more uneasy. He asked nervously, "What kind of tests?"

"To start, how about a resting EKG, an echocardiogram, and a stress test. This will give us some good baseline information. Then, when I see those reports we'll decide if you need more tests."

"What's an irregular heartbeat?"

"Well, as you know, when your heart is beating, it is constantly filling with blood and pumping that blood through your body. Most people don't realize how much work the heart has to do. In your case, something is making your heart sort of pause briefly. It's a very fast pause almost like a hesitation, and then it starts pumping again. This makes the rhythm appear irregular."

"Is it dangerous? Should I take it easy?

"No, I don't think you have to change anything. Of course, I wouldn't go out and run any marathons. Just be aware of how you're feeling and if anything starts telling you something call me. Meanwhile, I'll have my secretary make the referral for you. I'm going to send you to see Dr. Tanner. He's an excellent cardiologist and he specializes in sports medicine. You'll like him."

When he got home his family was waiting for him at the door as soon as they had heard the garage opener cranking the door up and then back down. It was his daughter Jenna that hugged him first. "Daddy, daddy, I missed you."

His son Will squeezed in and said, "Me too, I missed you too daddy." Paul hugged them both, closed his eyes, and for a moment felt truly blessed. A warm feeling came over him as if he realized for the first time the loving treasures he held in his arms. As they wiggled free, he released them. They ran down the hall yelling, "Daddy's home. Daddy's home." And as Paul stood up, he noticed Linda waiting, holding back Nugget, their golden retriever. She hugged Paul and whispered, "How did it go?"

"I'll tell you the details a little later, but it's not something to worry about."

She released him and added, "Go get changed, I'll have dinner ready soon."

He smiled and looked at her affectionately "Sure sweetheart." And as she started to turn away he said, "Hey, honey."

"Yes?" She asked with questioning eyes.

"I love you."

Hearing those words made her smile, "I love you too Paul."

"And you too Nugget" he said, bending down to pet the ever happy golden retriever.

Paul went upstairs to change and while halfway up, he tried to listen to his own heart. It was a new hobby for him. Whenever he exerted himself, Paul would focus on what his heart was doing. And as usual, his heart sounded to him as strong and regular as usual. Come on Paul, he thought. You just have to shake this thing off; you'll get it checked out. All of this reminded him of what had happened to his own father. Paul's dad had died of a heart attack at age fifty-five, an unexpected heart attack. He smiled thinking, that's such a silly term, are they ever expected? He looked at the few items of mail on the dresser and was happy to see his runner's magazine. He figured at least he could read about running; that is, until this medical thing was over.

The kids were sitting at their usual chairs around the dinner table as he sat down. They held hands and Paul spoke, "Oh Lord, please bless this food we are about to eat. May we come to appreciate the many gifts we have received. Amen."

"Amen" Linda and the kids echoed.

Paul passed the serving plates around as Linda helped Will with his. Will was the youngest; he had just enjoyed his fifth birthday. He was a happy little boy who had a way of finding joy in everything he did. Linda had marveled at this child ever since he was born and Paul thought the world of him too. She would often say in amazement, "Paul, that boy has a special way of finding a pony in the manure no matter what, he's a blessing that one." Paul had always wanted a son and William, named after his own Grandfather, filled that wish wonderfully. They loved everything about Jenna too; she was nine and very much a little doll. They had found the name Jenna searching through some books of names and fell in love with the name, as soon as they had found it. Jenna means *pure of heart* and they often said it fit her perfectly.

"Daddy," Jenna started.

"Yes, sweetie?"

"After supper, can you look at my artwork from Camp? I made it for you."

"Yes, I would like that."

"Daddy," Will asked. "How about my favorite story, can you read it at bedtime?"

"Sure Will, I can read your story. The one called, *Bears in the Night?*"

"Yes, that's the one. Thanks daddy."

It didn't take long for Dr. Gilford's secretary to make the referral to the cardiologist. Paul had the appointment for his tests, the following week on Wednesday. A few days went by without another sensation; actually it was Sunday morning when he felt another slight tug. They were attending church services and he was sitting there in the pew between his two children during the sermon when it happened again. Paul found himself closing his eyes and praying that the heart trouble he was experiencing would turn out to be a minor inconvenience and nothing more. Jenna must have felt something because she squeezed her father's hand tighter and Paul gave her a loving smile in return.

After church service, they went for a visit with Paul's mother who lived in a senior citizen complex in the harbor town of Oyster Bay on Long Island. It was an upscale community setting that offered beautiful surroundings with all the amenities one would look for at any age. There was a golf course, an indoor pool, clubhouse, tennis courts, a weight room with a total exercise facility, and as many parties as one wished to attend. His mother thrived there and even though

Paul's father had died suddenly, she found a way to adjust and refocus whatever time she had left. That's what she would tell Paul, You can't live in the past you know. Life is what you make it . . . and I choose to make mine happy. She was especially happy when Paul and his family paid her a visit. It made her feel so alive whenever the grandchildren were with her. Linda recognized some of Paul's traits in the way his mother lived her life. She was robust and cheerful, with a wonderful sense of humor. She was simply a delight to be around and it was the same way with Paul. Whenever she recognized these things, she figured she knew where it was that Paul inherited those positive attributes. Linda counted her blessings as well, two special children and a man everyone envied. She too enjoyed a very happy life.

While helping his mom in the kitchen, Paul took advantage of the moment.

"Mom," he started wiping dry the last of the dishes. "I had a visit with Dr. Gilford."

"How is that old crow doing these days?"

"He's fine, but I have a little problem with my heart." As he said that, he noticed the happy smile fell off her face and he wanted to reassure her right away. "Nothing to worry much about, Mom. It's a little irregular heartbeat that's all."

"You mean, it happened all of a sudden like?"

"Yes, I never had anything like that before."

She felt a bit lightheaded and reached for a kitchen chair for balance. She said sadly, "You know I can't help but think of your father, his heart trouble was sudden too."

He stepped closer to his mother and told her, "It's a simple thing mom, they just restart my heart and the beat gets corrected."

"Restart your heart? My, how do they do that?"

"A small electric shock that's all."

"A shock Paul? Is that painful?"

"No, there's no pain because they put you to sleep, just like during an operation."

"When will this be happening?"

"Dr. Gilford wants me to see a cardiologist and have some tests, then we'll see."

She put her arms out to hold Paul as she explained, "Paul, you and your brother, you're all I have left."

"I know mom, but don't worry, this is nothing, really."

Before they knew it, next Wednesday rolled around and it was time for Paul's appointment with the cardiologist. Linda asked if he wanted company and Paul felt he could use the support. He made sure she didn't mind waiting around during the testing and she said she would feel more comfortable waiting in the doctor's office than at home. So, they went together. Linda drove her white Range Rover giving Paul a chance to relax.

His visit started off with a three-page questionnaire including his overall health status and family medical history. Paul checked off just about every no box on the form. What got his attention and stopped him cold was the question; does anyone in your immediate family have heart disease? He stared through the papers at the memory of his father being lowered into his grave. I'd say, he thought with a little anger, when your father is fifty-five and taken away by a sudden heart attack, yes sir, that qualifies as heart disease in your immediate family.

About fifteen minutes later, Paul watched an elderly man; using a cane for balance, take slow steps over to the reception desk. He leaned toward Linda and whispered, "Oh boy, first you find out you have heart trouble and then you look like that." She just smiled and placed her hand on his.

At the same time he was thinking about that old man, a nurse came out and called his name, "Mr. Simms? The doctor will see you now." As soon as he stood up, Paul wished he had a cane to help him feel more balanced. Steady now. You can do this, he said to himself trying to rescue the moment. The nurse led him into a small exam room and told him he could take off his shirt and sit on the examining table. While he sat there he had an eerie sense of how quiet the place was. The nurse came back in and proceeded to check his blood pressure. She asked him to step on the scale while she measured his height and weight. Then she started to collect some items placing each on a sterile drape she had placed next to him.

"We have to do some blood tests Mr. Simms. This will only take a minute; you'll feel a little stick." There wasn't much of a reaction as Paul watched the nurse go through her motions and then there was his bright red blood filling a tube and then another. Soon after, the nurse opened the door and before leaving said, "The doctor will be in shortly." Occasionally, he could make out some talking in a distant room. Then there was silence and as he recognized the quiet, the door to the exam room opened and there was Doctor Tanner chart in hand.

"Hello Mr. Simms, my name is Doctor Tanner. Do you mind if I call you Paul?"

"Sure, no problem."

"So, Dr. Gilford referred you. He sent a note saying you're athletic and generally in excellent health. So, what's the problem Paul?"

"A couple of weeks ago, I sensed a feeling in my chest, here by my heart. It was like a tug inside. In shows up sudden like and then disappears."

"Do you feel dizzy when it happens?"

"No."

"How about medications, are you taking anything?"

"No."

"What about sports."

"I'm a runner, but no, it never happens then."

"The note from Dr. Gilford explains that during a physical examination he detected an irregular heart rhythm."

Yes, that is what he explained to me and the reason I'm here."

"How about I listen too?"

"Sure."

Dr. Tanner placed his stethoscope in his ears and listened in to Paul's heart sounds. After a few minutes he continued, "Well all right, let's start you off with a resting EKG, then, we'll work up an echocardiogram, and finish with the stress test. Do you have any questions before we start?"

"No, but maybe I will later on."

"Very well, I'll tell the tech to bring in the EKG machine. It'll just be a minute."

About two hours later, all the tests were completed and Paul and Linda Simms were waiting in Dr. Tanner's office for the results. Dr. Tanner was not tall and he didn't have a big frame, but he had a way about him that left you feeling confident in him. It was as if he had an aura of great healing surrounding him; maybe it was his walk or the soft comforting way he spoke. Paul felt it the very first moment he met Dr. Tanner; an incredible feeling of trust and confidence in a small package. Then, the waiting was over and in walked Dr. Tanner. He had Paul's ever thickening medical chart in his hands open to the EKG printouts as he sat down behind his mahogany desk opposite Paul. It's funny Paul thought, the waiting seems to make my heart flutter more than a fast paced walk on the treadmill. How stressful is this? Dr. Tanner looked up from the medical chart, took off his reading classes and commenced his explanation.

"The good news is there doesn't seem to be any blockages, nothing showed up in the imaging. The echogram showed your heart function is normal; your heart valves have no visual defects. Now, usually, when we compare a person's resting EKG, when the heart is functioning without a workload, to the stress test EKG, which is when the heart is working hard, we are able to detect problems. In your case, when your heart is working hard, the way it was on the treadmill, your cardio-rhythm was excellent. The bad news isn't so bad, it is pretty much what we expected. In the resting EKG, when your heart is beating without any workload, there is a very slight disturbance, a sort of hiccup to your heart's rhythm. The EKG printout here shows it occurs about every four beats, not always every four, but just about."

"What causes that to happen?" Paul asked hoping for a simple enough reason.

"Well frankly, we don't know. Some people have these sorts of problems from the time they are born and they don't show up until years later. In other cases, a life event will create the problem."

"Is Paul's case serious, I mean life-threatening?" As she asked that, Linda's right hand tightened into a fist.

"Well, no, it's not like a major defect in a heart valve or a blockage in an artery."

"Can it be fixed?" Paul asked feeling his breathing increase.

"Yes, there is a procedure we use in cases like yours. It's called electrical cardioversion."

"That's what Dr. Gilford had mentioned, cardioversion? Up until then, I've never heard of it."

"Yes, it doesn't usually make the headlines. Except, back in 2003, England's Prime Minister Tony Blair had the procedure to correct fluttering of the heart. His medical problem is called superventricular tachycardia or SVT for short. These types of medical problems involve the electrical activity of the heart. However, in your case, your heart's not fluttering it's skipping."

Linda asked, "Did Tony Blair have the cardioversion?"

"Actually, yes, he did."

"How does it work Dr. Tanner?" Paul inquired moving forward on his seat.

"Cardioversion is a rather simple procedure where we, under general anesthesia, use a defibrillator to restart the heart's cardio-rhythm. Kind of shock the heart into a different rhythm."

"What about risk? Is there a risk involved for Paul?"

"It's referred to as a low risk procedure, but there is always a risk whenever general anesthesia is used and in rare cases the cardioversion causes the heart to stop beating. There are occasions when the heart goes into cardiac arrest from the shock and we are unable to restore a normal rhythm. The number we use is approximately one point five percent chance of mortality."

"What is your experience?"

"I do about one hundred cases a year . . . and experience about ninety-five percent success rate."

Is there a chance of my dying during the procedure?"

"You're as healthy as an ox with just a little irregular heartbeat. I don't see any problem."

He sat back and asked the question that's been on his mind the most. "What if I don't do anything?"

"In your case Paul, there are no guarantees. We can't tell you that you will not have a cardiac event and we can't tell you, you will. I can only make a recommendation and that would be to arrange for the cardioversion procedure as soon as you can to protect yourself and your family."

"I don't know Dr. Tanner, the idea of purposely shocking my heart sounds sort of creepy. I'm not at all comfortable with the idea. Let me read up on it, do some research on the Web and talk things over with my wife."

"Very well, Mr. Simms, if you have any questions or if you want to discuss the procedure please do call my office."

"Thank you doctor."

Paul decided not to go directly home, and instead asked Linda to take a walk with him over to the Sayville docks. He loved the water and knowing that it always had a calming influence, he thought it would be a wise place to take a stroll. On the way they stopped for some coffee on Main Street and headed over to the parking area near Land's End. They had lived in Sayville for the last twelve years. Sayville was once a thriving shell fishing community, supplying fresh shellfish to New York City and the rest of Long Island. They had purchased an old turn of the century Victorian home and restored much of its original character and its charm. The rear of the house faced south off the water's edge and they had spent many summer evenings on their deck sipping wine looking out at the Great South Bay. Some would say they lived the American Dream. Paul owned his own successful accounting firm, Linda was an elementary school teacher, and they had Will and Jenna, two beautiful healthy children. They also enjoyed Nugget, their lovable golden retriever.

Except, now Paul was thinking of his own mortality and what would happen to his family if things went bad for him. "Paul," Linda started, "why don't we talk about what Dr. Tanner discussed?"

"What? You think I should go ahead with the cardioversion?"

"What choice is there? You can't live the rest of your life like you have a time bomb ticking inside your chest."

"No, but what about the downside? There is a chance that . . . ."

She interrupted him mid-stream, "But what Paul? How can you not have this procedure and make sure you're with us years from now?

Paul took Linda's hand in his and explained, "You know how I am, I need to research this. To learn more about the pros and cons."

Linda took a deep breath, sighed and offered her thoughts. "But Paul, this is not very complicated. And the doctor already explained the procedure is not very risky, if at all."

As she turned to embrace him, Paul noticed a large seagull gliding gracefully in the air above the water. He let his breathing slow and allowed his mind to clear. They stood there for a while locked in each other's arms feeling the warmth of the sun. Then, Paul decided, "All right, I'll call Dr. Tanner and set it up. And I'll arrange for a couple of days off at the office." They walked back to the car holding hands with a peaceful quiet.

Almost a week later, Paul was sitting in the conference room next to his business partner, Roy Wilkins while their dozen or so employees found seats for the impromptu meeting. "Thank you all for joining us on such short notice," he started looking into the familiar faces around the room. "This will be a brief get together. I just wanted to explain a few things before any rumors were invented." There was some whispering in the back of the room and a few employees around the table exchanged surprised looks. "There is some minor news to share that's all. I'll be taking some time off next week for a little medical procedure and while I'm gone Roy here will be running the show."

"What's happening?" one of the accountants asked.

"I am having a procedure to help my heart return to its normal function."

"Is it surgery?" one of the secretaries asked.

"No Sally, it's not surgery. I have been experiencing a skip in my heartbeat and they plan on using a little electric shock to restart my heart. It's not serious at all. And I'll only be away from the office for a few days."

"Paul," one worker asked, "You're always so healthy, when did this happen?"

"Well Steve, the cardiologist told me I may have always had the problem but they can't really explain what triggered it now."

One of the computer experts yelled out, "Anything we can do boss to help, you let us know and we'll take care of it."

There was a chorus of responses like that one. The employees as a group liked Paul Simms, some would even go as far as to say they loved him as a boss. He was considered by most to be extremely fair, kind, and compassionate; always asking about their loved ones at home and about their personal interests. While he ran a tight ship, the atmosphere in the office was relaxed and highly productive. This news about his heart condition surprised them and they were genuinely concerned for him and his family. "Well, thank you," he responded, "I knew I could count on all of you for your support. That's it then, we'll keep you posted." As he turned to speak with Roy, the room slowly emptied with an occasional friendly backslap and a word of encouragement.

Marybeth, his secretary since he opened the company walked over. "Paul, please tell Linda if she needs anything, or any help at all, she should call me."

Paul smiled and told her, "Thanks Marybeth, I'll let her know."

At home the night before his procedure, Paul tucked William into bed and read *Bears Into the Night* to him until he fell asleep. He looked in on Jenna, gently kissed her forehead, and pulled the covers to her chin. He lingered there for a moment, looking at the angelic, peaceful expression she wore on her face. Closing the door he went downstairs to spend time with Linda. They sat curled up on the couch with soft jazz playing in the background. Linda sipped a chardonnay while Paul did his best to forget the next day's agenda. He still had reservations about the cardioversion procedure, but kept them to himself. He closed his eyes and put himself on a beach with the sounds of the waves rolling onto the shore mimicking the waves of thoughts in his mind. Soon after they retired to bed and to Paul's surprise he fell off to sleep without trouble.

"Mr. Simms, Mr. Simms, you're all done. You can open your eyes now."

"Where am I?" he moaned.

"You're in recovery Mr. Simms." The nurse said waking him gently. "The procedure is completed and Dr. Tanner went to speak with your wife. Can you sit up a little for me now? That's it, very good. You rest now and I'll check back in a few minutes."

Paul looked around the large room noticing a number of other patients among the busyness of the room. He felt groggy, as if caught between not completely awake or completely asleep. He knew he had been under general anesthesia, but he was aware of a noticeable soreness in his chest as if he had been whacked with a baseball bat. Oh yeah, I can't wait to feel this after the anesthesia and painkillers wear off, he thought sarcastically. Soon after, he realized he must have dosed off because as he awoke he found Linda standing at his bedside. She kissed him hello and took his hand in hers.

"You're okay Paul, the doctor told me everything went well. How are you feeling?"

"I feel awful," he barked, "How the hell do you think I feel?" Hearing him snap at her like that made her take a step back and reflexively release his hand. Hearing Paul speak so sharply to his wife, the nurse came over and whispered to Linda,

"Don't worry, the anesthesia can do that. It'll wear off in a few hours."

"Thanks," Linda responded. "I wasn't expecting him to be so grumpy."

A couple of hours later, after the hospital's discharge procedures were completed, Paul was being pushed in a wheelchair to the sliding doorway and Linda's Range Rover parked nearby. As the attendant helped Paul out of the wheelchair and into the backseat Paul shouted, "Ouch, watch out for my head you idiot!"

"Of course Mr. Simms," the attendant remarked, visibly shaken as he closed the door.

"I'm so sorry for his bad temper," Linda told him.

"What's irking him?" the attendant said turning to leave in a huff.

Linda slid behind the wheel and started the engine. She looked in the mirror to check Paul and found him starring out the window. She noticed dark uneven shadows surrounding his facial features as if he had a scowl on his face. "Okay Paul, we're on our way home, let me know if you need anything." She checked the mirror again and he hadn't moved ignoring her homebound comment.

They sat quietly during the ride back home to Sayville. Linda pulled the Rover into the driveway and walked around to help Paul. She opened the door and extended her hand. To her surprise he whacked it away and snapped, "I don't need a hand, I'm no cripple."

"I know Paul," she said feeling the hurt on her hand and her heart. Paul found his way into the house and there was Nugget excited with her tail wagging as usual. He kicked the dog to the side and growled,

"Get out of my way you stupid mutt." Nugget whimpered and hid beneath the hall table. Linda watched the incident in disbelief. What's gotten in to him, she wondered? Paul grabbed onto the banister and dragged himself hand over hand up the stairs and over to the bedroom to lie down. Linda couldn't decide should I leave him alone or offer to help him? The way he was acting, she didn't know what to do. As she was contemplating what to do, the phone rang and it was Paul's brother checking on him.

"Hello Linda, so how did it go?

"Hi Jonathan, it went well. And everyone at the hospital was terrific." As Linda told him that she couldn't help feel maybe she should warn Jonathan about his brother's foul mood.

"Did he survive the shock?"

"I think so?"

"You think so? Can't you tell?" Jonathan said with a little laugh.

"Well, it's just . . . I think he's in a lot of pain?"

"So, can I say hi?"

"Let me check if he's sleeping."

"Sure, thanks Linda."

"I think he could use some cheering up, I'll just be a minute."

Linda took the portable phone with her and walked upstairs hesitating outside the bedroom for a few seconds before opening the door. Paul was lying on his side and she couldn't tell if he was sleeping or not, so she leaned over him and softly spoke his name.

"Paul? Paul, are you awake?"

"What do you want?" he shouted opening his eyes and lifting his head off the pillow. "Don't you know I need to rest?"

She was startled, like a deer in headlights, until she found her voice. "I'm sorry Paul, it's your brother on the phone. I didn't mean to . . ."

He grabbed the phone from her hand interrupting her in mid-sentence. "Yeah, well just give me the phone and leave me alone."

She backed out of the room as if on tiptoes not wanting to upset him anymore that he already was. My goodness, she thought, it must be the pain. I better check with the doctor about some pain pills. As Linda closed the bedroom door she could hear Paul speak to his brother on the phone.

"And what do you want this time shithead?"

"What do you mean I shouldn't speak that way to her? She's my goddamn fucking wife and I can talk anyway I want to her. Yeah, well, you go to hell!" Then, standing on the other side of the door, she reflexively ducked down as the portable phone hit the door. Paul yelled her way, "If you want to eavesdrop on somebody, go eavesdrop on your mother."

Linda moved away from the door and went downstairs to her purse. She nervously grabbed for her cell phone and found the cardiologist's card. She quickly dialed the number and decided to step outside the house.

"Doctor's Office," the receptionist answered.

"Hello, my name is Linda Simms and my husband had a procedure today and I need to speak about something with Dr. Tanner. Is he in?"

"Well Mrs. Simms, he is seeing patients now."

"I know, but it's real important, something's happening and I need to talk with him now."

"Is it an emergency?"

"It is to me, please can you just ask him?"

"Hold on a moment and I'll see if he can pick up."

Linda's eyes were nervously darting all over the front yard and the gates on the side. She had never seen Paul behave this way and it had her frightened.

"Hello, this is Dr. Tanner."

"Oh, thank you for taking the call Dr. Tanner, I really need to talk with you."

"Is everything all right Mrs. Simms?"

"I think Paul needs some pain pills doctor."

"Pain pills? Is Paul in pain?

"He is very upset."

"Usually, just Tylenol takes care of the discomfort."

"Oh, I think he needs more than Tylenol doctor. He's yelling at everyone, and I mean everyone and everything. He is being very, very, grouchy."

"Umm, that's usual. I suppose I can call in a prescription to your pharmacy. I'll put my girl on and she'll take down the information. Does he complain about the way he's feeling?"

"No, not really, just about everyone around him though."

"Okay, give the drugstore a call in about fifteen minutes before you head over, that should be enough time. Listen, the pain pills are strong and will most likely make him sleepy, so, no driving while he's taking them, okay? And let me know if things don't get better."

"Yes I will, thanks again Dr. Tanner." As she disconnected the call, the idea of Paul sleeping for a while popped into her mind. Now, that wouldn't be a bad idea, really.

Upstairs, Paul was tossing and turning making a mess of the covers and without knowing it, a mess with everyone around him. He couldn't sleep and he was starting to feel more and more restless. As the burning sensation on his chest drew his attention he stood up and went over to the mirror unbuttoning his shirt, his eyes opened wide in amazement. What the hell, he thought starring at the large red burn over his heart, now look at that will you. Somebody's going to pay for that, oh yes; there'll be hell to pay for that. There was a light knock on the door and Paul shouted,

"This better be damn good, I really want to be left alone."

"Paul, sorry to bother you." Linda said opening the door only a crack. "I'm going to run to the drug store for pain pills. Dr. Tanner is calling in a prescription."

"Who said I need pain pills? I only need something for the pain in the necks who keep interrupting me. I need my rest damn it."

"Okay Paul, you rest, I'll be back as soon as I can." As she stepped away, the telephone rang and Linda rushed to pick up the portable phone still on the bedroom floor. She closed the door to the bedroom answering the phone on the way down the stairs.

"Hello . . ."

"Hi Linda sweetheart." Paul's mother answered in her usual chipper way.

"Oh, hello Mary."

"Linda is Paul awake? I won't want to bother him if he's sleeping."

"Paul is awake, but he must be in some pain because he doesn't seem like himself."

"Do you think he'd rather not talk? I can call back another time."

"Oh, I'm sure he'll want to say hi, just keep in mind that he's experiencing some discomfort."

"What about pain medication my dear, didn't the doctor take care of that?"

"Yes, the doctor gave him a prescription for pain, actually, I'm on my way to the drug store now. Hold on a minute and I'll bring the phone up to Paul."

"Thanks Linda, you're a dream."

As she stood at the door she swallowed hard, then knocked once and entered the bedroom.

"Paul, it's your mother. She called to see how you're doing."

"I don't want to talk with her now," he snapped. "Can't you just say I'm sleeping?"

"Too late Paul, now you say hello and be nice."

"Oh, I'll be nice," He responded obviously toying with her. Then he yelled, "Just give me the phone and give me some privacy, will you!"

Linda handed the phone to Paul and left quietly. She lingered briefly on the other side of the bedroom door. He took the phone in both hands and looked up at the heavens before greeting his mother.

"Hello mother, how are you?"

"I'm fine Paul, but how are you?"

"Considering what I've been through, I guess you could say I'm terrific."

His mother heard more sarcasm in her son's voice than she was used to. "You sound upset Paul, did it not go well?"

"Well? Yes, it went well and I'm not upset at all." His voice cracked and his tone changed as he angrily continued, "I'm just pissed off that everyone is treating me like a baby and I'm no baby."

"Paul? I know you're not a baby, but you don't have to raise your voice to me." Surprised by the manner in which her son spoke to her, she stood and felt hurt by Paul's lack of respect.

"Well Mother, this is the new me and if you don't like it, don't bother calling here anymore. How about that?"

"Paul, I didn't raise you to be so disrespectful. What has come over you?"

The only answer Paul gave her was the click of a disconnect and then silence as he hung up the phone. Linda ran off shaking her head in disbelief, she had never heard Paul speak to his mother that way. Paul's mother sat back down looking into the phone for answers. Paul smiled and mumbled out loud, "It's about time someone put that old biddy in her place."

Linda handed the prescription to the pharmacist and asked, "How long will that take, I'm in a hurry?"

"Not long, give me ten minutes."

"Oh, thank you, you're so kind."

"My pleasure Mrs. Simms. Oh, I see this medication is for your husband, is he all right?"

"Yes, he just had a little medical procedure, that's all."

"Well, you give him my regards Mrs. Simms, he's such a nice man."

Nice man? She thought, it seems that's more in the past tense. You mean more like, Yes, Paul used to be such a nice man. That is until; he had his cardioversion procedure. Oh my god, could it be?

While standing on the cashier's line at the pharmacy a sudden scary thought entered Linda's mind, the thought made her feel panicky. She looked at her watch confirming her fears; the kids would be home from camp soon and what about the mood Paul is in. Oh god, no, I better get home. In a panic she bolted leaving the Cashier holding her change, ignoring the Cashier's voice calling after her.

When Linda pulled into the driveway, her heart was racing. She couldn't gather her things fast enough. As she opened the front door there on the hallway table were the children's camp backpacks. "Jenna? Will?" She shouted and nothing, no answer. Linda ran up the stairs to the bedroom as fast as she could and there outside in the hall sitting on the floor next to the door was Will sniffling.

"Will, are you okay?" While asking that question, Linda was doing everything to hold back her emotions.

"Daddy, called my book *Bears In the Night* stupid mommy, why did he say that? I love that book, he's a mean daddy."

"Oh Will," she started, "I'm sure daddy didn't mean to say that. You know he's not feeling well."

"Is he sick?"

"Yes, he is sick and I have some medicine to make him feel better. Will, where is Jenna?"

"After daddy yelled at me, he yelled at her too and then we just ran out. I think she's in her room."

"Okay, you sit here and I'll go check on Jenna."

Linda walked over to Jenna's bedroom door and knocked a few times before entering. There on the bed was Jenna crying clutching her pillow around her head. Linda sat on the edge of the bed and placed a gentle hand on her shoulder.

"Jenna honey, what happened?"

"Daddy yelled at Will about his favorite book and then when I showed him my painting he tore it in half and called me dumb. He told me I better do better or else. Or else what Mommy? He scared me."

"Jenna, I told Will that Daddy is not feeling very well right now. I'm sure he didn't mean to make you cry."

"I think daddy hit his head or something because he's not the same daddy he was yesterday. I want my old daddy back." Jenna started to sob holding a tissue to her runny nose.

Linda took her into her arms. "Come on Jen, let's get Will and go downstairs to have some hot chocolate. Then, I'll give daddy his medicine."

The whistle of the kettle signaled it was time for hot chocolate as Linda filled the cups with hot water. She handed the can of whipped cream to Jenna first and reminded them, "Be careful of the hot water, we don't want any burnt tongues." Jenna pointed the can and giggled when the whipped cream spiraled into her cup. Licking her fingers, she handed the can to Will. "Your turn Will," she said while she spooned the whipped cream and hot chocolate into her mouth. Will pressed the spout and watched the whipped cream mostly miss his cup dripping down the side and leaving a pile on the table. He looked up at his mom thinking he would be scolded, but Linda just laughed with them instead. Then, seeing the children enjoying themselves she figured they could be left alone for a little. It was time for her to face the ogre in the bedroom. "Okay guys, you enjoy the hot chocolates, I'm going to go upstairs and give daddy his medicine. I'll be down soon."

Linda took a glass of water and the painkillers up to see Paul. She had already decided not to confront Paul about the situation with the children. Instead, she decided to ride out this painful mood thing he was going through. After all, she had reasoned with herself, there would be time to review that little experience. Linda knocked and as she opened the door was very surprised to find Paul sitting in the chair with his hands over his face sobbing. "Paul, it's okay, I have your medicine.

Here take these two and here's some water." Even more of a surprise to her, instead of arguing or yelling he just took the pills and sipped the water without a hint of the expected resistance. Linda said, "You should rest now Paul. The doctor said that the pills would make you sleepy so, come on, into the bed and up go the covers. Good! Anything else I can get for you?" Paul just rolled over and closed his eyes. He was exhausted.

The next morning, Linda prepared a breakfast of cereal, toast, and juice for the kids. She hurried them along to dress and out the door to the camp's bus stop. Linda feigned the need to rush; she didn't want their father who was sleeping upstairs to yell at them again, that's all. Five minutes after the children were out the door Paul walked into the kitchen dressed in a suit and tie ready for work. Taken by surprise Linda asked, "Paul, do you think you're well enough to go to work already?" He nodded as he poured himself some juice. Nugget had been lying on the cool kitchen floor by the cabinets and when Paul walked in, the dog stood with his back up and a menacing growl escaped through her showing teeth. Paul had no reaction; he placed the glass in the sink, grabbed his briefcase from the kitchen desk and walked out of the house car keys in hand. Linda's eyes had darted between Paul pouring the juice, the growling golden retriever, and the closing door as Paul silently departed. Reflexively, she scratched her head and wondered out loud, "Now, what was that about?" And no kiss goodbye or a cheery have a great day. That was not like the Paul she knew. Then she recalled her daughter's comment from last night, I want my old daddy back! And she added, I want my old husband back too.

It didn't take long for Paul to get angry again, cruising along in his corvette on the Southern State Parkway, a driver of a BMW cut him off and that triggered a response in Paul. He reflexively downshifted and over-accelerated bringing the engine close to red lining. As he came along side the BMW, the driver swerved cutting the wheel to the right and exiting off the Parkway before Paul could even say a word. Paul was livid and wanted to get even with someone, but whom? As he scanned the road ahead of him, he moved his car forward within a foot of the car in front. Serves him right, Paul thought. If you're going to go slow this is what happens. The driver must have heard Paul's anger because he switched on his signal and moved to the right lane freeing Paul to hit the accelerator and zoom ahead. He swerved right and left, shifting and maneuvering his corvette around the cars in front of him, as if he needed to arrive at work in record time. As he exited at Route 110 North, he left a trail of upset drivers giving him obscene gestures and cursing him down the road. Paul just laughed and continued along his path like some cartoon villain.

Paul was still laughing as he entered his firm's office building. He ignored the well wishes of the receptionist, Helen and his secretary, Marybeth as he hustled to his desk. Within a few minutes his buzzer went off and as he picked up the receiver, he questioned the call in a troubled voice,

"What? What do you want now Helen?"

"Oh, sorry Mr. Simms, sorry to interrupt you."

"Yes, you interrupted me. So, what is it?" he snapped.

"Mr. Cooperman is on line two, he's asking about his company's quarterly taxes and why they're so high? No one else is here; I thought you would want to take it." As Helen said that she swallowed hard, feeling the pressure.

Paul snarled, "Well, all right, but whose account is it anyway?"

"Amy," she responded in a timid voice. "It's Amy's account, sir."

"I see, well she'll get hers," he responded angrily. "For now, tell Marybeth to get the file and bring it in right away. Do you understand that Helen?"

She paused not knowing how to respond to his demeaning tone. So Helen just surrendered, "Yes sir, right away."

As he disconnected the call, a smile grew on his face as if he was pleased to have rattled another person.

Then, as he glanced at the blinking light of the line on hold he thought, m *aybe* I should just keep you waiting eh? You fat tub. Changing his mind he pressed the extension button and answered the call sarcastically.

"Mr. Cooperman, now what is it that you want?"

"Hi there Paul. Long time no see, how is everything? Oh, and how is that cute little missis of yours?"

"Listen you asshole, you can stop the make believe shit as far as I'm concerned and you can leave my wife alone. What business is it of yours anyway?"

As Paul looked up there was his secretary, Marybeth, staring at him in disbelief at what she was hearing. She wondered, Well I never, first he ignores us as if we didn't know him for years. Then, he makes sweet Helen cry and now, he's being so mean to a client? He was always so polite and pleasant to everyone. Jesus, Joseph and Mary, what is he, some sort of Jekyll and Hyde? I wonder what's gotten into him? Looking back at the phone Paul continued,

"Oh, shut up . . . and I don't care if you take your business somewhere else, you're a pain in the ass anyway. Fine, yeah, yeah, yeah . . ." He didn't wait for Mr. Cooperman to finish his sentence, as Paul hung up the phone he said to Marybeth, "Don't bother saying anything and when Amy gets around to showing up, tell her I want to see her now, not yesterday." He looked up with such a menacing look on his face he actually made Marybeth feel frightened and he added with a snarl, "Is that understood?"

"Yes, sir." And she left nervously shaking her head.

An hour later Paul's business partner Roy Wilkins found Amy crying as she was placing her personal things in a small cardboard box.

"Amy", he started, "What is it? What's going on?"

She plopped down on the chair and blowing her nose looked at her hands and pleaded, "What did I do? I had an appointment this morning and had been excused. And just because he's in a particularly bad mood, I don't see why I should be fired like that, as if I was a crook."

"You're not a crook Amy, I'm sure Paul thinks he's doing the right thing. Look, I'll speak to him, you just go home and I'll call you later this afternoon."

"Thank you Roy, but I don't think it'll do any good, he sounded serious enough."

"We'll see Amy, just go home and try to rest."

As Roy Wilkins was on his way to speak with Paul about Amy, Marybeth asked him if he had a minute.

"Well, Marybeth, I don't have a lot of time. Is it important?"

"I'd say so, it's about Mr. Simms. He's acting a little strange since he came back."

"Strange? I know he's a little grouchy, but after all, he rushed back to work after his medical procedure."

"Well, I heard him yelling at the receptionist and he's been unusually mean to me. And he called Mr. Cooperman an asshole and told him he didn't care if he took his business somewhere else. Doesn't sound like he's much in control now does it dear."

"I was on my way to speak with him, let me see if I can help."

"Thanks Roy. After you speak with him, let me know what you think, okay?"

"Sure Marybeth."

Roy Wilkins politely knocked once and walked into Paul's office. He found him sitting hunched over staring out the window. Roy closed the door behind him and pulled a chair up next to Paul.

"Listen, I want to talk with you about the way you've been treating everyone since you came back." Seeing no reaction Roy continued, "I mean firing a good employee, making Helen cry, being downright mean to Marybeth, and then telling a longtime client he's an asshole. What is going on Paul? Hey Paul? Can you hear me?"

He sat there in that same position without flinching, no response to what Roy had told him. It was as if he was in a trance. Roy was totally unsure of what to say and what do to. He sat there looking at Paul as if in doing that he could wake him.

He stood up and walked over to him. He gently placed a hand on his shoulder. "Perhaps you should be home resting . . ." Without warning, Paul shoved him to the wall knocking over some of the items on the shelves as he sunk to the floor. Paul looked down at Roy spitefully and yelled at the top of his lungs,

"Don't you put your hands on me you piece of shit. I'm Paul Simms and I own this company. You would be nothing without me, don't you forget it!"

"What has come over you?" he asked, as he pulled himself off the floor.

"Maybe your doctor needs to give you some medicine to help with these outbursts?"

Paul stood there in disgust and yelled back. "What outbursts? And nothing has come over me, just get out of my way and leave me alone you shit."

Rushing, Paul brushed past his business partner causing him to knock into the desk. Without looking back, he slammed the door shut. He hustled past his secretary Marybeth ignoring her well wishes. He found his way to his corvette and slid behind the wheel. As he started the engine he pressed his foot to the accelerator revving the engine feeling the power as the car rocked. As he sat behind the wheel a smile grew across his face; then he slammed the clutch down, shifting into reverse. He backed up scraping the side panels of two parked cars and shifted into first gear. As he slammed his foot down on the gas, he released the clutch feeling the power under him. The corvette raced ahead spinning wheels while leaving a rubber trail. The squealing tires signaled his power.

She picked up the phone on the first ring, "Paul? Is that you?"

"No, Linda it's Roy."

"Oh Roy, I'm so sorry. I was hoping to hear Paul."

"You sound worried"

"Well, I am Roy; he left the house this morning without a word. Tell me, was he at the office?"

"Yes he was here, but things didn't go very well. You know Linda, he's acting like a different person since he came back."

"Different, in what way?" As Linda said that, she could only imagine how badly Paul would behave at work.

"It's the way he speaks and the way he treats everyone. It used to be he was friendly and cheerful and he cared about everyone. But now, he's mean, treats everyone like they are worthless. Just this morning, he fired Amy, upset Marybeth, made Helen cry, called a client an asshole, excuse my French, and he physically knocked me out of his way twice"

"To tell you the truth, he hasn't been much better at home. He made the kids cry by saying really mean things to them, yelled at his mother and brother, and he's been very brusque with me too."

Roy hesitated, and then added. "It seems to me that all this started after he had that heart thing?"

"The cardioversion procedure? I know, it seems that way to me too. But the doctor never said anything about mood changes or about a personality shift"

"Can you speak with the doctor Linda? Ask him about this. Maybe he can help? We can't just sit around and let this happen to Paul."

"Yes, actually I'm rushing over to the hospital to speak with the doctor now. His office manager said they could squeeze me in on his lunch break."

"Please let me know what he tells you, we've got to fix this thing."

"I will Roy, and thanks for your support and for caring. You're a good friend."

"Well, you know we love you guys, everyone always envies the life you and Paul have."

"Thanks, I'll let you know what the doctor tells me as soon as I can. Bye for now"

"Bye Linda, and good luck."


Paul had quickly left the parking area of the Huntington Quadrangle swinging his corvette out onto Route 110 heading south to the parkway. He was impatient at every intersection jumping the gun as each traffic light changed from red to green leaving trails of black rubber skid marks behind him. As he neared a small strip of stores on the right, he noticed a man in a suit at the corner waiting to cross the street. There was a leftover puddle from the night's rain at the curb and Paul couldn't resist the temptation. He moved the corvette to the right lane and without warning zoomed through the puddle causing a splash that soaked the man from head to toe. Looking back in his rearview mirror, Paul laughed out loud and banged the steering wheel in excitement at the sight of the man standing there cursing. Just down the road, he spotted the Route 110 Diner and decided to stop for something to eat.

The hostess smiles and asks, "Table for one, sir?"
"What do you think? He responds in a dreary voice.
"Right this way, sir."

While she escorts Paul down the isle, he frowns at everyone looking up at him.

"Here you go." She says, handing him a menu while pointing to a table in the corner.

Paul sat there without opening the menu already knowing what he would order. While he sat in the booth, his mind was busy counting the minutes before the waitress came by.

"So, what' it'll be? She asked, chewing gum at the same time.

"Hey, tell me," he started to ask in a sarcastic voice. "If I order a burger a certain way, am I gonna get it the way I want, or the way the cook wants?"

"I just tell him what the customers want; I don't tell him how to cook. If you tell me, I'll tell him. How's that sound?"

"I'll have a cheeseburger, medium rare, and a side of fries. And will I have to wait forever or what?"

"Would you like something to drink, sir?" she said, ignoring the wise guy reply.

"A chocolate shake now, and if you can remember, a coffee later."

"You got it." She said, starting to walk away ending the conversation.

Paul reached out and grabbed her arm, yanking her back. He looked up at the waitress, and with a menacing voice told her, "You make sure that cook makes the burger the way I want. Is that clear?"

"Yes sir." She responded, trying to pull her arm free. Quickly walking away, she thought, It's just a burger for goodness sakes.

The receptionist buzzed her into the office, "Thank you for taking the time to see me, Dr. Tanner."

"Yes, well my secretary told me you were very upset on the phone and wanted to come in. It's about Paul, she said."

"Something happened to him doctor. And I wanted to discuss it with you. I'm just beside myself with worry."

"What seems to be the problem Mrs. Simms, is Paul still in pain?"

"I'm not sure it's pain. Well yes, at first that seemed to be the logical explanation for the way he was behaving, but now, I'm not so sure."

"What do you mean behaving?"

"Let me ask you this Dr. Tanner, is it possible for someone to have a personality change from the cardioversion?"

"People don't change their personality from a change in their heart rhythm."

"Well that may be, but I'm telling you that since Paul had the procedure, he has had . . . I'm sorry, this is very difficult to put into words." Linda hesitated, feeling the tears fill her eyes.

"Take your time Mrs. Simms." Dr. Tanner told her sympathetically.

"Well, as strange as it sounds, he has had a change of heart."

Dr. Tanner looked deeper at her and added, "I'm not following you Mrs. Simms."

"Since the cardioversion procedure, my husband has become some kind of mean monster. Before the procedure, Paul was a sweet, loving man; and now, he's turned on me and our kids. And he used to adore those kids. He has also yelled at his mother and his brother." Not giving him a chance to interject, Linda continued, "Wait there's more. His business partner told me he's yelled at his workers, fired one, and even told an important client he's an asshole. Does all of this sound normal to you?"

"It sounds to me like he's upset about something, is everything going well with the business? Or, has something happened at home?"

"No, nothing is different, except that since you shocked his heart, he has not been the same man. And I want you to fix him."

"Excuse me?"

"Give him another shock, change him back to the man he was before."

"Mrs. Simms . . . I can't give him another cardioversion procedure based on some whim, or some idea that he's not as nice as he used to be?"

"Why not? You did this to him and now you can undo it."

"I don't think you understand? I need a medical reason to do the procedure."

"Haven't I given you enough of a reason?"

"No, but I can recommend an excellent psychiatrist. Perhaps Paul needs some group therapy or someone to talk to."

"This is hopeless, don't you see? If he doesn't get changed back something bad is going to happen and I don't want it to happen to me or my children. You've got to help him get back to the way he was. What's wrong with you doctors?"

"Please Mrs. Simms, don't leave . . . I can't do anything, you have to understand . . . Mrs. Simms?"

He zoomed from the diner exit turning southbound back onto Rt. 110 weaving around the afternoon traffic. At first, Paul had no idea where he was heading. He was just enjoying the power of his car and the devil within him. He wheeled around the sharp turn of the parkway entrance speeding eastbound, whizzing by unsuspecting drivers. Then, as he neared Bayshore, he had an idea, a notion that this might very well be a good time to select a car and play chicken with the driver. He exited at Fifth Avenue and found his way onto Merrick Road. Paul looked ahead and spotted a silver BMW and in his mind, this was the same driver that had cut him off earlier on his way into the office. Paul thought, now I'll get even. I'll show him who has the nerves and who is the chicken. Paul took the first opportunity and moved across the solid yellow lines separating the oncoming traffic from the eastbound side heading directly for the BMW. Some drivers started honking their horns; some moved to the curb while others looked on with disbelief. Paul felt the exhilaration of a teenager misbehaving out of school, setting his sights on the BMW approaching him. The driver of the BMW was simultaneously talking to his fiancée on his cell phone while tuning in a satellite radio station. The music blasted from the speakers while they discussed their evening dinner plans and where they would meet. If he had been paying attention to the road, he would have seen the approaching corvette closing in.

At that moment, Paul wasn't thinking of what might happen to him. He felt the rush of excitement build as pushed down on the accelerator even more. His corvette zoomed ahead on a definite collision course; Paul mouthing to himself, "Come on, come on, you chicken. I got you now."

While the driver of the silver BMW was telling his fiancée "Of course I love you, you know I do!" Just then, he looked up at the road and seeing the corvette about to crash into him head on, he defensively steered the BMW to the right avoiding the direct hit. Paul's corvette smashed into the BMW's rear fender causing Paul's dream car to spin counter-clockwise across the road slamming into a parked delivery step-van. Paul felt his head smash into the door as the glass shattered and he heard the crumpled sound of fiberglass and metal before he passed out. The steam of the leaking radiator poured out of the crumbled hood giving the accident scene a Hollywood look. Onlookers were stunned at the incredible sight they had witnessed and several wondered out loud what had gotten into that driver's mind.

The siren signaled the ambulance's arrival at Southside Hospital. The paramedics rushed the two patients into the trauma unit of the emergency department. Behind the curtains, there was a commotion of medical experts attending to them. The emergency department's staff was yelling instructions for care punctuated with their new patient's conditions. Then, a trauma nurse yanked the curtain opened and said in desperation, "This one's pressure is dropping!"

While a young doctor replied, "Call cardiovascular, who's on call?"

One of the techs yelled out, "Dr. Tanner's already on his way. He said to prepare the crash cart."

A nurse injected, "The cart's ready, let's get a fast track on his bloods, stat."

The patient's eyes were trying to focus, but all he could see was the bright lights above and the confusion of a thousand voices and a thousand hands.

"Anyone know his name?" Dr Tanner asked as he slipped on his protective gloves.

One of the techs replied, "They're trying to contact his family now."

The trauma nurse yelled out, I think we're loosing him, pressure's down to 80 palp."

The young doctor pleaded, "Let's get some Atropine going and I want 60 cc's of D5W."

"His name?" Dr. Tanner wanted to know. "If it's not too much to ask? What's his name for Christ sakes?" Then suddenly, the monitor screamed a steady tone as the flat line appeared on the screen. Dr. Tanner mechanically picked up the paddles, set the charge and heard the machine start its familiar charging sound.

"Doctor?" The trauma nurse wanted to know. What are you waiting for?"

The clerk yelled over from the desk, "His name is Paul Simms doc, and the guy's wife is on her way." As he heard the name, Dr. Tanner turned and was able to see through the bruised and bloodied face of the victim. *Oh, my god . . . it is Paul Simms.*

"If you're not going to do it, move out of the way." The young doctor pleaded, "we don't have much time, do it now."

Dr. Tanner yelled out, "Clear," and thought, this one's for Linda and your kids Paul. As he placed the paddles on his chest, the spike went through Paul's chest to his heart causing his body to rise. Everyone's eyes went to the monitor as the flat line bleep continued. Dr. Tanner added, "Increase the joules and recharge." Dr. Tanner's eyes followed the nurse's hands at the defibrillator. Dr. Tanner warned once again. "Clear!" A second charge invaded Paul's chest, giving his heart a strong shock. The flat line bleep on the monitor switched to a slow but steady beep as the emergency staff recognized the sound. Dr. Tanner feeling relieved added, "Okay, let's inject 30 cc's of Epinephrine, push more Saline into this guy, and sew up that gash on his forehead. As soon as he's stable, I want a complete MRI work-up; let's see if he's got any skull damage."

A few hours later, Paul was lying in the Intensive Care Unit. As he slept, the monitors quietly displayed his steady heartbeat. He had been through the painful experience of the emergency department's trauma unit, scanned internally by the MRI suite, and now he was resting in the ICU. Paul's head was bandaged, the head wound suffered in the accident stitched and treated. Several IV's were stacked on the attached pole providing fluids, antibiotics, and medication to help his heart and his pain. Linda sat at his bedside waiting and hoping. After the hospital called her cell phone, she was unsure of what condition she would find Paul in. The staff had been so evasive about what had happened and not very forthcoming with a prognosis. As often happens in the hospital, there was a reluctance to predict the future. It was Dr. Tanner's comment to her that gave her hope. "He got his shock again Mrs. Simms. It was what you wanted."

As Linda held Paul's hand, she felt a tug and as she squeezed his hand, Paul reacted by squeezing back. She stood to move closer as Paul's eyes blinked open. He pulled her gently toward him and as she came into focus, Paul smiled and said, "Hi beautiful, I love you sweetheart."

Linda looked at the emotion in his eyes and instantly knew the results were good. "I love you too Paul, we're all happy to have you back."

Later, while Paul was resting, Dr. Tanner asked to speak with Linda. He brought her into the radiology reading room. She wanted to thank him for changing her husband back, back to the sweet, loving man he always was. That is before the cardioversion procedure turned him into some kind of ogre. She stood there; in front of the light box looking at the MRI scans of Paul's brain, wondering what this was all about. Dr. Tanner gave her some time to absorb the images before her; he was ready to offer the only explanation possible.

"Linda," he started, "The best I can think of is nothing short of amazing. This dark area here, in the frontal lobe of Paul's brain, this is an arterial malformation. It resembles a small grape stem. It's a brain aneurysm, a tangle of blood vessels that blocked the normal blood flow to this particular area of Paul's brain. Now, I've conferred with one of the best-known neurologists, and our guess is that this malformation was the cause of Paul's recent bizarre behavior. Frankly, if it weren't for the cardioversion and the accident that followed, we would probably never have learned of this malformation." Linda stood there silently. The idea had stunned her. She looked deeply at the images of Paul's brain while Dr. Tanner added, "And, I'm afraid to say Paul could have died of a stroke. Small wonders," Dr. Tanner added, "having nothing to do with *a change of heart.*"

# ONE WEB,
# OR
# ANOTHER

*"The tragedy of life is not in the fact of death,
But in what dies inside of you while you live."*

Norman Cousins

J oey Capella walked into his bright-white studio
apartment with his usual fast pace, closed the door
and flicked on the lights. He took off his jacket and threw it
over the armchair. He went directly to his Sony Viao desktop
computer, turned on the machine and while it was booting
up, he opened up the new CD he bought. One eye always
seemed to be stealing a glance toward the computer waiting
for its ready state. Joey was as full of excitement this time
as he was the very first time. Anticipation was never an easy
thing for him, the more he looked forward to something, the
harder it was for him to be patient. He grasped the wireless
mouse in his right hand moving the curser among the familiar
desktop shortcuts. He clicked on the AOL symbol sending
the program into its start-up mode. He knew he had a short
minute or two before he could sign on, so he pored himself
a glass of Merlot and reached for a bag of cheddar flavored

Chex mix before heading back to his computer desk. Just as he moved in front of the computer screen, the sign-on menu appeared. Joey selected his usual screen name, GoodStuffNY and typed in his six-letter password. He hit enter and walked over to the CD player, powered up the stereo and placed the new CD in the slot.

Just as the music started to play from the speakers, the AOL voice announced, "You've got mail!" Joey smiled; it was a little game he played. He would always leave some leftover mail in his mailbox so that whenever he signed on, there would be some mail there and he would hear the AOL voice announce, "You've got mail!" There was a time when he would sign-on and nothing new would be in his mailbox and there would be no announcement telling him he had mail. Why have nothing and feel bad, when you can fool AOL and always have mail, he would tell himself.

Smiling at the idea, Joey sat down in his computer chair, took a sip of wine, a handful of Chex-mix and reached again for the mouse. He clicked on the new mail symbol and up they came. He looked from one e-mail address to the other until his eyes spotted KWisconsin. He double clicked to open it up wondering what it would say.

> Hey Joey, I've missed u. What have u been up 2? And how was that new Nora Jones CD u picked out at the store? I went shopping 2. Yup, after u asked me about it, I went 4 that new Victoria's Secret wonder bra and French cut string bikini panties we talked about. You would definitely like the way I look in it. I mean hot, hot, hot! Maybe, later in the week I'll take a digital photo and send it to you. Would u like that? Oh, and did u get to check out that old movie I was telling you about. You remember, Pure Luck with Martin Short and Danny Glover, one of the

funniest movies I have ever seen. I'm home tonight,
maybe we can IM? Would you like that?

TTYL

*Kate*

Joey sat there reading the e-mail note over and over thinking how lucky he was to have found Kate on the Internet. It wasn't through a single's club or a dating service or anything like that. They met in a chat room for Jazz music lovers and their conversations spilled over into a private chat room where they exchanged personal profiles. Kate had explained she ran her own Public Relations firm in a small town outside Madison, Wisconsin. Joey told her he was a medical lab supervisor at Stony Brook Hospital on Long Island—one of the hospitals operated by New York State. Joey was forty-two and divorced without children. Kate was thirty-nine and a single Mom with one six-year-old son.

Since his divorce four years ago, Joey had been in and out of many romances. He always had an easy time attracting women; it was just a problem working out a long-term relationship. There was always something that doomed the relationship; a wacky quirk, an unexplained habit, something that bothered him or just a wrong fit. He liked talking with Kate on the Internet; he felt safe. It was a virtual relationship and for Joey, much easier than a real in-person one. They had been sending e-mails and IM-ing for three months. They had tried telephone conversations, but since they missed each other so much and ended up leaving phone messages, they decided to send e-mails instead and to use the Instant Message feature of the AOL service when they were on-line at the same time. It seemed less complicated and more exciting. At first, their conversations were mostly about Jazz music. Then, their chat turned to their careers exchanging information about their work roles, how their careers developed, and their future ambitions. After that, their conversations turned personal with Kate explaining about her being a single mother and what her son Josh was like. Joey discussed his first marriage and the theories about its failure. Lately, they crossed into sexual joking and sharing sexual fantasies. Joey was hoping to explore computer sex with Kate wanting to make a jump to exchanging sexual pleasures over the Web.

Frankly, it was all he thought about. And all he talked about with his co-worker and best friend Pete Simpson. When they had lunch, Joey would fill him in with all the latest details about what he and Kate had talked about and where Joey wanted things to go. Pete had seen his friend go through his divorce and just figured the Web thing with this new friend Kate was harmless enough. His thinking was, if no one got hurt what would be the harm? Often, they would end up laughing about all sorts of possibilities with Joey's budding Internet friendship. Pete would say, "Maybe you can both have web cams set up in your apartments and send each other live camera views of yourselves." Joey used to talk about having sex with her over the Web. One time, Pete asked him half joking,

"So Joey, why don't you go visit her for real?"

Feeling a little embarrassed Joey hesitated and then replied, "What, you mean just get on a plane and fly to Wisconsin?"

Pete kept the banter going by responding, "Sure, then you can really get to know her."

Joey thought about that idea, smiled and said, "Yes, and even touch her."

They laughed a while about that idea. "Imagine that" Joey would say. "Fly out to Wisconsin to meet Kate?" Except over time, Joey started to think more and more about the idea of flying out to meet Kate. The idea intrigued him; it was as if his friend Pete, had planted a little seed in Joey's brain and it was growing.

Joey sat there reading the screen thinking about what he would write back to her. He was more than a little nervous when it came to typing e-mail notes to Kate. Even though she was a virtual friend, he felt some pressure to not screw up this relationship. Joey took a couple of sips of the merlot and grabbed a few more bites of the Chex-Mix. He clicked on the e-mail reply button and typed in the subject box. *Exciting Idea . . .* Then continued,

> Hi Kate, Thanks for writing. About the Nora Jones CD, it is great and I'm listening to her right now on the stereo. I can understand the reviews she has been getting, she's awesome. And what color is that Victoria's Secret outfit anyway? U know, I am very partial to red, black is a great choice too. I did rent the *"Pure Luck"* video you told me about and look forward to seeing it Fri. It sounds like a pisser. Say, how does the wonder bra make you look? How about telling me your measurements? At 5'5" and 110 pounds you must have a great bod. BTW, the photo is an exciting idea; do you own a digital camera? I'd really like to see you in that outfit—or should I say, see you out of the outfit (lol). I'll look for you on-line tonight around 9.
>
> > *Bye for now,*
> > *Joey*
>
> *PS: I miss u 2*

Joey read the e-mail note over again and couldn't believe that he had been able to actually write like that. He wondered where those words came from? And how daring he had become to ask about her underwear and about her body. He just figured typing into a box and sending something over the Internet was easier than talking with someone directly. With e-mails he could step outside himself and be more daring, after all he thought, what was the harm; it wasn't as if you had to face someone.

Pete Simpson wasn't really Joey's best friend he was his only friend. For reasons Joey never talked about, he just didn't like people much. Joey's parents had died when he was a teenager and since he came from a very small family, he was the only one left. An Aunt had cared for him until he went off to college and she passed on some years after that of cancer. *No living relatives* he would sign whenever he filled in an insurance form at work. His ex-wife had remarried and moved to California, long out of sight and out of mind. For Joey, Pete was it. Except now there was Kate. Joey had such a crush on this woman from Wisconsin. For him, she was fun, sexy, uninhibited, and as he often thought, she liked him too. In one of his therapy sessions a while back, he had learned that often people in a new relationship find the experience exhilarating, and the feeling becomes almost a drug. The feeling, sort of a natural high of the heart, leaves the person addicted constantly wanting another contact since each contact was another feel good high. Joey often thought about that because his on-line experience with Kate was truly addicting. When he was at work he couldn't wait to get home to check his e-mails and when he was at home all he wanted to do was sign-on and talk with Kate. It didn't matter to him much whether it was healthy or not; he wasn't going to stop exchanging e-mails with her any time soon.

Then one night, Kate was especially uninhibited on-line. She used the Instant Messenger feature of AOL to tell Joey she was lying naked in bed with something in her hands. Kate asked if he felt the vibrations? She asked Joey to tell her what he would like her to do with it. When Kate IM'd the suggestion it practically made him orgasm right then and there. Sometimes, when he felt the sexual tension between them, it made him shaky and he could hardly type. Often, he ended up pressing the wrong keys as he tried to respond as fast as Kate was able to. Seeing so many typos in his notes just made him even more nervous.

When Kate asked a second time, what he wanted her to do with the thing in her hands, he typed.

> Slide it between your legs and imagine me there.
> Kate wrote back, you mean like this, ahhhh.
> Joey jumped at that line and added, Slowly let it fill you a little at a time.
> Kate responded, I might need your help?
> Joey stared at those words feeling himself becoming aroused. He took a deep breath and carefully typed, Lie back and feel the vibrations deep inside of you.
> This time she replied with only one word in the IM, . . . Moan.
> Joey closed his eyes, and imagined hearing the moan from Kate.

Joey's mind was racing from the IM's they were sending each other. He couldn't believe how real this simulated sex act was. At the same time he felt sexually excited, he wondered how far he could go. The combination of reality and fantasy often brought him to the edge.

> The IM screen opened and Joey's eyes flashed to the words Kate typed, Wow, that one was a 10 +, ooooh.
> Joey smiled and typed a response; I guess that one was off the Richter scale, eh?
> Kate only responded with, lol.
> And Joey really did laugh out loud.

Then they chatted about the news and about the country's continuing political unrest, and they shared more details about their lives. As they typed their instant messages back and forth, Joey realized how close they had grown. It amazed him that they were able to feel so trusting and open even though they lived nearly a thousand miles apart and never met in person. It made him realize the power of the Internet and how this technology opened up the world to anyone with a computer and a modem. Then, they signed off with the usual, TTYL—*talk to you later.*

The next day at lunch, Joey could hardly contain his excitement as he told his buddy Pete of the latest wild computer sex experience he had with Kate. Pete asked,

"She actually said she was using a vibrator?"

"Well no, not exactly."

Pete took a minute to collect his thoughts. He was curious about their on-line relationship, but at the same time, he didn't want to take anything away from his friend either.

"So, Joey how do you know?"

"Know what?"

"How do you know anything happened."

"Hey Pete," Joey started sounding annoyed, "I just know! Kate and I have become close, we have a special relationship."

"I know, I know, you've told me. But, how can you tell if she was really performing these things or she just said she was doing them? After all, you're on the computer here in New York not sleeping with her in Wisconsin."

"I'll tell you Pete, it doesn't matter if she's faking it or not. I mean, what difference does it make? It is what it is."

Pete looked at his friend and could see the hurt in his eyes. So, he asked gently, "So what now Joey, you mad at me?"

"Of course not, but why can't you just be my friend and not cause trouble for me and Kate?"

"Hey Joey, I didn't mean to cause trouble, I was just asking, that's all."

Then they sat there quietly at the small table in the Hospital's cafeteria, Joey eating his grilled ham & cheese sandwich with a side of potato chips and Pete having his split pea soup. A few minutes went by and as Pete sipped a steaming coffee he asked Joey,

"How about we go see a movie on the weekend? There are a couple of action flicks opening."

"Sure, I'm up for that. It doesn't matter to me, so pick one out and we'll go." Then there was more silence. A little later Joey broke the uneasy feeling when he laughed out loud and said, "I guess the only real way to prove anything is for me to buy a ticket and go fly out to Wisconsin and see things for myself, right?"

Pete looked at his friend and smiled, "Would you do that really? Would you Joey?"

"Hey Pete, it was your idea, remember?"

Then they both laughed as Pete placed one tray on top of the other and headed over to the lunch tray disposal racks. Joey refilled his coffee cup, placing a lid on the container and met up with Pete at the door.

Later that night, Joey signed on the computer while thinking about how he would pose the question. He couldn't decide if he was better off having a computer relationship with Kate or possibly changing everything by actually visiting her. Sure, he was curious and he thought about the merits of real versus simulated. Except, there were some nagging doubts about what would happen. Maybe he was better off just keeping things status quo. He entered his screen name and password and continued the debate in his head while he watched the AOL software go through it's start-up. He knew he liked what he had so far, and what he had was a fun relationship that gave him something to look forward to. At the same time, it was working for him and while he felt a special closeness to Kate, he also felt safe. Then there was the sexual stuff, the type of activity he never experienced in any of his real relationships. The other side of the argument was simple; maybe he could have all of this and more? The more would be the benefit of having a real relationship. Yes, he realized, but at what cost? It always came down to that. Except this time, he was leaning toward the more.

"You've got mail" the computer speakers came alive. Joey felt a rush as he clicked the Instant Message box. He hurriedly typed in Kate's screen name and selected "Available?" His lower lip signaled a sad response, as the reply told him Kate was not yet signed on. So, he decided to write her an e-mail note and maybe even practice the wording to suggest he would visit her in person? Maybe? He stared at the empty send mailbox as if the words could jump from his brain into the computer. Then he decided to start with, "Hi Kate, I was looking for you on line and since you're not signed on, I decided to write you a little note to let you know I was thinking about you. If you have some time to say hello, I'm here waiting for you." Joey stared at the screen again thinking about how best to phrase the big question.

He typed, "Kate, we have grown real close and I was thinking, wouldn't it be real nice to have an in-person visit with each other?" He re-read the line and thought, not bad Joey just keep it going. He continued to type, "I had this idea that maybe I would just take some vacation time (I have a few weeks coming to me) and hop on a plane and fly out to visit with you. We could spend as much time as you would like, a few days, a week or so? Whatever fits in with your schedule?" As he read the lines over and over trying to decide if he worded the big question correctly or not, the AOL Instant Message popped up and the computer speaker signaled with the Instant Message audio sound. The sudden surprise startled him a bit until he realized who it was that IM'd him.

He typed in the reply box, "What Pete? What's urgent?" and clicked send.

And Pete responded in the IM, "I figured out what movie to go see."

Joey didn't like being interrupted and sent Pete a slap, "That's it? That's what you interrupted me for. About the damn movies?"

A few seconds later Pete replied, "Well sure Joey, we made a plan remember?"

"Of course I remember, stupid."

As Joey sent that IM note, another Instant Message box opened. It was from Kate, "Can you talk a little?"

Joey typed in, "You bet. How are u?"

When Joey hit send, a reply popped up from his friend Pete, "What time do you want to go out Saturday? The movie is playing at 7:20, 9:40, or 11:50. What's your pleasure?"

Sometimes, Joey liked having two Instant Message sessions going on simultaneously. He found it fun and challenging to keep two conversations going, but not this time. This time he wanted to concentrate on the big question with Kate. He typed an IM to Joey,

> "hey listen, kate signed on and I'm gonna ask her about having a visit. So, just pick a time and I'll see ya at work tomorrow. ok?"

There was no answer and Joey knew his friend Pete did not like being second fiddle to anyone. Joey figured he'd straighten it all out tomorrow at work.

Joey clicked on the reply button to Kate's IM and typed, "So how was your date kate?" and clicked send.

Within a few seconds Kate responded, "Hey Joey, what do you mean date?" What kind of date?"

Joey read that IM and didn't know at first what Kate was referring to. His thoughts were all over the place and he felt a slight wetness under his arms; a sure sign he was feeling nervous. He was ready to type a response, but nothing was clear in his mind. Joey looked back at what he typed in the IM window and realized what had happened. He typed,

> "That was quite a slip Kate, to be honest while I meant to ask, how was your day? I was actually thinking of a date."
> "What kind of date Joey?"
> "Uh, I was thinking of a real date with you silly."
> "Joey, how would we have a real date? You live in New York and I live in Wisconsin . . ."
> Joey took a big breath and continued, "Here's what I was thinking. I was thinking I would take a week or so off from work and fly out to Wisconsin and meet you in person. How does that sound kate?"

There was no reply, and Joey could feel the perspiration under his arms again. His mind went blank at first and then he started to come up with all sorts of questions. Maybe she doesn't really like me? Perhaps the whole thing was a lie after all? Why did I ask that stupid question? Joey went on and on thinking all sorts of crazy reasons why Kate would not answer. And then a reply popped up in a large bold font,
**"I WOULD LOVE THAT SO MUCH!!!!"**
And Joey felt more excited than ever. She likes me, he thought. She really likes me and he started to laugh out loud as if he was a teenager.

Joey typed in the reply box,

> "It will be so cool to finally meet you. I bet we're going to have a great time. Unless for some reason,

the whole experience just goes to my head, but
not much chance of that. I'll behave myself, I
promise."
And Kate typed back, "Now Joey, you don't have
to do that?"
"Which one," Joey quickly typed. "Loose my head
or behave myself? lol"
"Well, you might loose your head from all the
attention, but I don't expect you to behave
yourself—lol"

Joey felt some sexual excitement pass through him at the
idea. And he thought, maybe I'll fly out tomorrow. He smiled
and typed,

"So, when do you think I should come out?"
"Anytime. Really, why wait?"
"I can probably arrange everything in two weeks,
how does that sound?"
"Two weeks would be good for me too."

Joey decided to try something out and typed,

"so kate, what are you wearing?"
"ha ha," She wrote, "Would you like to choose?"
"how about just telling me . . . ?"
"okay, i have on a pair of very tight jeans that show
off my long legs and my wicked figure. on top, i'm
wearing a pink, light to the touch, soft cotton tee
that's cropped short exposing my tiny waist. nothing
under the tee and french cut string panties under
the jeans. my hair is tied back to a ponytail and i'm
wearing very light make-up to give me a healthy
glow. how does all that sound?"

During Kate's description, Joey's right hand found himself
hard through his pants while his mind thought of the image

Kate created. It also scared him because what excited him more than the visual Kate described, or the narrative of the description itself, was Kate's willingness to have some sexual fun. At that moment, he wanted to grab his coat and run all the way to Wisconsin without stopping.

At lunch the next day, Joey filled Pete in with the details of the big question. How at first he was so nervous, how Kate was so open to the idea, and how it all worked out in the end.

Then Pete asked Joey, "So, you're going after all?"

"Yup, nothing's going to stop me now. In a couple of weeks, I'll be looking at my sweet Kate face to face. You know what she told me Pete?"

"No Joey," he asked sarcastically, "How would I know what she told you?"

"She told me that she was looking forward to making me breakfast after our first night together. She said she would make me a great breakfast; eggs, home fries, pancakes, fresh squeezed orange juice, and Hazelnut coffee too."

"Sounds too good to be true. I bet you're happy as can be, eh?"

"Oh yeah! And I already put in for my vacation time—shouldn't be a problem at all."

"That's great, I'm happy for you."

"Yeah, me too." And they both laughed.

Then Pete asked, "So, what time Saturday night, Joey?"

Joey had a blank look on his face as he asked, "Time?"

Pete folded his arms across his chest and looked off in the distance. He was more than a little standoffish as he replied,

"Oh, you forgot our plans, eh?" Pete could see that Joey really had no clue as to what he was referring to, so he just continued, "What time? How about what time for the movie? Duh . . . ?"

"Hey Pete, cut me some slack, I have a lot on my mind."

"Sure Joey, can't you tell that I'm just kidding around with you? I mean really, I wish it were me heading out to meet a sexy beautiful woman in Wisconsin."

"You mean that Pete?"

"Yes Joey, of course I mean it."

But he didn't really. Pete was just plain jealous of his friend Joey; and inside somewhere the idea crossed his mind that he wished Joey had never met this girl Kate.

A couple of weeks later Pete Simpson was driving his best friend Joey Capella to LaGuardia Airport. An old Elton John song was playing on the radio, "Don't Go Breaking My Heart" and the lyrics, sung in a duet style, made Joey think about his feelings for Kate and he wondered, would she end up breaking his heart after all? What did they feel for each other anyway? Was it just infatuation or was it love? Joey found himself staring out at the traffic passing them on the road and paying no attention at all to his friend's conversation. His thoughts completely engulfed him. Joey started to think about how many hours of his day he spent either e-mailing her, having IM conversations with her, talking with his friend Pete about her, or just thinking about her, and he knew it was a good chunk of his day. How could it be just infatuation? And what about the excitement he felt whenever he had a connection with her? Those feelings were not imaginary; they were real. He thought too, that love was a very tricky and difficult emotion to understand. After all, who could ever understand love? He had a flashback of his ex-wife announcing the end of their marriage as he ended up biting his lip.

"Hey Joey," Pete asked, "What terminal did you say?" Pete glanced over and found his pal Joey staring out of the window. He shoved Joey's shoulder hard and asked, "Hey man? Come back from where ever you were visiting and tell me again what terminal are you flying out of?"
"Sorry, it's Northwestern."
"Hey, where did your thoughts take you anyway?"
"I guess I was spaced out thinking, that's all."

"Well, you sure do have a lot to think about. When are you coming back Joey? I'll make sure I'll be available to pick you up when you return."

"I'll have to let you know. Kate and I decided not to have a planned return trip. Maybe I'll stay the whole two weeks or maybe it'll just be for a few days. We're keeping things loose and hoping for the best."

"Just let me know Joey and don't worry, I'll make sure I can pick you up. I mean I'll want to hear all the details of this adventure."

And they both laughed as Joey pointed to the terminal entrance. Pete helped his buddy with his bags from the trunk and hugged him farewell. As he got back into his car, he watched his friend walk away, enter the sliding doors of the terminal, and disappear in the crowd.

A week later, Pete was having lunch outside the Hospital sitting by himself at a table in the cafeteria's patio thinking about his friend and how his trip to Wisconsin might be going? Pete had tried hard not to count every day that went by, but he couldn't help himself. It had been seven days since he dropped Joey off at LaGuardia Airport and Pete was figuring he would be hearing from his buddy soon. He had thought about calling Joey's cell phone and debated the idea not wanting to interrupt or upset his friend. He took his cell phone out and placed it on the table staring at it while he took another bite of his sandwich. What would be the harm, he wondered? He would just have a short call to check on his buddy that's all. Pete's hand slipped over the phone at the same time the person at the next table asked, "Hey, you using the ketchup?"

Pete passed him the ketchup bottle and said, "Sure, no problem." Pete picked up his cell phone and hit the keys to open his phone's address book. He watched the curser move down to his friend Joey's number and then he pressed send. The cell phone rang three times and went to Joey's voice-mail.

"Hi, this is Joey, leave a message and I'll call you back."

Pete heard the beep and answered, "Hey buddy, what's going on out there in Wisconsin? Give me a call back here in New York when you can. Hope all is well? Pete." He hit the disconnect button and slipped the phone in his pocket and walked back to the hospital not knowing exactly what to make of that.

The days went by slowly, and every day that passed Pete wondered about his friend Joey out there in Wisconsin. He usually smiled at the idea of Joey hanging out with his new interest, Kate. He thought, I wonder how that first home cooked breakfast she had promised him worked out as he visualized the sexy scene in his mind. Pete just figured his buddy must be having a grand old time out there in Wisconsin. Later that night, Pete signed onto his Internet account and sent Joey an e-mail note.

> "All right now, ten days have gone by and it's time to surface and get back in touch with your old friend here on Long Island. I've left a few voice messages and now here's an e-mail request too. Give me a quick call so I can stop worrying. Pete"

As the days totaled fourteen, Pete thought it very odd that Joey never did return any of his phone messages or his e-mail note. While he tried hard not to let the fact that Joey did not get in touch with him back at home bother him, the idea that something was going on nagged at Pete. Then one day at work, Pete had an idea. What if, he wondered, what if Joey contacted his boss to extend his vacation time? Yeah, he thought. That could have happened and it would explain everything. During the next break, he walked over to Joey's Department Head's office and asked her secretary if Joey had recently contacted her? The secretary's name was Florence and while Pete was standing there at her desk, asking about Joey, in walked the Department Head.

"Excuse me," Pete asked, stopping her in mid stride, "My name is Peter Simpson and I'm Joey Capella's friend and if you don't mind, could I ask you if Joey has been in touch about his vacation."

Florence tried to explain, "I'm sorry Ms. Jackson, I tried to tell him that this is personal information and we can't divulge any personal information without . . ."

"That's okay Florence," Ms. Jackson interrupted. "I have a few questions about Joey Capella too. Come into my office for a few minutes and we can talk. As they entered the office, Ms. Jackson motioned to a chair and asked, "Excuse me, I'm sorry, what was your name?"

Pete sat down and responded more nervously than he imagined, "Simpson Ma'am, my name is Pete Simpson and I work in the radiology department. I'm Joey best friend and well, I'm concerned about him because I haven't heard from him in two full weeks."

"Um, I see," Ms. Jackson started. "It's interesting because we haven't heard from him either. He took five days from his permanent vacation and slotted in another ten days if he needed the time. I gave him some freedom because Joey has been very dedicated here in the lab and I felt after all the work he's done, he could use the stress break. He had told me that if he would stay away for more than five days he would contact me. He hasn't, and well, I'm starting to worry too. It's not like Joey, usually he is very reliable and trustworthy."

"I know Ms. Jackson," Pete replied getting excited. "It's just not like him to be out of contact for so long. I mean I knew he was going off on a sort of adventure, but I still thought he would keep in touch and let me know what he was up to out there."

Ms. Jackson sat up and squared her shoulders back as she continued. "And you haven't heard from him?"

"No I haven't heard from him since I dropped him off at LaGuardia. And that's not the Joey I know."

"Did you say adventure?"

"Yes, he went off to meet a woman from the Internet?"

Ms. Jackson looked puzzled and asked, "A woman from the Internet? What is this some science-fiction movie?"

Pete felt a bit nervous and squirmed in his seat. "I'm sorry Ms. Jackson, I forget. Let me start from the beginning. Joey was writing e-mails back and forth with a woman in Wisconsin called Kate. A woman he met on the Web in a chat room and after they started to have feelings for each other they agreed to meet. So, Joey flew off to Wisconsin fourteen days ago to actually do it . . . to meet her in person. I took him to LaGuardia Airport on the morning he flew off and I haven't heard from him since. Not by phone or by e-mail, nothing, nada."

"Umm, I see. And why are you here?"

"I just figured he might not want to be calling back home in front of the woman of his dreams, and I thought that perhaps he was in touch with his supervisor at work. Tell me, did he?"

"No Pete, he has not. But, of course, that doesn't mean anything bad has happened to him either."

"I know, but still I'm worried." Pete stood and started to thank Ms. Jackson for her time, when he turned back around as Ms. Jackson was picking up the phone. He interrupted her, "I'm sorry to bother you Ms. Jackson, but can you let me know if Joey does contact you?"

"Of course I will, leave your contact information with Florence."

"That's great, thanks."

As Pete left her office, Ms. Jackson dialed her husband's number at the Fifth Precinct. On the third ring it was answered,

"Homicide, Detective Jackson speaking."

"Hi honey."

"Oh, hi sweetheart, what's going on?"

"Well, I don't know what to make of this, but I have a situation and could use your help."

"Sure sweetheart, what's on your mind?"

She giggled and said, "If you call me sweetheart one more time, I'll just be melting over here ya know."

"Come on Hun, what's up?"

"It's a little involved, do you have a few minutes?"

"Sure, go ahead."

"Well, one of my lab supervisors went off on a vacation of sorts and hasn't come back or called. It's like he just plain fell off the earth."

"Now Gloria, is that really a big deal?"

"I think so because it's out of character for him to not be in touch; he's too responsible for that. And I just spoke with his best friend who took him to the airport and he was asking about him. It doesn't feel right, that's all."

"How long has he been gone?"

"Fourteen days."

"Umm, that is a long time. How about his family? Did you try contacting his family?"

"Well, that's another reason why I have this uncomfortable feeling."

"What's that?"

"He doesn't have any family, they're all gone."

"I see, well Gloria I'm not sure that homicide is the right place to start, maybe missing persons would be better? But if you want me to, I can talk with the missing guy's friend and take it from there?"

"Would you sweetie? That would be a big relief."

"Have him get in touch with me and we'll set up an appointment, okay?"

"Thanks big fella. Are you coming home late tonight?"

"Just a little, I have to finish some reports before I leave." Then he added in a loving voice, "What do you have in mind?"

"Oh, you just hurry home big fella, I'll be waiting for you. Love you sweetie."

"Yeah, me too. And thanks for the tease."

Gloria giggled as she hung up the phone and pressed the intercom. As her secretary answered, she asked, "Florence, did Pete Simpson leave his phone number?"

"I have it right here, would you like me to try to reach him."

"Yes, I would, I need to speak with him. Thanks."

Ms. Jackson sat back in her chair trying to make sense out of the situation. She filled her mind with all sorts of thoughts. What would make Joey Capella not call in, she asked herself? A responsible person like him would never do that. Except, if he couldn't. And what would cause that? Maybe he was in a serious accident? Maybe, he just wanted to disappear? Wouldn't be the first time some guy found a way to fall off the earth if he wanted to. But, her mind kept telling her, that's not Joey. Then the intercom rang.

"Yes Florence,"

"It's Peter Simpson on the line."

"Oh good. Thanks."

She picked up the call and explained, "Peter, I wanted to ask if you would be interested in talking with a detective about Joey Capella?"

"Sure, of course. But the police, do you think it's that bad?"

"Like you, I don't know what to think? But, before you get too worried or too excited, you should know it would be unofficial, the detective's my husband."

"Your husband's a detective?"

"Yes, a homicide detective."

"You think it means homicide?"

"Let's not jump to conclusions Peter. I asked my husband to help and he suggested he would speak with you and take it from there. Okay?"

"I understand, what should I do?"

"Just call him and set up an appointment."

Ms. Jackson passed along the phone number and explained that if he called right away, her husband would be at his desk. Pete placed the phone on its cradle and sat back in his chair a moment to collect his thoughts. He felt frightened for his best friend, and couldn't help but think the worst. He picked up the piece of scrap paper, held it in his hand and stared hard at the detective's phone number he had hurriedly jotted down. Pete couldn't help but think that this would be the first time he ever got involved with the police. His thoughts flashed to the image of Joey walking through the sliding doors at the airport and disappearing into the crowd and how that scene resembled the opening of the television show, *Without a Trace*. Joey swallowed hard, picked up the phone and dialed the number. He closed his eyes as the phone rang several times in his ear.

"Fifth Precinct, Detective Jackson speaking."

Pete sat there wanting to speak, but no words escaped from his mouth.

"Hello? Who's there?" The detective asked sounding miffed at the annoying silence.

Finally, Pete muttered, "Detective Jackson this is Pete Simpson. Your wife, uh, I mean Mrs. Jackson, gave me your number and asked me to call you."

"Yes, this is about the guy who works for her, eh. Joey, Joey Capella? And you're his friend, right?"

"That's correct, sir. Except, it's more like I'm his best friend."

"Sir?" Detective Jackson echoed, "Please don't say that again, you'll have me laughing to the floor."

Pete felt the heat fill his cheeks as he realized the embarrassment of the moment. "Sorry sir, I mean Detective."

"Well Pete, if you have some time in the morning, could you come down to the station and talk with me about Joey so I can size up the situation?"

"Yes, no problem. I mean I would do anything to help Joey. What time should I come in?"

"How about eight in the morning. Oh, and bring a picture of your friend if you have one? And any other personal information too, okay?"

"You said the Fifth Precinct? I'm sorry sir uh, detective, where is that?"

Detective Jackson had given Pete the directions to the station house and explained before they hung up, that anything he could think of would help; even if he thought it might be unimportant. As Pete took out a few sheets of notepaper and a pencil from his desk, he tried hard to recall any of the things Joey had told him about. He wrote down everything as the thoughts popped into his mind. Her name was Kate, she lived in a small town near Madison, Wisconsin, Joey flew Northwest Airlines, and she ran her own public relations firm. As Pete starred at the list, it dawned on him that he didn't really have a whole lot of information about her. This isn't going to be much help to anybody, he realized. Pete reached over to the top shelf and took hold of the frame that held a photo of Joey and him in front of one of the wineries they had visited together on Long Island's North Fork. He took apart the picture frame and placed the photograph down with his list.

The next morning he arrived at the Fifth Precinct and went looking for Detective Jackson's office. As he walked along the corridor, he looked down at the visitor's badge they had clipped on him when he signed in. Thinking about the lost souls who were locked behind bars, he was happy his badge just read visitor. As he stood there, one of the uniformed officers asked him, "Need some help finding someone?"

Pete asked, "Yes, can you tell me where detective Jackson's office is?"

The officer pointed into one of the office suites and told him, "He's right in there. The second cubicle on the left."

Pete walked up to the entrance and knocked timidly on the file cabinet. Detective Jackson looked up and asked,

"Pete? You must be Pete Simpson?" Pete nodded and took a small step backward realizing how large a man this detective was.

"Come on now Pete, you have a seat right over here and don't be feeling scared or anything, I won't bite." Detective Jackson motioned over to the only seat in the cubicle while he had this big shit-eating grin on his face. "All right, let's start from the very beginning. What's the skinny on your friend Joey Capella? Pete took a deep breath and explained everything he knew. How his friend Joey met Kate in a Web chat room and how they e-mailed each other every day and how they talked on the phone too. Detective Jackson asked about the nature of their relationship and what this woman meant to Joey? He wanted to know everything and Pete felt shy to explain the sexual encounters Joey had told him about.

"I think he loved her," Pete added timidly. "Ever since his wife divorced him four years ago, Joey was lonely inside. I mean he dated, but he never had that special feeling toward a woman until he met Kate. She made him feel more alive than anyone else I can remember. And he was always excited about her, never a dull moment with that Kate."

Detective Jackson hesitated and then requested information about Joey. "Tell me his phone number and his cell phone number too. And his home address. Oh, and Pete, do you have a key to his place?"

"Yes, I have a spare key."

"How about we ride over there and look for some more of the details?"

"Sure, no problem."

As they rode over in detective Jackson's unmarked car, Pete felt strange to be riding with a cop in a cop's car. It was a *Twilight Zone* sort of feeling that was more unreal than he was prepared for. Detective Jackson helped the situation by normalizing the experience as best he could. When they arrived at Joey's small apartment, they could see there wasn't any sign that someone had been there recently. No dishes in the sink, no fresh food in the refrigerator, or clothing out of place. They went through Joey's papers on his desk and Pete tried to start up Joey's computer. He couldn't get past the sign-on screen without Joey's password and the detective told him he would send one of his buddies, a police computer expert over to see if they could learn about Kate's e-mail address and check out their e-mail correspondence.

On the way back to the station house, detective Jackson explained to Pete what the next steps would be. "I can't really do much without any evidence of a crime. If we can find out her address, I'll send a request for assistance to the Madison, Wisconsin Police Department along with his photo. We can ask if there has been any police activity concerning Joey Capella and ask if they would also check the local hospitals too. Usually, police departments offer professional courtesy on cases like these. I'll also run his driver's license through the police system for identification purposes and we can request a printout of his phone calls for both his landline and his cell phone numbers. I can send a request to the airline and ask for information and we can relay a request to the car rental companies where he landed. Maybe we'll get lucky and find out more information about this Kate including her home address. Who knows?" They shook hands and Pete thanked him for his help. Detective Jackson told Pete he'd give him a call in a few days to update him on the things they found out.

Pete drove back to work and spent the afternoon half trying to forget what was happening and half trying to remember any additional details to add to what they already knew. Forgetting what was happening was practically impossible. Even working with the patients that lined the Radiology waiting area couldn't clear his mind of the thoughts and not all of them good ones. One of the not so good ones was the idea that something really bad had happened to his best friend Joey and when all was said and done it was his fault. Pete figured it was his fault for not being a bigger influence and getting Joey to put off the trip until he knew more about who this Kate really was. Then, just as he was helping a very overweight old man onto the x-ray table, Pete stepped away into the shadows of the procedure room and froze. A dark thought passed through his mind as he remembered what he had told Joey, "Why don't you fly out to Wisconsin and meet her in person Joey?"

"Hey," the man on the table yelled, "are you going to take this x-ray or just stand over there all day?"

Joey heard the man's upset voice and snapped out of it. "I'm really sorry sir, I have a personal problem and it has been weighing heavily on my mind. I'll work on the images and have you out of here right away."

Later that night, Pete sat at his home computer scanning down the list of e-mails from Joey in the AOL personal filing cabinet looking for one that might have included Kate's e-mail address too. He was also trying to figure out her Internet provider. If he could uncover either one, Pete figured he'd be able to turn it over to detective Jackson and they could track her down for sure. It was a time-consuming chore, but an important one. Pete tried to be patient as he opened each e-mail one at a time and looked to see if there was an address in the copy box containing Kate's information. Pete was thinking too, thinking about the kind of person Kate might be. Could she be some horrible monster? Or was she the sweet caring person Joey thought she was, or something in between? Yes, he realized, the Internet opened up a world, but what kind of a world was it?

A few days later, Joey got a call from Detective Jackson. He had wanted to fill him in on what they had learned. "Well, it isn't a whole lot," Jackson started. "Yes, the airline confirmed that a Joey Capella had purchased a one way ticket to Madison, Wisconsin. But, the car rental agencies had nothing in their computers about a Joey Capella renting or leasing a car. Verizon looked into his cell phone account and told us that Joey's last cell phone call was the day before he left and nothing after that. The Madison, Wisconsin Sheriff's office looked into any reports that mentioned Joey's name but nothing showed up. It was the same story with the hospital emergency room check, no record of a Joey Capella needing medical attention. We followed the lead on her phone number and that turned up a home address in a small town called Berona about twenty miles North of Madison. The Madison, Wisconsin Sheriff contacted the Sheriff who has jurisdiction in Berona, which is in Dane County, and he went a knocking at that address. No one answered the door and there was no sign of mischief either. Pete, there's no indication that Joey was ever at that address and no evidence of any crime. The Berona Sheriff, Dan Blackstone, told us he couldn't really take any more action unless we can show him something."

Pete's mind was racing at full steam and he nervously asked Detective Jackson, "What about the Internet? Did you get her e-mail address and look into what she was writing about?"

"Yup, it turned out she is an AOL customer and they let us look into her e-mails to Joey. Harmless stuff mostly, the usual kind of information swaps and a little computer sex thrown in on occasion. Nothing to illustrate any foul play."

"Where does that leave us detective?" Pete asked feeling down.

"It leaves us in limbo Pete. Sheriff Blackstone did tell us he'd have a patrol car go by her place every once in a while and maybe even knock on her door. But nothing promising Pete."

Pete was feeling like the answers were slipping away so he tried to appeal to him, "I know, except Detective Jackson, I can't help but feel something happened to him and we have to find out what it was."

"There's nothing I'd like to do more Pete, but my hands are tied. I'm a Suffolk County homicide detective on Long Island; I have no jurisdiction out in Wisconsin. I have no power there and anyway, we still don't have any evidence of anything."

Pete feeling frustrated, tried a different tack. "Well, he is a missing person, can't we go to the FBI with what we know?"

"You know what they'll tell me Pete" They'll sit behind their desks and just explain, lots of times someone gets on an airplane and just flies off. There are hundreds of cases on the books of someone disappearing and many of them are children. Frankly, unless you come up with some evidence of a crime, there's not much the FBI would do either. I'm sorry."

Pete, disappointed at the lack of enthusiasm, felt angry and raised his voice, "Well, that's not good enough. We have to do more than that. I mean can't you go out there and bring her in for questioning or something?"

"No, I can't. Like I said, I have no jurisdiction in Wisconsin and my captain won't let me go off on some wild goose chase."

"Well, what about me? I have no captain to worry about and I'm free to travel anywhere I want to. How about that?"

Detective Johnson paused a moment. He liked the idea but couldn't let on, "Now what do you know about police work? You'll just be wasting your time."

Pete took another deep breath, more to control his emotions than to calm himself down. "Looking into what happened to my buddy would not be a waste of time. No sir, it would be a good thing all around. And as far as not knowing anything about police work, how about you teach me? You help me by running down what I should do."

Detective Jackson was impressed with this young man's drive; maybe he could pull it off. "Are you sure Pete? You sure you want to tackle such a dangerous job?"

"Yes, I can do it. How about you make a list for me, coach me on what I should do and who I should see and I'll make the arrangements for time off and get a plane ticket to Madison, Wisconsin?"

Detective Jackson started to have mixed feelings about this and more than a little worry. "Sounds like you are one determined young man. Let's talk tomorrow around noon?"

"Okay Detective, until tomorrow."

There was an uneasy silence as Pete hung up the phone. He felt such emptiness, such loss. And he felt pleased that he wasn't just sitting around anymore doing nothing.

The next day, Pete went to his Department Head to arrange the next 5 days off. He made up some story about a sick relative and got what he wanted. With the weekend in-between, he'd have seven days to play private eye. Then he phoned Detective Jackson who wasn't at his desk. Pete left a voice-mail message explaining how he could be reached either at work or on his cell phone. Next, he went on his computer to find a flight to Madison. There were seats available for a direct flight, JFK to Madison in the late morning: he booked a one-way ticket since he was unsure when he would be finished. He took care of some work-related duties and mentioned to a couple of colleagues that he was taking an emergency family leave and would be away for a week. On the way home that afternoon, Detective Jackson called Pete's cell phone.

"Yes, hello?"

"Hi Pete, Detective Jackson here. So, you got the time off and plan on going ahead with the trip?"

"That's right and I also booked my flight on Northwest Airlines for late tomorrow morning out of JFK."

"That doesn't give us much time now, does it?"

"I can come by now and see you if that'll help?"

"Sure Pete, come on over, I have some things for you. Except, instead of meeting here, let's go have a bite to eat. It's best to keep this on the q.t. When you pull into the parking area call my desk and I'll come right down. Okay?"

"Yes, that's fine."


A short time later, Pete pulled into the Fifth Precinct's parking lot and called Detective Jackson to let him know he had arrived. Within a few minutes he was downstairs struggling into the front seat of Pete's Toyota Corolla asking Pete if he wouldn't mind driving?

"When you pull out, make a right, there's a diner a couple of miles down the road on the right side. How you doing? Feeling nervous?"

"Not really, more excited than nervous. Should I be nervous?"

"Beats me? I just figured you might be. No harm intended. So, listen Pete. I put together a list of questions for you and a list of places to go, to try to get the answers. There's no right or wrong way to go about this. For us detectives it's experience that makes the difference you know. When a detective goes out on his first case, he's as green as can be and usually makes a ton of mistakes."

"What advice do you have for me Detective?"

"Mostly Pete, I would tell you to trust your instincts. If you are feeling weird about something, you probably need to get out of there. I put the name and number of the Dane County Sheriff I talked with on that list. Sheriff Dan Blackstone and if you get into a jam contact him pronto. There's the diner Pete, on the right."


They entered the diner and found a quiet booth in the rear. They ordered up some burgers and fries and continued to talk. Detective Jackson looked across the table at this young man sizing him up as best he could.

"Look Pete, I don't want you to be having any grandiose ideas that you'll be able to solve this mystery. You just ask some questions and when you get some answers, go see Sheriff Blackstone and let him do the real police work, Okay?"

"Sure, but where do I start? Should I go to this woman Kate's place and ask about Joey and let her know I'm his friend?"

"Yeah sort of, except don't tell her you're his friend. Tell her you're a relative, his cousin or brother. You'll get better results if you're a relative, that's for sure.

As Detective Jackson handed Pete a few pages from a steno pad he continued,

"Her address is on the list too. She lives just north of Madison in a town called Berona. You said your flight's to Madison right?"

"Yeah, direct from JFK."

"Well, when you get there, go to the car rental desks, show them the photo and ask if anyone has seen your brother? Maybe, you'll get a lead. Then, you can either rent a car or take a taxi. That is, if that hick town has taxis. While he laughed at that idea, Pete was starting to feel nervous. How was he going to get around and how would he manage without knowing much about where he was traveling to?

"Detective Jackson, if you were handling this case, what would you ask her?"

"It isn't so much as what I would ask as much as how I would watch her reaction. We know Joey Capella went to see her, we know he flew out there. We know he arrived in Madison. What we don't know is what happened to him after that. So, you have to make it clear that you know he came to see her. You have to confront her, and then watch her reaction. The idea is to make her feel comfortable and then watch if she reacts in a nervous way like she did something wrong or she knows something."

"I see," Pete said. "Sort of trip her up."

"Exactly, and at the same time don't put yourself in any danger. I mean we don't know for sure if anything really happened to Joey. Perhaps, he got tired of her and traveled somewhere else? Or, maybe she knows something and will act strange. You have to watch her eyes. If you ask her a question and she looks down while she answers, that's a give away what we call a tell. The more she does that, the more suspicious I would be."

"What else? What else should I look into?"

"You have the photo right?" Pete nodded. "Go see the neighbors if there are any, ask if they saw your brother around in the last two weeks or so? You'll be surprised what people in these small towns will notice, especially when something happens out of the ordinary. Another thing on that list to check out are the convenience stores. It might be that Joey went into one of them to buy something last minute. Or a florist, or a liquor store." Detective Jackson reached inside his jacket pocket while he told Pete, "Oh, and here's the best part. A photo of Kate, my friend the computer expert was able to pull it off Joey's computer's hard drive. Good looking girl that Kate. If it was me, I might have flown out there too, if I was single of course.

Pete was looking carefully at that photo of Kate, just as the waitress brought their burgers to the table. He realized immediately how attractive Kate was and how she was just Joey's type too. He placed the photo down with the other papers and sat there looking at his burger. Detective Jackson, was dripping ketchup over his fries and placing the tomato and lettuce on top of the burger. He looked over at Pete and remarked, "You gotta have your strength Pete, you're heading out on an adventure and you'll need to be fortified. So eat up."

The pilot's announcement that the flight was making its final approach to the runway at the Madison airport awoke Pete from his restful sleep. He smiled briefly at the businessman in the next seat and looked out of the small window at the vast farmlands simply astonished at the emptiness of the land. The steward interrupted his thoughts when he tapped Pete on the shoulder,

"Excuse me sir, the Captain asked everyone to buckle up. Thank you."

Pete hurriedly grabbed for the seat belt replying "Oh sure, of course." He looked outside and could see the airport looming ahead. It wasn't anything like Kennedy in New York, he thought. He could see the control tower and a few runways that crisscrossed in front of a few small buildings that he assumed were the airport's terminals. Before he knew it, the plane was stopped at the terminal and the pilot was announcing,

"Ladies and Gentleman, thank you for flying Northwest Airlines. Enjoy your stay in Madison, Wisconsin."

Pete found his way to the baggage claim area and within fifteen minutes he was looking down the row of rental car agencies that lined the far wall. As he surveyed the situation, Pete could see that Budget Rental had a few people on line, but the attractive blond women at Hertz was all alone moving some papers around on the counter. He headed in her direction and found his mouth becoming dry. He walked up to the desk, placed his bag on the floor and asked her if she had a few minutes to help him. She looked at him with a company smile and answered in a cute voice,

"Of course sir, that's what I'm here for."

"Well Ma'am," Pete started, "I know this sounds a little strange, but my brother was supposed to meet me and well, I was wondering if I showed you a picture of him maybe you could tell me if you have seen him here. His name's Joey, and he flew out here two weeks ahead of me and now he's not here." Pete slipped the photo out of his pocket and placed it down in front of her. He had no clue as to what to do, so he just continued. "Yeah, we're moving here from New York and he was supposed to get us an apartment to stay in. Joey's the one on the right." She picked up the photo of the two of them and looked at the picture carefully.

"No, I can't say that I've seen this man before." She giggled a bit and added, "Not that I would have minded, he's cute!"

"Are you sure you haven't seen him? Take another look, it's real important."

"No, I would have remembered him. I've never seen him."

Pete put the photo back into his pocket, looked up at the girl and told her, "Thanks, thanks anyway. I'll just ask over there."

It was the same thing at the Budget Car Rental counter and the Alamo desk. No one remembered seeing Joey. All Pete got for his questions was a lot of head shaking and sorry we can't help you remarks. Pete picked up his bag and slung it over his shoulder. He walked out of the terminal building and spotted a short line of three cars with a taxi sign at the curb. He opened the door of the lead taxi sliding his bag on the seat following it in. He closed the door telling the driver, "I'm heading over to Berona. Do you know of a reasonably priced motel in town?" The driver, a black man in his sixties with an unshaven face, wrote down some information on a passenger log that was hanging onto a clipboard tied by rope to the dashboard. He slipped the car's transmission into drive and rolled away from the terminal building.

"A reasonably priced motel? Shit man, you're going to Berona sir, no Trump Palaces there. There's only one place and that's the Green Tree Motor Lodge just outside the town and within walking distance of Main Street. Not much of a Town you know. It's about fifteen miles from the airport and a million miles from a real city."

Pete turned to look out the window as the taxi left the airport road turning onto a four-lane highway. "Green Tree?

Okay with me." There was some silence as the taxi sped along. Pete noticed the houses off the highway were becoming less frequent and the clusters of trees were turning into open fields of cornrows. As they headed for Berona, they ended up passing acres and acres of farms and an occasional small dairy farm set back in the hills.

Then the driver asked, "Mind if I smoke sir, it's a habit I can't seem to break?"

"Go ahead, smoke if you want to. It doesn't bother me."

"And if you don't mind me asking, where you from? You look like a city boy."

"Me, a city boy? Naa, I live in a small town too, it's called Miller Place on Long Island about sixty-five miles east from New York City.

"Long Island eh? I was there once. I went to see about work at a racetrack called Belmont. But, that was over thirty-five years ago. I guess a lot has changed in all those years, eh man."

"How did you end up here in Madison, Wisconsin?" Pete asked curiously.

"The horse track didn't need any help at the time, and my wife had a family that farmed here not far from the airport. Except back then, the airport was just a dirt runway with one crop dusting plane. They shut down the farm years ago and I started driving a cab for cash. It hasn't been easy."

"No, I guess not."

The driver turned up the country music playing on the radio as Pete spent the remaining time staring out of the window. The taxi turned off the highway and soon after found the gravel road entrance to the Green Tree Motor Lodge. Pete looked at the rows of modest cabins set back in the trees on one side and the main building with about eight matching green doors on the other side. There were a few cars parked in front of the doors of the main building and Pete noticed two young boys playing with a dog in front of one of the rooms.

He paid the driver and asked if he could get in touch with him if he needed another taxi?

The driver slipped him a business card and told Pete, "You just give me a call when you need a ride and I'll be here lickety-split. Ask for Sammy, they'll let me know you called."

"Sure Sammy and I'm Pete, thanks again."

Pete grabbed for his bag, closed the door, waved and headed for the motel office. He watched Sammy head the taxi out down the gravel road. He checked in and told the heavyset woman in the Motel Office he'd be about a week, maybe. Pete asked, "Is there anyplace to get something to eat?"

The woman told him, "There is a restaurant in town called Mother's Cafe, about a quarter mile away. Just down the road a piece."

He took the key for number six, "Okay, thanks."

"You have a nice afternoon now."

The room was clean, very bare but comfortable enough. He placed a few shirts in the closet and hung up the two pairs of pants he brought with him. He put away his socks, underwear and pajamas in one drawer of the pine chest that hugged the wall on the opposite side of the bed. He decided to use the bathroom before heading out and felt relieved and glad that he did. Pete made sure the room door was locked, slipped the key into his pocket and started walking toward the town. Once down the road he took out his cell phone and looked to see if there was any signal available. The display showed only one half bar next to the roaming symbol and even that was flickering. Umm, he thought. Maybe that's why I never heard from Joey. Not much of a cell phone signal out here.

Pete started to feel the unused muscles ache and throb in his legs as he walked a quick pace on the main road to Berona. It seemed like more than a quarter mile, but then over a small hill he saw the buildings begin to line up just ahead. There was a church. A Baptist Church with a long white steeple and at the very top, a large bell dangled from ropes. Once he reached the Church, the sidewalk started and as Pete stepped up with a little moan, he could see a hardware store, a small redbrick building with a sign that read Berona First National Bank. There was a butcher, an antique shop, and a bakery in a cluster. There were several pick-ups and a few cars driving through the town and a dozen or so people walking about. Not like tourists ambling around the shops, but like people with some business in mind. He noticed three older gentlemen sitting on a wood box seat outside the Barber Shop having a smoke like they had all the time in the world. Pete stood there thinking he was watching some movie about a bank robbery in the mid-west. Any minute he expected Bonnie & Clyde to race up the street in a 1932 Ford with guns blazing. As he got closer, Pete spotted a convenience store standing alone next to a service station, and across the street was Mother's Café. When he arrived at the door of Mother's, Pete noticed a tractor kicking up dust around a farm stand down the block near the end of town.

Mother's wasn't much of a restaurant, it looked more like a country diner with a few small booths in front of the windows and a long counter with a dozen red covered vinyl stools. About half of the stools were occupied, and the folks sitting there all seemed to take a look at this stranger in town. As Pete took a seat in one of the booths, a young woman smacking on some chewing gum handed him a menu and asked, "Hi there, can I get ya somethin to drink?"

"A glass of iced tea would be nice."

"You bet you, be right back."

Pete decided on one of the specials, the half a roasted chicken dinner with mashed potatoes and carrots. When the waitress came back with his drink, Pete ordered his meal and decided to make inquiries about Joey. He took out the picture while he asked,

"Excuse me, you seem very nice." The waitress blushed and crossed her legs. "Would you mind looking at this photo of me and my brother? He came into town a couple of weeks ago and well, it would be helpful to me if you could tell me if you remember seeing him."

The waitress took the picture and held it up staring at it while she remarked, "Nope, I don't recall seeing him around these parts. What happened to him?"

"Don't know, except he came to Berona to find us a place to stay and now, I can't find him."

"Did you go see the sheriff? He could help you find someone who's missing."

"I plan on it, but thanks anyway."

"Anytime."

As the waitress started to turn away, Pete had an idea. "Excuse me Miss,"

"Yes, did you forget somethin?"

Pete smiled and asked, "I was thinking, maybe you saw his girlfriend? Here's a picture of her, have you see her around?" Pete had taken out the photo of Kate that Detective Jackson had passed along to him. He figured he had nothing to loose and everything to gain.

"My, my, she is a purtty thing now isn't she? But no, I haven't seen either of them around Mother's. You mean they're both missing?"

"Well, I don't know that they're really missing? I'm just trying to see if anyone recognizes them. That's all. Thanks for your time Miss."

After dinner Pete paid his check and went along to the other stores in town showing the two photos and asking the same questions. Not one person mentioned seeing either Joey or Kate. No one showed any positive signs or nervous reactions either. As he left the farm stand and began the long walk back to his room at the Green Tree Motel, Pete started to have that empty feeling again. He had a few thoughts in his mind that he couldn't shake. What am I doing out here in Wisconsin? What do I know about police work anyway?

While he was nearing the end of town, a police cruiser slowed to a stop along the road. "Excuse me there young man, can I have a word with you?" Pete, surprised to see a local police car, froze in his tracks. It took nearly a minute for him to finally close his dropped jaw and walk over to the open window. "Sheriff Blackstone here and I'd like to know if you need help with something?" As Pete looked his way, he figured it didn't take very long for someone to call the Sheriff. The Sheriff slowly opened the door and stepped out of the cruiser. Pete Simpson took a deep breath and tried not to show his obvious nervousness.

"Hi Sheriff. My name is Pete Simpson and I'm from New York. Just asking the folks here if they saw my brother, Joey Capella."

"Got some ID on ya Pete Simpson?"

"ID? Sure, and I think one of the Long Island Detectives called you about this case? Do you remember speaking to a Detective Jackson from New York?"

"Jackson ya say, well yes, I do. And I guess they sent you down here because we couldn't find any trace of this guy Joey?" The Sheriff asked pointedly.

"No Sheriff, it wasn't anything like that. Joey's part of my family, he's my half-brother and I felt like I needed to look into things, that's all."

"That explains the two last names, but tell me Pete, have you found out anything?"

"No, nothing. I just got into Berona and all I had a chance to do was ask around here in town if anyone has seen him?"

"And?"

"No one has."

"Well, I'll tell you what Pete. You go ahead and poke around. Just don't rattle anyone too much otherwise I'll get a few more phone calls. And as a favor to Detective Jackson I'll be around if you get in any trouble and if you do find some sign of him or worse, you call me right away. How does that sound?"

"Sounds good, Sheriff. And I appreciate your willingness to help, thank you kindly."

"All right then, you have a nice evening now."

The Sheriff got back into his car and picked up the radio as Pete started the trek back to the Green Tree Motor Lodge.

The next morning Pete asked the clerk if he could he use the office phone to call over to New York. He dialed Detective Jackson's number and got his voice mail. So, he just left a long message about his experience and how no one recognized Joey's picture and how he met Sheriff Blackstone. The Motel Clerk listened in wondering what that was all about and who this Pete guy was anyway, some government agent or FBI man? Pete asked if he could call the local taxi company and the clerk nodded okay. She offered Pete some coffee and a still oven-warm corn muffin. Pete took them both happy to see some country hospitality.

About an hour later Sammy pulled up in his taxi raising some dust among the gravel. Pete wondered if that long wait constituted being there lickety-split as he had said? He got into the taxi with a cheerful, "Good Morning Sammy, am I glad to see you. My feet are tired and sore from all the country walking I've been doing."

Sammy, answered, "I'm glad you called Pete, where we off to today."

"Here's the address Sammy. It's where one of my brother's friends lives and I wanted to check it out and see if they have any information for me."

Sammy looked at the address, smiled and said. "I know that place, it's an old house about three miles from here. It used to belong to one of the farming families in the area. I guess they're renting it out or decided to sell it off.

About ten minutes later, Sammy turned the taxi off the main road and drove slowly up a narrow and twisty pot-holed driveway. As the taxi pulled up, Pete could see the house. It was an old rundown converted farmhouse. The first thing Pete noticed was how everything green around the house was overgrown. The front of the house was covered with darkened oil-stained cedar shakes. The forest green paint around the windows was chipped and peeling off. The roof was stained with leaves and the black shingles worn away in spots. One of the windows was cracked and another had broken glass in one of the windowpanes. On the right side of the house, sitting in tall-uncut grass, was a rusted up Ford Fairlane resting on flat tires. Pete sat there looking at the house wondering how he could keep the taxi waiting. He remembered an old trick and took out a twenty-dollar bill from his pocket. He ripped it in half and told him, "Sammy, here's half of a twenty, the other half is in my pocket and it's yours if you wait for me while I say hello to an old friend."

"Plus the fare?" Sammy asked as he reached for the half-torn bill.

"Yes, and a good tip too."

Pete opened the door of the taxi and stepped out while quickly looking over the property. As he approached the house, he spotted someone peeking through an old yellow curtain in the front window. He wavered, turning around briefly to make sure that Sammy still had the taxi sitting out front before taking a few more steps forward. Pete avoided looking into the window again and took a careful step up onto the porch as the old wood planks gave slightly under his weight. He knocked on the door and felt his heart pounding in his chest. The door creaked open and standing in the doorway was a woman looking close to forty. She was a short stocky woman about five feet three inches tall and easily two hundred pounds. The first thing he noticed was the three chins hanging down from her mouth and the fluff of hair forming on both her cheeks. She was dressed in bib-top farmer style overalls over a yellowing oversized tee shirt. Her dark brown hair was cropped very short and uncombed. One thing for sure, Pete quickly realized. This is not the girl in the photo.

"What can I do fa ya there fella?" She asked sarcastically, as if the knock on the door interrupted her beauty treatment.

Pete swallowed with a very dry throat, coughed, did his best to clear his throat and responded. "My name is Pete and I'm looking for my brother." At that moment, Pete looked right into her eyes as he continued, "His name is Joey Capella. Have you seen him?"

The woman placed her hand on the door and looked down at her feet when she responded, "Never heard of any Joey Capella, why ya askin?"

"Joey came out here from New York to meet this woman." Pete pulled the photo of Kate out of his jacket pocket and held it out. "Her name is Kate and she invited Joey to visit her."

"Why you knocking on my door, I don't know any Kate and never heard of any Joey from New York?"

"Why? I'll tell you why." Pete started raising his voice in frustration and anger. "Because this is the address he had. This is the house he came to meet Kate in and why don't you start telling me the truth?"

While the woman at the door began to answer Pete's question, her eyes became fixed on the taxi out front. "I told you, I don't know either of those people and you, Mista Wise-ass New Yorker, ya better get off my property before I call the Sheriff on ya."

"You mean, Sheriff Blackstone? Oh yeah, call him. He knows I'm here and wished me good luck too."

The woman slammed the door causing Pete to step back abruptly losing his balance and almost falling off the porch. He knew he had been very brave speaking to her that way and he also knew he was totally out of his element. Pete climbed back into the backseat of Sammy's taxi with mixed emotions, felling shaky with a mind that was racing with thoughts. Sammy pulled slowly away as Pete glanced up at the window, noticing once again the unattractive heavyset woman peeking through the front window at them.

Sammy asked, "Hey, what was that all about? That lady there didn't seem very welcoming."

"No, she wasn't and I'm glad you were waiting for me too. Who knows how crazy she would have become?"

"Say man, you got that other half of the twenty? Gas is expensive you know."

Pete handed the other half of the twenty to Sammy commenting, "Here Sammy, and a small price for insurance."

Later that day, Pete tried to use his cell phone but couldn't once again because of a weak signal. He went to the motel clerk and offered to pay to use the phone a second time. He called Detective Jackson and filled him in on what has been going on here in Berona. Pete held back his anger at the woman he encountered explaining to Detective Jackson why he felt she was lying. Not being able to keep eye contact, looking down and appearing so nervous about the taxi outside. Detective Jackson complimented Pete and reminded him to be careful.

"You can't do much with suspicions and ideas Pete."

"Pete felt excited and asked, "Do you think the Sheriff would go back to that house with me?"

"That's hard to say Pete, maybe, maybe not. You can call the sheriff's office and ask?"

"I'll think about it and let you know what happens."

"Okay Pete, take care and remember, don't overreact and do anything stupid."

"Sure, I'll remember that. Bye for now."

The next morning Pete did telephone Sheriff Dan Blackstone to discuss what happened at the door. The Sheriff was intrigued enough or annoyed enough to go along with Pete's request. He told Pete he would pick him up at the Green Tree Motor Lodge in a couple of hours and they would go look into the situation at the lady's house.

Before long, Pete was climbing into the passenger side of the Sheriff's car and as they rode over, the Sheriff asked a lot of questions about Joey. And then, recalling what Detective Jackson had told him over the phone, the sheriff asked Pete what Joey was doing visiting some stranger he met on the Web? Pete tried his best to explain how something like that might have happened to Joey. About his divorce and about how Joey was feeling particularly lonely these days. The Sheriff also explained something very odd to Pete and it took him by surprise. Sheriff Blackstone told Pete that he wasn't the only one coming into town asking about a missing person. Actually, in the last year alone there were three inquires plus his. Except, Pete was the only one with an address to knock on. This time he felt he had to take more action and look into this woman's situation at the farmhouse.

Then the Sheriff pulled his car up the narrow dirt driveway and all Pete could do was look ahead and wonder. This time Pete didn't see anyone peeking out of the window. They walked up to the door of the farmhouse and knocked a few times. No one answered as the Sheriff called out, "Hello? Hello, anyone home? This is the sheriff here, hello?" The sheriff tried knocking again and then said to Pete, "Okay come on, let's take a look around back."

They passed a small overgrown garden and looked into an open garage made of rotting long planks. As they were about to give up the search for the woman, Pete spotted the entrance to a shed that was stuck into the side of the hill and asked the Sheriff,

"What is that shed there?" Pointing toward the tree line to the more than half-buried shed behind the garage.

The Sheriff responded, "Years ago, when they grew potatoes and corn here, they used to store the vegetables in there. Sort of a natural icebox and a great way to keep the leftover crops from spoiling." They walked over and as the Sheriff pushed in on the mildew stained door, it fell to the side hanging on one hinge. They could see a narrow tunnel in front of them. Sheriff Blackstone called out, "Hello, anyone down there?" He took out his flashlight from its belt clip holder and nodded to Pete to follow him in. The tunnel became narrower a few feet in and they needed to duck under an overhead railroad timber support. There was a small water drip into a puddle that gave off a musty odor. Just to the right was an opening and the bright beam from the flashlight revealed a sight they weren't prepared for. What they saw frightened Pete Simpson to the bone.

On the far wall were a few wood shelves sitting between stacks of bricks. On the shelves were skulls, about a half dozen on each shelf. They appeared to be human skulls. Eighteen in all and all lined up in order with the same distance in between and the same angle facing straight as can be. Pete immediately felt nauseous and wanted to run out of that cave as fast as he could. Sheriff Blackstone motioned to him to back out carefully. "All right Pete we found something here that needs more experience than I have. Let's not disturb anything and I'll call this into the State Police. They'll bring a Forensic Team over here to determine what it is we have uncovered."

They backtracked out of the tunnel and into the daylight. Pete found himself doubled over behind a bush as the Sheriff called for backup. When they searched the farmhouse room by room they concluded that the woman who was living there apparently left in haste. There were unwashed dishes in the sink, food in the refrigerator and clothing scattered on the bed. A power cord and a phone line laid across a small wood desk in the bedroom offering evidence a computer may have been used there. They figured whoever was living in the farmhouse either left on some errand or flew the coup. Whatever she did, she did in a hurry.

Later that evening, Pete telephoned Detective Jackson and was full of excitement filling him in on what he and the Sheriff had found.

"What will you do now Pete?" Detective Jackson wanted to know.

"Well, Blackstone said the State Police would want to question me. But, after that there doesn't seem like there's anything left for me to do here. The Sheriff explained he would contact you after all the forensic examinations are finished and the investigation is complete. So, I guess I'll be flying home late tomorrow on the next available flight to New York."

"Okay Pete, let's talk in a couple of days?"

"You bet I'll call you."

"Have a safe trip back."

"Thanks, I will."

About a month later, all the reports were in and Pete was sitting in Detective Jackson's office back on Long Island. "Well Pete, we have most of the answers, not all, but most. And I'm afraid it's not very good news. After the forensic examinations of the skulls by the experts from the FBI and an investigation by the Wisconsin State Police, here's what they found. The skulls are human and all are males between thirty and fifty years of age. The tests show that the men were all murdered over the last twenty-four months and a very powerful form of sulfuric acid was used to dissolve their bodies. They found a steel tub further back in the shed that contained the acid. Next to the tub was an old worn down butcher-block table with an assortment of butcher knives positioned in the table's slots. There were traces found of human tissue and blood but no evidence of anyone's remains. Only the skulls were found and Pete, I'm sorry to tell you this, but the DNA findings prove that the last skull on the shelf belonged to Joey Capella. He fits the profile they developed for all the victims, no family and no one to look into a missing person. Except, she never counted on you Pete. You proved to be the one to ruin her nest."

"The FBI and the Wisconsin Sate Police concluded that the woman called Kate that Joey thought he was meeting probably never existed. She didn't run her own Public Relations firm, she didn't look like the pictures she had e-mailed Joey, and she wasn't a single mom as far as we know. Instead, the woman you met was a strange and rare case of a female serial killer, a woman who attracted unattached single men with no family in Internet chat rooms. She used the Web as her contact method and lured her victims to visit her by fooling them to think she was a sexy beautiful woman. It appears she faked everything including caring for them and ultimately teasing the men with make believe sexual play. AOL's parent company, Time/Warner cooperated completely with the FBI who looked into details of the woman's AOL account and found numerous e-mail notes to many men all over the country. There were photographs of the victims, their e-mail addresses and in many of the cases, phone numbers to lead the investigators to uncover their identities. What the e-mails exposed was a pattern of lies and deceit that revealed her true nature."

"The FBI investigators have been able to locate records of the men she murdered and have looked into their pasts. They have found an incredible trail of deceit and with DNA tests have discovered who most of the victims were. What this woman does is terrifying. Like the black widow spider, she lures these perspective mates in, and kills them. Except, this killer does even more. She butchers their bodies and uses acid to burn away everything but the skulls. Whoever she is, she's long gone. The FBI is on her trail and perhaps they will catch up with her at some point. For now, they need to warn the public and Internet users everywhere of this black widow spider of the Internet who uses the web as her lair. One might say for her—it was one web, or another."

# SEEING

## IS

# BELIEVING

*"Trust everybody, but
cut the cards."*

W.C. Fields

The sand felt cool under her bare feet while the morning sun glistened off the perspiration beading along her shoulders. The ocean waves curled their way onto the sandy shore with thunderous roars of power. Melissa loved her morning run along the ocean stretching from Southampton, Long Island on the east to the County Park at Moriches Inlet on the west. She loved the sights her eyes took in and she loved the sounds of the ocean as she made her way west. It was her usual exercise routine, combining a beach run beside the ocean with a return trip along Dune Road on roller blades. She carried her blades, two water bottles, an energy bar and an iPod music player in a small backpack strapped around her shoulders. As she ran along, she never tired of the views of the mansions first from the ocean side and then from Dune Road. Those mansions, long a symbol of wealth, always reminded Melissa of her own humble beginnings. What she could see was home after home rising from the sand in various architectural designs one more beautiful than the other inspiring her to make her practice not only a medical success, but a financial success as well.

When she reached the Park, Melissa sat at a roadside picnic table just inside the Park's entrance; she donned socks and slipped on her roller blades snapping the buckles into place. She found her hand reflexively moving to her left eye feeling the itch and the burning sensation once again. Of course, she knew she shouldn't rub her eye, but yet she couldn't control the impulse either. The burning reminded her to stop procrastinating and to finally make that appointment with her eye doctor not putting it off any longer than she already had.

Feeling the warmth from the sun, she sipped some water and looked out at the fisherman casting their rigs into the channel waters. A dozen or so seagulls circled above the water taking turns diving down like kamikaze pilots into the chop to snatch unsuspecting baitfish. She could see the commotion of the seagulls and how they attracted the attention of the boat skippers converging on the area. Melissa smiled and after a brief rest, she placed a Yankee baseball cap over her head, adjusted the iPod's earplugs and set just the right volume before heading out down Dune Road. She waved to the Park Ranger as she skated past the gate knowing his eyes always followed her out. It was more than the way the spandex shorts showed off her tight buttocks and slim hips, it was the complete look of a beautiful woman exercising that drew attention.

Melissa leaned forward and folded her hands loosely behind her back as she slid her blades along the smooth blacktop settling into the rhythm of the music playing in her ears. She could feel the ache in her thighs as her legs pulled her entire weight along without the benefit of an arm swing. For a short while, she had found a way to escape the daily pressures and forget the unhappy situation at home. Except, somehow the thoughts found a way to pop right back into her mind. She recalled for the thousandth time the phone call on that dreadful day that changed her life when the nurse from the hospital announced her mother had suffered a stroke and was in intensive care. Eight days later, Melissa was walking out of the funeral home carrying a small pure white shopping bag. The white bag contained a plain cardboard box that held her Mother's ashes, the result of her cremation. Nothing had prepared her for the cold matter-of-fact handling of her mother's remains by the funeral home director. Sure, she thought, being cremated was her mother's wish, but who expected it would go like it did. The entire experience left her withdrawn and sadder than she could ever remember. Even now, two months later, her mother's passing so suddenly left her feeling empty and with an extraordinarily heavy heart.

The beep, beep of a construction truck horn driving by too closely snapped her back to reality and to the pain in her thighs that had grown. She decided to hold up a few minutes at the wood path called Munn's Point that jutted out from Dune Road along the coast ending in the bay. She rolled along the planks noticing a young couple embracing at the water's edge. Melissa took a deep breath and felt a pang in her own heart. She shook her head with a chill recalling the memory of her husband packing his suitcase and heading out the door. She gently removed the iPod's earplugs from her ears and thought, no more husband, no more mother, what's next? She turned her head toward the giggles from the couple seeing them chase each other playfully around the sand. *Yes,* she realized, love can make you giggle at one time and it can make you cry at another. Enjoy the moments kids, while they last.

A few hours later, Melissa was showered and ready to head out to her office. She walked into the den of her parent's house and checked on her dad. He was sitting comfortably in a La-z-Boy lounge chair watching a golfer drive a ball to the cheers of the crowd. "Hey Pop" she softly shouted, "I'm on my way out to the office. I'll see you later for supper, okay?" Her dad's eyes never left the TV while only an arm and a small wave of his hand acknowledged her departure. Melissa let the door close quietly behind her as she made her way to the red Jeep Wrangler parked in the drive. She started up the engine and felt the tires spin on the gravel bed driveway as she entered the main road. Melissa quickly shifted the gears of the manual transmission increasing her speed. She enjoyed having the top down as she felt the early summer breeze lift her hair.

She parked the Jeep and quickly read the sign reserving her spot in the small parking area. Dr. Melissa Speyer, Speech Pathologist. She smiled to herself with pride knowing what she had overcome to reach this stage even with the odds against her so great. That little sign always gave her a reminder, always gave her a lift. Melissa felt the irritation in her eye again as a tear slid down her cheek. Damn, she thought as she looked in the rearview mirror at the redness in her eye. All right all ready, I'll call the optometrist and have that looked at. This itching is really annoying. She reached for her bag and slipped out of the jeep walking briskly to the entrance of her Hampton's Pediatric Speech and Language Center. As she entered past the large white door, she glanced over at the waiting area. There, her first scheduled patient was waiting playing with the dollhouse, as her mom read a magazine with a bored look on her face. Melissa stopped by the reception desk,
"How are you today Jeanette?"
"Oh, I'm doing fine Dr. Speyer." She gestured to the waiting area and added, "They've been here about ten minutes now. Little Anna is first up and Jason is expected in forty minutes." Dr. Speyer blinked a few times, as if that would clear up the burning in her eye. Jeanette added, "I can call Dr. Biddle about that eye if you'd like and set up an appointment for you?"
Melissa grabbed for a tissue to blot the tears and answered her, "Okay, sure, call Dr. Biddle for me. I think he has evening

hours tonight, so ask him if he can see me this evening around seven."

"No problem Dr. Speyer, now you go take care of Anna."

Melissa slipped on her white lab coat as she heard Anna and her mom enter the treatment room. Anna was one of Dr. Speyer's success stories. Anna was born prematurely weighing only three and three-quarter pounds. Of course, as in most premature infants, there were developmental delays that needed intervention. Anna's pediatrician, Dr. Gross from Southampton Hospital had referred her to Melissa Speyer from the very beginning. At first, Anna was part of an early intervention program and Dr. Speyer consulted as a member of the interdisciplinary team. Soon after, Anna was also seen by Dr. Speyer privately to increase the therapy by spending more time with Anna one-on-one. Anna's parents could afford it and why not? Having money was part of living in the Hamptons and Anna's parents would do anything to help return little Anna to normal function. The intervention made a difference. Anna was speaking almost normally for her age. It was three years of intensive speech therapy; three years of working closely with Anna. Dr. Speyer felt great about the progress and great about the difference she was able to make.

Her second patient, Jason was not as lucky. The same low birth weight and premature delivery, the same intensive intervention; but, not the same result. For some reason, unknown to everyone involved in the case, Jason hadn't improved much at all. While Jason could identify the letters of the alphabet, he could not sound out many of the letters or put those sounds together into syllables to form words; never mind complete simple sentences. He had the cognitive ability, but not the vocal skills. He was behind in his age appropriate development by at least eighteen months. Dr. Speyer tried; she tried everything she knew. In Jason's case, there was something wrong with his brain function and not just a developmental delay. Jason's parents would not give up; especially his mom who insisted on private sessions at their lavish Watermill home in addition to the scheduled office visits. Each visit made Dr. Speyer wish she could do more. But she couldn't and Jason, unlike little Anna, would most likely not take part in a normal school or a normal life.

After the children's therapy sessions, her office assistant reminded her of her schedule. "Excuse me Dr. Speyer," she said with the usual admiration. "You have an evaluation scheduled at the Hospital in thirty minutes."

Dr. Speyer looked up at Jeanette and replied in a soft voice, "Yes I remember, one of Dr. Gross' patients, right?"

"That's right, a newborn delivered over the weekend. Small too, just barely three pounds."

"They're so tiny Jeanette, so fragile and yet these premature babies are strong enough to fight for their life."

Jeanette was beaming in admiration of her boss when she said, "It's amazing what you do. I could never manage to work with these little babies."

"Sure you could, if you had the training and experience you would have no problem."

As Jeanette took a deep breath, her head sank forward causing her shoulder length hair to fall in front of her face blocking the view to her hazelnut colored eyes and her increasingly pink cheeks. Melissa recognized Jeanette's sadness and let her own kindness show through.

"Well look," Dr. Speyer said warmly, "never mind anyway because I'm glad you're my office assistant. I wouldn't want to give you up."

Jeanette lifted her head and replied, "Oh, thank you for saying that, but you better hurry up now or you'll miss your appointment. And by the way, I set up an evening appointment to have your eyes checked by Dr. Biddle at eight-fifteen this evening. Are you still feeling that itchy eye?"

"Oh yeah Jeanette, it's still bothering me, but the itch comes and goes. If it is an infection of some kind, I'll be glad to have some medication to clear up whatever it is. You can't imagine how annoying this irritation is."

Just then the phone rang and as Jeanette answered the call, she waved to Dr. Speyer to go ahead and Melissa, recognizing the window of opportunity, waved back as she left the office heading over to Southampton Hospital. Once the Jeep was pointed down Montauk Highway toward the hospital, the thoughts in her mind focused on her father. What is the best thing for him after all, she wondered. Without Mom to look after him, he isn't able to live independently. And I can't stay with him indefinitely, but where would he be the happiest? Her mind raced through the options; an adult home or assisted living, wondering where he would fit in and where he would receive the best care? After all, her Father was only sixty, but since that work related back injury and the disability that followed, his options were limited. It wasn't his mental ability, just his limited mobility. At least in these settings, he would have opportunities to socialize and to join in on the planned activities. She knew he would have a much better life than just sitting in front of the TV watching baseball all alone.

The rest of her afternoon was taken up with several home speech therapy visits and another group of office appointments. Before she knew it, Dr. Speyer was parking her Jeep at her parents' house and rushing in with two takeout dinners. She and her dad didn't spend much time together these days and their dinnertime was about the best quality time they had. "Hi Pop," she yelled from the kitchen trying her best to be upbeat. "Come on in, we've got a good one for supper." Her dad entered the room and Melissa embraced him with a warm greeting.

"So, how's the doc doing this evening? He asked with his usual sarcastic tongue.

"Oh Pop," she replied ignoring the sarcasm. "I worked with another preemie today; a little girl just barely three pounds. And she was sooooo cute."

"Yeah, well, better it's someone's else baby and not mine. I had my hands full just raising you and that devil of a brother of yours."

"Now Pop," she started sternly. "Don't you be trying to make me feel bad again. We've been through all that before."

They sat down to eat and left all the bad thoughts alone for a while. She knew how bitter her father had become and tried hard not to provoke him. At moments like these, Melissa felt the sadness knowing very well that her father loved her and would do anything for her. It was just his anger that got in the way, but at that moment she didn't want to think about that family pain.

Later that evening, Dr. Biddle was examining Melissa's eyes. "So, tell me. How long have you been feeling the irritation?"

"About a week," she answered. "First it was the left eye and I guess whatever bug was causing the problem jumped over to the right eye too because now they're both bothering me." Dr. Biddle placed his scope down and explained he needed to take a wipe from her eye fluid to determine what was causing the problem.

"It looks like an infection growing in there Melissa; we'll be able to identify it after it's cultured. My best guess is there's some bacteria at the root of it. It'll take twenty-four hours or so to know for sure."

Melissa blinked a few times and asked, "Can you give me something for it now or do you have to wait?"

"I can write a prescription for an ocular antibiotic that will help clear up any infection and lubricate your eyes at the same time to minimize the itching."

"That's great," Melissa started. "And thanks so much for squeezing me in tonight."

"Sure, no problem Melissa, happy to help."

He took out his prescription pad and wrote up the medication order. As he handed it to her he explained, "So, we'll call your office with the results in a couple of days. If the irritation gets worse, call and let me know. This medication should have an immediate effect, but let's keep an eye on it. Okay?"

"An eye on it?" she asked tongue-in-cheek and they both laughed. Melissa looked at her watch and figured if she rushed over she could make it to the Main Street Pharmacy before they closed.

As she entered the old time pharmacy, Melissa thought, it's so great to live in a small town where everyone knows everyone. Especially when it's five minutes to closing and you need a prescription filled.

"Hi Howard," she said with a coy smile on her face. "Can you do me a favor and fill this?"

Howard Westfield smiled back as he looked over the wire-framed glasses tilted down his nose. "How can I say no to a beautiful girl like you Melissa? I mean even if it is closing time and I still have several prescriptions yet to go. Give it here now." As he reached for the half folded piece of paper he added, "And I suppose you'll want to wait for it eh?"

"It's for my eyes and I can't take the itch anymore, Howard"

"Oh, it's for you? I just assumed you needed something for your father."

"No, not this time. This time I have the problem."

He looked at the prescription studying the medication order for a minute.

"Ah, so you have a bit of an eye infection?"

"I have no clue where I picked it up either."

Howard Westfield, PhD started mixing the drugs as he explained, "Picking up an infection isn't that unusual for someone who works with children and don't forget you're in and out of the hospital too. Lots of nasty little germs hanging around hospitals you know." Just then, there was a clang of a large bottle dropping onto the counter as the glass canister slipped through his grip breaking a couple of smaller vials making a chemical puddle and a liquid mess. He had a cuss word or two for the experience as he blamed himself. "Gosh darn these old hands, look at this mess." He wiped the counter with some paper towels dropping them into the small garbage receptacle he kept under the counter. "I'm so sorry Melissa and embarrassed."

"Don't you worry about anything Howard, I made you rush and things happen when you rush."

Doctor Westfield slowly entered the medication information into his computer and printed out the label for the eye drops Doctor Biddle had ordered. He attached the label and placed the vial with its dropper into a small bag and handed the package to Melissa. She signed for the medication thanking him once again for filling the prescription even though it was late.

"You're welcome, anytime. But listen, don't overdo the drops Melissa, just two or three every four hours, okay?"

"Sure Howard, I'll be careful.

Later that night, Melissa was in the bathroom reading the warnings on the printed insert that came with the medication. Oh my god, she thought. It's amazing how many cautions they list for these medicines. If everyone followed those contra-indications, I bet no one would ever take their medicines. She shook the medication vial, unscrewed the cap and dunked the eyedropper into the medicine. She squeezed the dropper bulb pushing the air out and when she let go, the medication rushed into the dropper. Melissa leaned her head back and with one eye staring into the mirror, she held her left eye open and positioned the dropper over her eye. She watched one, then two drops fall from the dropper into her left eye. She blinked reflexively and then blinked again to help spread the medicine. She switched the dropper over her right eye and held the eye open as a couple of drops fell out of the dropper into her eye immediately soothing the burning. She closed both eyes expecting to feel some relief from the burning and instead, she began to feel the strangest sensations. It started with an uncontrollable trembling moving throughout her body. The sensations made her grab hold of the vanity top to steady herself. Her heartbeat thumbed intensely inside her chest as she wondered what was happening. Even though her eyes were closed she saw flashes of colored lights before her blending with a hundred bright white spots flickering in a black background.

Melissa sat down on the toilet seat and placed her head down between her legs hoping the episode would stop. And it did, slowly. She blinked her eyes a few times seeing fewer bright spots while the flashes of color became less and less noticeable. Then the trembling subsided as her heartbeat slowed returning to normal. She regained control of her breathing as her brain had one thought, what was that she wondered? She tried to stand and found her legs weak, so she sat back down again and called out to her father, "Hey Pop, can you help me? I'm in the bathroom and feel dizzy."

Her father appeared in the doorway and nervously asked, "Melissa, are you okay? What's going on?"

"I don't know Pop; I put the drops in my eyes and had a reaction. There were flashes of light, I saw white spots flickering and my entire body started trembling. Then, within a few minutes whatever was happening passed. Now, I just feel lightheaded and nervous. Can you help me into my bedroom so I can lie down?"

"Sure Missy," he said. She heard that and had a flash of her childhood. It was what her father called her back then. It was his way of being affectionate and she smiled at the memory even with this strange experience still lingering.

Her father stood in front of her and offered his hands to help her up. Melissa started to grab hold of her father's hands and reminded him, "Now don't you go and pull your back out. Nice and easy Pop." As he slowly pulled her up to her feet their eyes met and she smiled as she looked deeply into his eyes. Suddenly, there was a strong electrical charge between them and Melissa closed her eyes tight as she felt a surge of energy pass through her hands into his and then back to hers culminating in her brain. When she was brave enough to open her eyes, she felt like she was floating in air. It was as if there was a suspension of time, as several flashes of light sparkled around several fuzzy images. She tried to focus her mind's eye and could see in a distance her father lying in a hospital intensive care bed wearing an oxygen mask and there was a respirator hooked up to an endotracial tube in his throat. Another surge of energy and a flash of color brought her eyes to his chest and suddenly she could see inside his chest cavity directly into his lungs as they expanded and contracted with each urgent breath he took in. What she saw frightened her to her core, because there was disease there inside her father's lung walls. Reacting to the horror before her, she yanked away and finally pulled her hands from his fixing her eyes on the bathroom floor as she sat back down.

He went to reach for her again and she recoiled, "Don't Pop, just let me be a minute. I saw something frightening and I don't understand what it meant." Her father stood there puzzled wanting in someway to be able to help her. He felt helpless as he watched her. Melissa started to regain control of her breathing again feeling the nervous trembling pass through her. "I don't know Pop, I saw you in intensive care and you were connected to all sorts of tubes. And you were breathing with a respirator. It was horrible. I could see inside your lungs and your lung walls were covered with blackened tissue. Oh, my God! It could be emphysema or cancer? And Pop, you looked much older, like seventy or eighty and I think you were dying. Did you see what I saw?"

"No Melissa, I didn't see anything. I only felt your strong grip on my hands and several strong tugs. The whole thing was weird."

Melissa looked at her hands and was surprised to see some small burn marks on the inside of her palms. "Hey Pop, she said in wonder. "What do you think this is from?" And she held out her hands to show him the burns. As she looked up into his face, her father drew back a bit and told her in a hesitating voice,

"Your eyes Melissa, there are streaks of bright red blood in them. Now, that's scary." She struggled to her feet and looked into the mirror with wide eyes.

"Will you look at that. I never had blood in my eyes before. Oh, shit . . ."

"Do you want me to call for an ambulance?"

As she looked again at her eyes and then her hands she responded slowly, "I don't think so Pop. There's no pain in my eyes, only that same itchy feeling I had before. What could they do for me in the ER? How about I just lay down for a while and then I'll see how I'm feeling."

Slowly, she took some steps into her bedroom leaning up against the walls. Her father followed behind, careful not to touch her. As she lay down, Melissa told her dad, "I'll tell you one thing though, I may not feel any pain, but boy, I am pretty exhausted." She took another deep breath and continued, "It's as if that episode, whatever it was, drained my energy." She closed her eyes and said, "Give me a couple of hours Pop, then we'll see. Okay?"

He pulled the afghan over her and said softly, "Sure Missy, you rest now."

The next thing she knew, her morning alarm was awakening her to another day. She turned off the alarm on her way to the bathroom and wondered if what she remembered from the night before was real or a dream. She turned on the light and immediately looked into the vanity mirror at her eyes. Except for a minor redness, the streaks of blood were pretty much gone. Melissa raised her hands to the light to take a good look at her palms and the burn marks were pretty much gone too. Now what, she thought. I have these vivid images from last night and yet, without the physical signs, how do I explain what happened to anyone? As a matter of fact, how do I explain it, or for that matter, believe it myself?

She spent the next few minutes recalling the shocks she felt and the flashes of light. She remembered the images of her father in the ICU and then, the dreadful pictures of his diseased lungs. She had no idea what brought on the whole thing or what it meant. Then, there was a shadow of doubt that made her reflect on the experience. Was it true, she wondered, or was it just part of her imagination? But, if it were true, what would cause something like that? Was it the eye drops I used or some kind of energy thing? As she thought about these different scenarios, another thought popped into her mind that gave her pause. Is it possible that this is a gift? That being able to see someone's future would be a good thing? The thoughts kept rolling around in her mind until, in the end she settled on the idea that it would be easier if what she thought happened, was just something she had dreamed, easier for everybody else too.

Melissa walked into the kitchen looking for her father and saw him sitting in a chair at the table with one hand under his chin, the other hand holding a coffee cup with the most worried look on his worn out face.

"Pop, from the expression on your face, I guess that what I was hoping was only a dream, really happened, eh?'

Her Father took a moment to gather his thoughts and replied in a nervous voice, "Oh yeah, it happened all right. And I've been worried ever since. What's going on Missy? Are we in some episode of the *X-Files*, the *Twilight Zone* or what? Don't touch that dial, there's nothing wrong with your TV."

"I have no idea Pop. Except, I feel fine now. A little shaky, but okay. And soon, I have to get ready to go to the Center." Maybe, I should call Dr. Biddle and ask him if he has any clue to what happened? Except, I don't think he or anyone else would be able to explain it away. I think we would get a lot of left field looks. And by the way, how come you didn't wake me up earlier?"

"I tried last night, but you kept moaning and ignoring me so I figured, hey, you must be tired."

Her father got up and poured a little more coffee into his cup. Then he suggested, "Here's an idea, maybe it's better not to say anything at all, sort of just forget the whole thing? What do you think about that idea?"

He brought over a mug for Melissa and filled it with coffee. She took the cup and sipped the coffee feeling the warmth flow inside of her. "You know Pop, my first reaction is to agree with you and just forget the entire thing. Then, there's the other side of the argument."

"What's that Missy, what other side?" He had replaced the coffee pot on the stove and sat back down again wondering what his daughter had in mind.

"I guess I'm curious."

"Curious?" He responded, as if there was some loaded gun built into that idea. "About what? Curious that the shocks and light flashes could end up hurting you?"

"No Pop, curious about two things. First, if what I saw in the future, your future; means we can do something about it before you get real sick and we can save your life. And second, if what happened could be replicated?" She looked at him and recognized that he was not following her line of thought. "Pop, I'm not a mad scientist or anything like that, I'm talking about the good that could come from such an ability. I mean, if I could take a few drops of medication in my eyes, touch someone and then be able to see something in the future that could end up helping that person, wouldn't that be a good thing? Wouldn't you want me to use such a power to help people?"

"Missy, what, you're thinking you have some superpower?"

"Maybe I do have a superpower Pop, and what would be wrong with that anyway?"

"I don't know Missy, I just don't know?"

They sat there for a minute or two being quiet just taking turns sipping their coffees. They both had so much to process, so much to digest. Melissa's Father broke the silence with another question. "What makes you think that what you saw was a good thing anyway?"

She sat there thinking about that question for a few minutes and then responded, "Here's what I think. How about we go arrange for you to have some tests; chest x-rays and a CT Scan. If it turns out that you are sick, and we can intervene and get you well, then I would have to say it is a very, very, good thing to have detected it early on. If there is no diseased tissue and you're not sick, then, I guess we'll know that what I saw meant nothing."

Her Father didn't hesitate even though he wasn't at all fond of hospitals or doctors. He finished his coffee, put the cup into the sink and told his daughter, "Okay, I'll go along with that. Will you set it up for me?"

"Yes Pop, I will and if I can, I'll arrange for the tests this afternoon." Melissa finished her coffee and decided to ask her Father for an opinion. "Well, one thing for sure, I better not use those drops again until I speak with Dr. Biddle about that medication reaction."

"Why Missy, do you think the drops caused it all?"

"I don't know if it was the drops or some combination of things. I can't ignore the timing, but it is heard to believe that some antibiotic would have that kind of effect?"

"Where did you get those eye drops Missy?"

"I went to the Main Street Pharmacy last night after my appointment with Dr. Biddle. Howard Westfield filled the prescription for me, you remember him right Pop?"

"Oh sure, I remember him, an older gentleman though, well into his late seventies, right? Wasn't he planning on retiring?"

"He likes to work, at least that's what he says."

"Gosh, I hope he's careful when he mixes up those medications."

Melissa heard those words, *I hope he's careful* and remembered the glass canister that dropped and the noise of glass bottles breaking. Then it hit her, could all of those drugs have gotten mixed up and ended up in her vial? Could that have caused the chemical reaction in her body? Melissa kept those ideas to herself not wanting to frighten her Father anymore than he already was.

"Well listen Pop, we're not going to figure this thing out right now, so I'll go shower and change and then I'll get in touch with Dr. Biddle and find out what he thinks happened to me? How about you relax for a while and I'll call you after I see him, okay?"

"Sure Missy, except, don't forget to call. You know I'll be worried about you, right?"

"Of course I'll call, right after I see Dr. Biddle. So rest up now and I'll see you later."

After her shower, Melissa stood in front of the mirror blow-drying her hair stealing several glances at the medication vial sitting on the counter. She wondered about the drops she used.

Was it the drops she placed in her eyes that caused her to have those visions? If it was the drops, what could have made them so powerful? All sorts of thoughts rolled around in her head. What would happen to her if she did take the drops again? What could be the worst thing that could happen? Maybe I would have another psychic experience and even see someone else's future? How bad could that be anyway? Then, she ended up having a little conversation with herself, "I guess that just depends on who it is? Or, nothing at all would happen? Look, how will you ever know that the eye drops caused what you experienced if you don't try them again? Really, girl."

Once her sandy blond hair was dry, Melissa picked up the vial and filled the dropper with the medicine. Then, she shook her head in disbelief, as she squeezed the dropper watching the medicine drip back into the vial. She thought, you guys look harmless enough, how did you ever become so powerful anyway? Then, she screwed the dropper on tight and went to dress.

As Melissa walked into her bedroom she looked up Dr. Biddle's pager in her address book. She dialed his pager, entered her cell phone number and disconnected waiting for him to respond. It didn't take long, her cell phone rang and Melissa answered the call, "Hello?"

"Hi, yes, someone paged me?"

"Oh, hello Dr. Biddle this is Melissa Speyer. I paged you."

"Is anything wrong Melissa?"

"Wrong? Well, not exactly, but yes, something isn't right either."

"What is it Melissa? What's the problem, did your infection get worse?"

Melissa swallowed hard and continued, "Dr. Biddle—listen carefully, I'm going to tell you something, something that happened to me after I used the drops you prescribed, but you can't laugh okay?"

"Laugh? Why would I laugh Melissa?"

"Because what I am about to tell you sounds like something out of a *Twilight Zone* episode or a Steven King novel, so don't laugh or call me crazy all right?"

"Sure Melissa, I'll just listen . . ."

So, she told him everything. About what happened after she used the eye drops. How there were flashes of colored lights and flickering white spots. Then, she told him what happened when her hands touched her father's hands and how looking into his eyes opened up some portal into the future and how she could actually see things. She also told him about the visions, seeing her father in an ICU bed and the diseased images of his lungs. She mentioned the burns on her palms and the blood streaks in her eyes. Then, when she was all done she asked Dr. Biddle,

"So, will the men in the white coats be coming to get me or what?"

There was a moment of silence and then Dr. Biddle responded, "Now, that is one of the wildest stories I have ever heard. Are you thinking of writing a book or a movie or are you just testing me?"

"I'm not doing any of that . . . it's all real and my Dad can vouch for me. He witnessed the whole thing. Well, at least he can tell you about the weird reaction to the drops."

Dr. Biddle hesitated, trying to organize his thoughts, and then he decided to take a look for himself. "I'll tell you what Melissa. How about you come into the office right away for an exam? Let me take a look at your eyes and your burnt palms and judge for myself. Oh, and bring the eye drops too."

"All right, it'll take me about thirty minutes to get ready and drive over. Will that be all right?"

"Sure, I'll meet you at my office in half an hour."

Melissa pressed the disconnect button on her cell phone and thought about that conversation. Now I know, if someone called me and told me that story, I would definitely think they were off their rocker or on drugs or something. Except, Dr.

Biddle knows me and knows my medical background. I guess I just have to explain the experience in a professional manner. She also decided to contact her brother and fill him in about what has been going on. Even though her father didn't have any contact with Craig, Melissa was close to her brother and stayed in touch with him frequently. She used her cell phone to call him and when he didn't answer she left a message that she needed to speak with him about an urgent situation.

Thirty minutes later, Melissa was in the eye clinic at Southampton Hospital showing Dr. Biddle her palms.

"The burns were darker last night, only these little marks are left," she said allowing her wrists to rotate from side to side so he could see the damage.

"I see and umm, they do resemble electrical burns. Look, they have a distinctive color and have not cut through the skin. I think we should have a specialist look at these burns just to help us gain some insights."

Dr. Biddle reached for his ocular scope and focused the light into Melissa's eyes. "Okay now, just tilt your head back a little and let me take a look. Well, I still see signs of an infection and the irritation you had the other day." He leaned a little closer and increased the magnification of the scope. "I also see that a few small capillaries have burst which could explain the streaks of blood you told me about."

"Dr. Biddle, what would cause the blood vessels to burst like that?"

"Sometimes that happens when a person strains too much causing the blood vessels to burst and the blood flows into the white of the eye. It could happen during childbirth or when an athlete strains. It's pretty common, but doesn't get much attention because it's not a serious condition."

Melissa flashed a memory of the experience last night and how the energy pulled and pushed her and her Dad back and forth with such force. "There was a great deal of power in that experience last night. I guess, it could have made me strain."

"And where are the drops I prescribed?"

She reached into her bag and handed him the small vial. He opened the vial and looked at the medication. Dr. Biddle shrugged his shoulders, took the dropper and placed some of the medication into a dish for a closer examination.

"I'm going to send that to the lab for analysis. Let's see what they tell us, okay?"

"Sure Dr. Biddle, I was hoping you would do that. There is something else I wanted to ask your opinion about."

"And what would that be?"

"Here's the thing, I know my story sounds far-fetched to say the least. And I have wondered how those two little drops in each eye could have had that effect?"

Dr. Biddle looked at her with a skeptical look on his face as she continued.

"But, if anything, I would like to know if those drops caused the reaction and I'm curious that if I was to use the drops again, would the same thing happen again and could I see into someone else's future?"

He leaned against the counter and folded his arms in disbelief, "So, now you're going from Dr. Speyer, the Speech Pathologist to Ms. Melissa the mad scientist?" He said it more tongue-in-cheek as opposed to an insulting manner, which made Melissa not grow impatient with him as he continued, "You know that sounds a lot like a Jekyll & Hyde story?"

"I know, I know, the entire episode is darn right crazy, but I can't stop thinking about the good that I could do. That is, if it did work again? Would you consider staying with me while I tried to use those drops one more time?"

"Wow, that's a thought. Are you sure you would want to give them another try? I mean really, what if . . ."

She cut him off by asking, "They're only an antibiotic, what possible harm would come to me if I used a couple of those drops anyway?"

"But Melissa, curiosity did kill the cat."

She lifted the vial off the counter, held it up to the light and in an excited voice told him, "Yes, but satisfaction brought him back. Come-on, help me with this, maybe I'll even be able to look into your future, would you like that?"

He turned away for a moment and thought about that idea. Wondering, What if anything she would see in his future? Oh my god, he realized, this is very exciting.

"I think I will Melissa, but only one time and one time only. Promise?" He watched her head nod in agreement as he continued, "and I want you to sit in that chair while I'm right here in the room watching you carefully. Are these acceptable terms?"

"Of course, here goes." She sat down into the exam chair and tilted her head back a little. Holding one eye open with two fingers of one hand, she let a couple of drops fall into her left eye. She quickly replaced the dropper in the vial and grabbed for the padded arms of the chair expecting another physical episode. She looked pretty funny there for a moment; her face muscles were drawn taut as she clinched her teeth tight together in anticipation. Her knuckles on both hands started to turn white from the pressure, but nothing happened. No flashing lights, no white spots flickering, no trembling, no electric energy or nervous twitches. Nothing. Melissa shrugged her shoulders in amazement, picked up the dropper and applied a couple of medication drops into the other eye. She instinctively prepared her body for the reaction, and once again nothing happened.

"Well, that's just what I figured would happen there Dr. Speyer, nothing! How do your eyes feel?"

Still stunned by the fact that there was no reaction, Melissa tried hard not to falter. "My eyes? They feel fine, actually the drops seem to have soothed the burning."

"Well, that's what they're supposed to do my dear." Dr. Biddle commented, holding out his hands to help her up from the chair. Melissa looked at those outstretched hands wondering if she had anything to fear.

"Come on now Melissa," Dr. Biddle commented trying to convince her that everything in deed was okay. "Really, you had no reaction, everything is fine."

Dropping her guard, Melissa slid partially forward on the exam chair and reached out to grab his hands. As she smiled in embarrassment, their eyes met and they felt the first jolt hit them hard. Dr. Biddle tried to pull away, but just as he tried another burst of energy held him in place as if an electrical shock locked them together. Their hands and arms trembled out of control. As Melissa's eyes closed tight, she once again saw the flashes of colored lights and white spots flickering on a blackened background. In the distance she saw the first image. It was an emergency vehicle, with its lights pulsing pulling up to a smoldering wreck of a car. The car, an expensive European import, was nearly bent in half facing the wrong way on the road. There was black smoke coming from what remained of the car's rear end indicating the fuel tank was on fire. Melissa experienced another jolt of energy as she blinked her eyes. This time, she couldn't make out the image, which was soft and cloudy. The red strobe lights brought the image into view for a couple of seconds at a time. As she forced herself to focus, she could see a man lying on a stretcher in the back of an ambulance being attended to by two emergency medical technicians who were yelling out vital signs and reacting with professional skill. Another flash of the red strobe gave light to the scene and she could just barely make out the bloodied face of the man on the stretcher as one of the EMT's covered his head with a white sheet. As she recognized the face, she yelled out, "Oh my god, I can't believe it."

Then, as quickly as the energy appeared it disappeared and Melissa broke free. The sudden release of his hands made Dr. Biddle fall backwards smashing himself into one of the eyeglass frame display cabinets that lined the wall. He slid to the floor in disbelief of what had just occurred. As he looked up at Melissa still sitting in the exam chair, he could tell she was hyperventilating. "A deep breath Melissa," he shouted to her as he gained his feet. "Yes good, and take another deep breath. Dr. Biddle raised a hand and explained to her, "Here Melissa, focus on my hand over here and deep breaths now. That a girl."

Melissa was shaking uncontrollably as her mind raced through the images she had seen. She tried to speak but only gagged.

"Are you okay?" He asked wanting to help her in any way. "Melissa, you look so frightened, what in the world did you see?"

She pointed to Dr. Biddle and told him in a trembling voice, "You, it was you in a terrible car accident and, and . . ." She was unable to voice the horror she had witnessed. She closed her eyes and slumped back into the chair as tears filled her eyes.

Less than an hour later Melissa was sitting in her Jeep Wrangler outside the Speech and Language Center trying to find enough willpower to see her first appointment. She was just finishing up the call to her father. Unable to tell him any of the truth, Melissa did the best she could under the circumstances. Actually, it was turning out to be less than half the truth.

"Yes dad, Dr. Biddle explained that I shouldn't worry about the reaction, that it must have been more of an hallucination than anything else. No, I'm not worried anymore. Okay, I'll see you later, bye."

After she hung up she felt sad that she had to lie, she had promised to call and she kept her promise. She figured that when it came to the lying, she would resolve that later on. It was funny how her relationship with her dad turned out. Sometimes he would appear sarcastic and insensitive, and at other times caring and affectionate. She knew the sarcastic insensitive part was an act, born out of his lonely unhappy life. Then in her head she heard his voice calling her "Missy" and she again realized after all, that was where his heart really was.

She sat there for a few more minutes still unsettled about her experience with Dr. Biddle. So, she decided to replay what had happened with the eye drops and Dr. Biddle over again in her mind. Melissa found the entire experience nothing less than troubling. Especially, the part where she told him about the vision she had of his future, she found it so hard to understand why he wouldn't believe her. He's so foolish, she thought; even if there is only a small chance that what I saw in my vision would come true, why risk your life? And why argue about what happened too. Just because he can't find enough reason to accept something, doesn't mean it won't happen.

Melissa closed her eyes and painfully recalled how they had argued violently with each other for some time. First, it was about the visions Melissa told Dr. Biddle about and then they had argued about the eye drops themselves. He wanted to take them so the lab could analyze their contents. Melissa had changed her mind deciding not to give up the drops to anybody, that is, not without a fight. Giving up such power was not something she wanted to do no matter how persuasive Dr. Biddle tried to be. Not only did Melissa doubt his motives about the laboratory analysis, she had her own suspicions about Dr. Biddle wanting the drops for his own personal gain. So they argued several points back and forth and when Melissa went to reach for her eye drops so did Biddle. They knocked the vial over and they both watched in horror as some of the medication slowly leaked out. She slapped his hand away and grabbed the vial tightening the top and placing it in her bag. In the end, she had stormed out of his office with what was left of those eye drops in her handbag as Dr. Biddle yelled after her.

Melissa let out an emotional sigh, took a deep breath and jumped out of her Jeep heading for the entrance to the Language Center. She looked up and saw a familiar sight, her brother's black Ford Pick-up parked at the end of the lot. Now what is Craig doing here? She wondered as she pushed open the door. Melissa looked into the waiting area and smiled seeing one of her young patients sitting on her mother's lap as she read a storybook. She walked over to Jeanette's desk and greeted her.

"Hey Jeanette, how are you doing?"

"Good, I'm doing good. How are you? And by the way, how is your eye infection?"

"The itch is almost gone, but if I told you what I have been through since I saw you last, you'd think I fell and hit my head or something. It's just been wild."

"Your brother's here you know? He's waiting in your office. Every time I see him, he gets better looking than the last time."

"I saw his truck in the parking lot, can you tell Mrs. Maitlin that I'll just be a few more minutes?"

"Sure, she's nice I'm sure that'll be no problem."

Melissa walked into her office and saw her brother Craig reading her diplomas along the wall above her desk. "What?" she started, "Don't you have anything better to read?"

Craig kept on looking over Melissa's wall of honor and replied, "Hey Sis, I'll never tire of reading these things. It just reminds me how smart you are and how proud I am of my kid sister." Then he turned, took one look at his sister and met her in the middle of the room as they embraced.

"You always have a way to make my heart smile Craig. But don't forget, we're all very proud of you too." He released her, and found his way to one of her leather armchairs.

He sat, looked up at her and replied, "Yeah, everybody except dad."

Melissa paused a moment and recognized the sorrow on her big brother's face. She knew that any mention of their dad always had the same unhappy affect on him. It started long before their mother passed. Actually, it seemed like all the while Craig was growing up, he and his father were always having one disagreement after another. Craig was a dreamer always looking for the next adventure and their father was the conservative one. It's just the way their father was and their home was no place for a young man looking to discover what life was all about. They disagreed about everything, dad wanted his son to play baseball, and Craig wanted to play ice hockey. If it wasn't about the way Craig wanted to dress, it was about the friends he had. Of course, Craig's schoolwork was never up to their father's standards. When Craig wanted to grow his hair long, his father wanted him to have a crew cut. And while Craig liked driving motorcycles, their father wanted him to drive a car. Eventually, their father just hardened on his son and gave up talking to him. The last big argument was just around the time Craig graduated from high school and more to do with Craig's college choice. Their father wanted him to go premed, always seeing his son as a doctor. Craig had other ideas, deciding long ago to turn to agriculture.

There was something about farming that appealed to the inner Craig. At first, Craig was unsure what exactly he wanted to do, but after a few semesters he realized his future was right here on Long Island, right here on the East End. He started to dream about becoming a vintner and maybe one day, even owning his own vineyard. He had read about the early success of the Hargrave family and the Palmer's who were among the first to recognize Long Island's rich fertile soil was just as suitable for grapevines as it was for potatoes. But back then, their father only saw a life of failure for his son and the two of them fought hard and long over Craig's decision to attend Cornell's School of Agriculture and not Cornell's School of Medicine. Their arguments soured them both and especially hardened his father. Over the years, they had less and less contact deciding that being apart was better than fighting all the time. After college graduation, Craig took the small amount of money he had saved up and a small loan from his mother; he purchased a fifty-acre farm and planted his first vines. Since then, his grapes have been in great demand and he added a second, slightly larger seventy-five acre parcel. It was hard work and yet, as successful as he had become, his father ignored the good in him still seeing the teenage Craig and their arguments. Then, when their mother died, so too did any chance of their reconciling their differences, that died with her too.

Melissa sat in the opposite armchair facing him with a perplexed expression on her face. She tried to smile and then told him, "I'm so glad you're here Craig, I need to talk with you."

"I got your cell phone call while I was out fencing one of the new sections. Sorry, I couldn't pick up."

"No problem, but before we talk I'll need some time to take care of my patients. Can you wait or should we meet for lunch?

"Listen Sis, how about I take care of some of my errands and I'll come by and pick you up for lunch. You can take me to Jonathan's over on Main Street for lunch."

"Sounds good to me, how about we meet there in a couple of hours?"

"Yup, see you then Sis."

She embraced him again and as she watched him walk out of her office, Melissa wondered, why their Father couldn't just let him be? If he did, she thought, he would have realized how much his hard work and dedication had accomplished. And maybe, he would have noticed how much his son took after his father. The reality was, the apple didn't fall too far from the tree.

During her morning speech therapy sessions with her two young patients, Melissa couldn't help think about her newfound power. At first, the idea of using this power seemed like a good thing; especially after the futuristic vision seeing her father's illness and knowing that if it were true, maybe they could do something about it now. Except, after seeing what was in store for Dr. Biddle, the doubts about using the eye drops weighed heavily on her mind and her conscience. It was part of what she wanted to talk over with her brother. He always had a good ability to listen and to see the pros and cons of any situation. A skill he had developed as a result of the long arguments with their father.

As she finished up her sessions she had enough time to call the hospital and set up the tests for her father. She spoke to Gail Lighter, the radiology manager and asked her if they could squeeze in a few x-rays and a CT scan for her father? Gail was a friend of Melissa's and told her if her father didn't mind going stand-by in the late afternoon, she could make sure the tests were done before her shift ended. They had chatted a while and Melissa explained to Gail that her father had a heavy cough he couldn't shake and she was worried that there might be something wrong. The reality was, Melissa knew the results of the tests would help her settle the questions in her mind. She wondered over and over about her psychic experiences. I need to know, she thought. The results of those tests will help me determine if what I'm seeing is something to believe or not. I mean if I can really see into a person's future I want to know, not keep guessing about it.

On the way over to the restaurant, she used her cell phone to call her father. She told him that the tests were set for later in the afternoon and that she would pick him up around four o'clock. When Melissa arrived at Jonathan's, she found her brother intently looking over the restaurant's wine list. She kissed his cheek and sat across from him, "Hey Craig, see anything worth ordering on that list?"

"Sure Sis, there are several wines I'd like to try, but I'm really fantasizing about having my own wines on that list someday."

"Craig, you're heading in the right direction. Be patient and someday you'll reach your dream. I just know you will."

"Thanks Sis, I can always count on you to steady my course."

The waiter came over to take their order and over the next ten minutes Melissa explained to Craig why she had called him. She included everything, starting with how she went for the eye exam because of the bothersome itch, how she might have rushed the pharmacist at closing time, and about the theory that maybe while he rushed to prepare the drops, one of the glass canisters slipped, knocked into some others and broke on the counter perhaps causing the various chemicals to get mixed up. She described the first time she used the eye drops and how there was an immediate reaction. She explained about the energy charges between her and their father and gave him detailed descriptions of the flashes of color lights and the white spots that appeared. She took a deep breath and asked, "So Craig, what do you think so far?"

Craig opened his eyes wide. Looked around and asked, "Okay Sis, what weird diet supplements have you been taking these days?"

Melissa was immediately hurt and asked, "Craig, do you think I would take the time and trouble to meet with you just to play some sort of game?"

"No Sis, I don't think that, but I mean really how could ordinary antibiotic eye drops cause that strong a reaction?"

Melissa's eyes were staring up to the heavens, as if she was looking elsewhere for the answer and then looking him straight in the eyes she continued, "That's just it, those drops are not ordinary. And if you don't believe that, wait until you hear the next part. Hold onto you hat mister, you're going for a ride.

She began the explanation about the psychic visions she had experienced including the images of their father in intensive care and what she saw inside his lungs. They talked a little about the ramifications of such a thing and how Melissa had set up a series of diagnostic tests for their father. They ordered another round of drinks as Melissa switched to the second experience with Dr. Biddle. How she had used the drops while he watched in his office. How at first, nothing happened and then after their hands clasped, how she had a vision of a serious traffic accident with police and ambulance lights flashing at the scene. And then she told him about the close-up she witnessed of Dr. Biddle's face, as they placed a white sheet over him. She also told him about their argument and how the eye drop vial had spilled over.

Their food order arrived and as she went on and on, the food just sat there getting cold. One would say they were both totally immersed. Then Craig put his wine glass down, leaned forward and asked, "Has it happened yet Melissa?"

"What? Has what happened yet?"

"Have you heard if Biddle was in a car accident?"

"Well no, I haven't. I mean why would I want to know?" A few tears slipped out of her right eye as she softly wept. Then, she added, "Who wants to be the one responsible for that Craig? Who wants to be the cause of anyone dying? I couldn't handle that. It makes me want to throw away that little vial and forget that I can see into someone's future, especially if it ends up being so damn tragic"

"What do you mean Melissa, why would it end up tragic?"

She lifted up her fork and pushed around some of the Lobster Ravioli she had ordered. "I'll tell you why, it's one thing to see your father sick and maybe, because of that vision you can get help for him. It's quite another to see someone end up dead in a car accident. Of course it's tragic and the whole thing makes me very sad."

Craig reached across the table and took hold of both of her hands. He squeezed them gently and explained, "Why Melissa, don't you see? That's the whole point you know?"

Melissa lifted her head as if directly connected to her heavy heart and took a deep look into her brother's eyes as if she was looking for the true meaning of his words.

"It's like this Sis. If you did have a vision of Dad and could see into his future and as a result you were able to help him, then that simply put, is a miracle. Now the same thing holds true for Dr. Biddle, if you had a vision of him and warned him about the accident you saw, but if he doesn't heed your warning, well too bad for him. You did your part; you gave him the information that is nothing short of another miracle. And what a wonderful power it is Sis, don't you see?"

It was as if a light bulb went off in her head and within the minute, a smile returned to her gorgeous mouth. "You're right Craig. Of course I didn't cause the accident I envisioned, I only foresaw it. You, my brother are a genius."

The waiter came by to check if everything was all right and noticing their lunch was untouched, he asked if they would like their plates heated up? As he took the dishes back to the kitchen Craig asked, "So listen, Melissa, I was thinking what if you took the drops and we touched hands, do you think you'd see into my future? Would you be able to tell me something about what's in store for me?" That question led them into another insightful and curious discussion. They found themselves laughing at some of their wildest thoughts especially about how they could market those eye drops to make a fortune telling people, especially the rich and famous, about their future. Then Craig stopped laughing, focused his eyes on her and asked Melissa, "Tell me Sis, would you use those drops on me?"

As she sat there unsure how to answer her brother's question, the waiter returned with their dishes and placed them down. There must have been something awkward in the air because he felt the need to quickly scoot away. Craig tasted some of the seafood pasta he had ordered and found that first taste to be absolutely delicious. "Now this pasta is just superb. How can they make something that tastes this good?" He was really enjoying his lunch taking turns sipping the Chardonnay from the Duck Walk Winery he had ordered and taking a portion of the pasta. At one point, when he tried a shrimp from his dish he told her, "This is by far the best tasting seafood pasta I have ever had. And this Alfredo cheese sauce is outstanding. What could be better than this, eh Sis?

And she replied, "Seeing into your future Craig."

He stopped the fork as it approached his mouth and asked, "Will you do it Sis? You'll use the eye drops on me?"

Melissa nodded in agreement which gave Craig a reason to exclaim a little to loudly, "Yahoo!" And then he added in a whisper, "That's just great Sis. I can't wait."

They hurried the rest of their lunch, settled the check and left the restaurant together. Craig followed her Jeep in his pick-up over to her office. Once inside, Craig asked, "Okay, what do I have to do?"

"You don't have to do anything silly. Just be ready to hold my hands when I tell you."

Melissa reached into her pocketbook and found the vial of eye drops. She held the vial up to the light and half squinting exclaimed, "You know there aren't that many drops left in this vial."

Craig squirmed in his chair and said. "As long as there is enough for me, that's all I care about."

When she heard that, Melissa began to think, she had created a monster. Then she realized, who wouldn't want what's left in this little vial all to themselves anyway? She unscrewed the dropper, squeezed the bulb and placed it square into the vial. They both watched the medication slide up into the dropper as she said, "Okay here goes. Please keep an eye out for me." She laughed as she tilted her head back and released a couple of drops into both eyes. She returned the dropper to the vial, tightened it and dropped it into her pocketbook. Then, she sat down to wait. She didn't have to wait very long because just then, she felt a little lightheaded and reached both hands out toward Craig. As he grasped her hands, their eyes met. The effect was immediate, as they recoiled from the first electrical charge. Melissa closed her eyes and the color flashes began. Then she witnessed the white flashes as another electrical charge jolted them. She looked deep into her mind and saw the images begin to unfold. In the first one she saw a group of people dressed in formal attire all standing around a middle-aged man in what appeared to be a large decorative wine cellar. There were a couple of bright flashes in the image and as the man turned to face her she saw a photographer checking his camera and then she recognized a slightly older Craig being given something. Melissa couldn't make out what it was he was holding, but she saw the smile on his face and knew it was a good thing. More color flashes occurred as the group of people surrounding Craig started to move away in slow motion. To her surprise she saw members of her own family and then she saw herself standing there next to Craig. The biggest surprise of all turned out to be her own father walking up to Craig and holding him in a gentle embrace including several back slaps. Another electrical charge made them tremble as the last image came into her focus. It was a newspaper unfolding to reveal a story with the banner, Craig Speyer Winery Wins First Prize For Best New York Cabernet Sauvignon. The Newspaper was the *Long Island Wine Gazette* and it had a black and white photo of

Craig holding up a glass of red wine in one hand and his first place prize in the other.

There was one last power spike that forced them apart and as they unlocked their hands Melissa sank slowly to the floor. Craig went to help her as she waved him back,

"I'm okay really, I just need a few minutes to rest. Each time I experience these visions it seems I can handle it better, except I get more exhausted than the last time. And let me tell you Craig, I'm really tired."

"That was incredible Sis, you were right. What a ride! Now tell me quickly, what did you see Sis? Was it good or bad? Don't hold back anything, I want to hear the whole nine yards."

Melissa smiled and told him, "Oh yeah, it was good all right. You are just going to scream when you hear what I saw."

And he did too; as she got to the part with the newspaper story he let out a yell of delight that had them both laughing with the excitement. Then, she asked him to quiet down for a minute and to sit with her while she described one of the images she witnessed. As she described how she saw their father walk up to Craig with everyone wearing the biggest smile and how he embraced Craig with the warmest fatherly hug one could imagine. Craig backed away with a look of disbelief across his face as he thought out loud, "I never thought that day would ever come." And then he sat down too filled with emotion to talk any more.

The next morning, Melissa was running along the beach and as one ocean wave after another crashed onto the shore before her, she realized it was the same for the thoughts that crashed onto her mind. First, there was the worry and concern over the results of her father's medical tests. They did several x-ray studies and a CT work-up, but her friend Gail Lighter wanted to also obtain some MRI imaging studies to take an in-depth look at his lung tissue and to rule things out. What would be the outcome of all of these tests, Melissa wanted to know? How sick was her father and what arduous journey would all of this send them on? Would there be chemotherapy, radiation treatments, or some horrible combination or would the test results simply point the way to the end for him if his condition was terminal?

As she moved further along the beach, there were the thoughts about her brother and the visions she witnessed of his future. To think his dreams of success would ultimately come true and with the addition of the happy ending with their father gave her spirits rise as she experienced jubilation for the future. Sadly, these happy thoughts were blunted by the fears for Dr. Biddle and the consuming worry about the deadly automobile accident she had seen. The worst part being, how to make him believe in what she saw was in store for him?

She also spent time thinking about those eye drops and the truly amazing power they contained? There was also a little laugh in her mind about her brother's crazy harebrained scheme to market and sell her ability to see into a person's future. Craig sure was keen on the money that could be made, she recalled almost laughing out loud at the idea. As she processed each thought and analyzed options she found herself going faster and faster along the ocean as her mind raced through each thought too. Where would it all end, she wanted to know and what would become of all of them?

Later that day, Melissa was in her office finishing up her afternoon caseload. She welcomed the diversion that came with her work. There were actually several occasions when the nagging worries and concerns she had fretted about earlier were forgotten. As her last patient entered the treatment room, Melissa was cheered by the size of the smile on Jason's little face. Oh, if only I could help him, help him in some way to improve his speech and ultimately, return him to be a normal kid, she thought as she took out the flash cards to begin the oral exercises they did together. Jason's mother released Jason's hand and told Dr. Speyer she would just wait outside. Melissa lifted Jason onto the wooden chair aligned it to the table and sat across from him. She showed him the first card and watched him grin; knowing he recognized the object in the picture. Melissa spoke out the name of the object and Jason tried his best to join in. Except, instead of carrrrrrr, it came out caaaa. Then, there was boat, and house, and dog, and tree and then there was frustration.

Perhaps it was all too much for her, too much to bare and too much to accept, because for some strange reason Melissa couldn't rationalize at the time; and without any warning and without asking. Melissa stood up, reached into her pocketbook and took out the eye drop vial. Jason watched in amazement wondering what was this new toy she would be showing him? Melissa leaned her head back and let a couple of drops fall into both eyes. Then, she knelt in front of Jason and reached out to lift both of his hands with hers. Jason's head titled somewhat, as if he could comprehend what was about to happen. The first electrical charge hit them suddenly nearly knocking Jason off the chair. Melissa held on increasing her grip and steadying him as their arms trembled. She closed her eyes and saw the flashing lights and the white spots started sparkling. In the background an image began to form and Melissa tried real hard to focus, to see the image. It was a classroom and in the center were a group of students sitting around a teacher reading a storybook. The image she saw started to clear and Melissa flinched as she recognized her patient Jason taking a turn to read the story to the class. She opened her eyes and looked at him while they still held hands. Melissa could see that Jason wasn't scared or upset at all. As a matter of fact, he was sitting there almost inviting her to look inside of him. Melissa blinked several times and focused her eyes on his forehead just as another electrical charge went through them. She closed her eyes again and saw another image coming toward her. She recognized an image of a brain and as she looked deeper, she could see inside and there in a far corner of one section was an extremely small mass pressing inward against a portion of his brain. The idea of such a thing made her shudder and she pulled her hands free in reaction. As she opened her eyes once again she realized what she had done and immediately embraced Jason, as if that would remove the instant guilt she felt.

They stayed like that for a few more minutes and then Melissa released Jason asking him if he was okay? Jason pointed to the red fire truck that sat in a pile of toys on the floor. Melissa reached for the truck knowing it was his favorite toy in the office and the one he always played with. He pushed the fire engine along the table as if nothing had ever happened. Melissa turned on the computer and watched the display brighten up thinking, obviously the experience didn't faze this little one at all. As the computer booted up, Jason heard the start up sounds and slid down off the chair to join her at the computer's keyboard. He liked this game they played on the computer. As he pressed the enter key, a picture opened up on the display and he had to speak the object's name out loud. Then, from the computer's speakers a mechanical sounding voice sounded out the object's name. Melissa watched Jason navigate the software, knowing that he was of high intelligence to follow the software and wondering if what she saw could be a brain tumor and the cause of Jason's true developmental problems? I need to call Craig and ask him his opinion.

That's just what she did once she closed up the office. His cell phone rang and he answered seeing the number information displayed on caller ID.

"Hey Sis, how's it going?"

Melissa heard those words and quickly thought; maybe it would be better to just keep quiet? But then again, why bother? So, she just responded. "Well, I'll tell you if you really want to know?"

Craig paused a brief moment and then answered, "Of course I want to know and remember, you called me. What happened now?"

"I used the drops again."

There was another pause while Craig digested the news. "With who Sis? And what did you see?"

"I was having a therapy session with one of my patients. It was this little boy Jason and he is so cute and I want to help him so bad."

"So, you used the drops to help him?"

"I don't know what came over me. It has been frustrating to be working with him for so many years and the results have been disappointing."

"Sis, I'm not following you at all."

"Well Craig, I always felt there was more of a reason for this boy's speech problems, so I thought if I used the drops and could see something I could believe in, then I'd really be able to help him."

"What did you see?"

"I saw him in the future reading a storybook in class and I saw an image, something inside his brain. It was a small tumor and it looked like it was pressing against a group of blood vessels."

"And you think this is causing his speech development problems?"

"I don't know for sure Craig, but it gives me hope. Do you think I was wrong to experiment? Did I make a mistake?"

"No, I don't think you made a mistake and if there is a chance you can help him, well, why not."

"I know, I know, that's exactly how I feel. Oh Craig, again you helped me stay my course. Thanks."

"Listen Sis, I didn't really do much? I only told you what you were thinking, that's all."

"Yes, except when I hear it from you, it makes me feel right. And how are you doing Craig?"

"Well, I'm okay I guess. There's a little trouble with one of the banks, but I'm hoping I can straighten that out. Hey, did you hear anything about Biddle?"

"You mean the accident thing?"

"Yeah, anything happen?"

"No Craig, Dr. Biddle is still A-Okay from what I hear. But if something happens, you'll be the first to know."

"Now Sis, don't say it like that. It's just, well, I mean I'd like to know that what you did see turned out to be the truth, that's all."

"Okay Craig, I'm not sure I fully understand you, but I guess you have your reasons. Let me go now, I have to get dinner set up for dad."

"Take care Sis."

"You too Craig."

A couple of days later, while Melissa was working with one of her patients, Jeannette knocked on the treatment room door and interrupted her.

"Excuse me Dr. Speyer, there's a call on line one from Gail Lighter."

"Oh, well, we only have another ten minutes left here, please tell Gail I'm with a patient and ask her for a number where I can call her back?"

"Sure, I'll take care of that."

When the call from Gail Lighter came in, it caught Melissa off guard and she needed some time to prepare herself for whatever news Gail was to deliver about her dad. She also wanted to be in a comfortable and quiet place for that conversation. She sat in her office staring at the telephone with the paper containing Gail's number in her hand. Finally, she decided to face the reality and dialed the number.

"Hello, Radiology, Gail Lighter's office."

"Hi, this is Dr. Speyer calling, I'm returning Gail's call, is she available?"

Yes, she told me she was expecting your call. One moment please Dr. Speyer and I'll locate her for you."

Then there was the music on-hold and to Melissa's surprise a Tony Bennett song, *Make Me Alive*. And she couldn't believe the irony in those lyrics. She also wondered why it was that when you were waiting for something important, it always seemed like time was standing still. The wait just gave her an eternity to revisit all the questions she had about her father's test results. Then the music ended with a click.

"Hi Melissa, and how are you?"

"I'm good except, a little nervous about the tests my dad had. Can you tell me what the findings were?" Right after she asked that question, Melissa could feel every muscle along her shoulders tighten, as if waiting for someone to strike her. For obvious reasons, she even held her breath.

"Well, this may surprise you, but everything came back negative. There was silence on the other end and it made Gail ask, "Melissa? Hello, are you there?"

"I'm here, but did I hear you right? Did you say everything's negative? No disease in my father's lungs?" Nothing?"

"Yes, it's good news. Your father's not sick after all. The report said there is a small amount of disease and recommended watchful waiting. And as you know, that just means let's keep an eye on things. But other than that, no, no cancer or emphysema. It's negative.

Melissa started to say, how could that be? But, left it all to herself. How indeed? Unless, of course everything she saw in those visions were just imaginary after all, just like Dr. Biddle had told her.

Sensing the pause, Gail asked, "Melissa, can I help you with anything else?"

"No Gail, but listen thanks so much for all your help. You're a good friend."

"You know, I hope you don't mind me saying this but, it doesn't seem like you're completely happy with the results? Is everything all right?"

'Of course I'm happy; it's great news for my dad and my whole family. Like you said, I'm just surprised. And thanks again Gail."

"Sure Melissa, you take care now, bye."

As she hung up the phone Melissa wondered, how it could turn out like this? How could her mind play such a game with her and fool her this way? There were, of course, no answers only more questions and Melissa didn't really want any more questions. Except she knew, you can't control that and the questions formed automatically in her mind. Could there be something wrong with the machines? Did the radiologist read the wrong studies? Was Gail holding back? When that last question popped into her mind, it made her laugh out loud at the ridiculousness of the whole thing. So, she took a deep breath, and decided to put the entire episode out of her mind for a while and to go home and tell her dad the good and confusing news. No disease? Indeed?

A few days later Melissa was sorting through the family mail when the phone rang. It was her brother Craig.

"Hey Sis"

"Hi Craig, what's up?"

"Well, I hate to tell you this over the phone, but I just need to get it over with."

"What Craig, what's going on?"

"I'm in hot water with the business."

"The business Craig? What happened to the business?"

"The trouble is financial. You see one of the banks I have a loan with is refusing to extend the terms and has decided to foreclose. If I don't come up with $125,000 by the weekend, I'll loose one of the vineyards and if that happens I'll end up taking a bath. I'll be forced to sell a second parcel just to handle the operating expenses of what's left. And I'm not sure there's a way to keep the operation afloat if I loose those two vineyards."

"Oh no Craig. This sounds terrible. Is there anything that can be done?"

"No, not really. I have tried to figure things out, but I keep coming up empty. No one I know can help with that kind of money. And there seems to be no out for me. It's sad, because I just keep thinking about that vision you had, and the idea that I thought I would become a successful vintner, and I feel real down. I had to tell someone Sis, thanks for listening."

"Listen Craig, we'll find a way. I'll talk with dad, maybe he can help?"

"Yeah right, that man will enjoy this news more than you know. Him help me? No way Sis, I can guarantee that."

"Let's see Craig, and I'll talk with you later."

Melissa hung up the phone and sank deeper into despair. All her visions were turning out to be false. With Craig's dream shattered and the news about her father's hospital tests being negative, reality hit her that the visions she witnessed were all just lies. That there was no need to cure her father, Craig was not going to be a successful vintner, Dr. Biddle would not be in a terrible car accident and young Jason would not have a normal life.

Over the next week Melissa did her best to return her life to normal. She did all the things she normally did, morning beach runs, daily therapy with her patients, reading medical journals, dinner with her dad and so forth. Except, the whole experience had cast a shadow over her life and the thoughts of what could have been left her more and more depressed. One day, as she was heading for a meeting with one of the pediatricians about a case, Melissa bumped into one of the child psychologists she knew from the developmental team.

She decided to ask for help, "Hi Stewart, how have you been?"

He looked up and smiled at Melissa, "Oh, hi there. I've been good, how about you?"

"Me? Good, things are good. You know it's funny that I ran into you."

He looked at her curiously and asked, "Why is that?"

Melissa looked down at her feet as if she couldn't look him in the eyes and told him, "Well do you have minute? I have been reading some articles on psychic experiences and have developed some curiosity. Would you know anyone here at the hospital in the psychology department that works in that area?"

"Psychic experiences, eh?"

Melissa nodded as he continued, "Well let's see, no not here at the hospital, but I do know a colleague over at the college who teaches a class in parapsychology."

She got excited over the prospect and raised her voice in response, "You mean at Southampton College?"

"Yes, except, it's owned by Stony Brook University now. His name is Professor Clarkson, William Clarkson. We went to college together and I think if you're interested in talking with someone local involving psychic experiences, he's your man?"

"Would you happen to have his number by any chance?"

"Why yes, I should have it in my book." Stewart lifted his briefcase and fumbled through several pockets before pulling out a worn out address book held together with a doubled up rubber band. As he slipped it off and opened the address book he mentioned, "I'm not one for those electronic gizmos you know. I'm a bit old fashioned."

Melissa just smiled and waited patiently as he located William Clarkson's entry. "Here, let me jot it down for you. This is his daytime office number; it's all I have. And you just tell Bill that Stewart James referred you, he'll help you I'm sure."

He handed the paper to Melissa and she thanked him. "That's really good of you Stewart."

"No problem Melissa, and how about we have lunch some time? I'd be curious what you two end up talking about."

"Yes, I'll call you and we'll set something up. I'd like to hear how your kids are doing too."

"Very well then, you have a good day now."

"Yes, and you too Stewart."

As she walked away she curled that piece of paper in her hand and slid it into her blazer pocket. A feeling of relieve came over her, still nervous, but pleased to at least have a direction.

Later that day, Melissa called Professor Clarkson explaining the referral from their mutual friend Stewart James and how she hoped he would be able to help her with some questions on the topic of psychic experiences. He agreed to meet with her and they set up an evening appointment a couple of days later. Melissa knew she needed to speak with someone about the haunting images and the futuristic visions she had seen. All of this was just getting to her.

During the meeting, Melissa told William Clarkson everything that happened. He encouraged her and reminded her not to leave any details out. He even asked questions and interacted with her explanation. Melissa noticed that at some point, he had moved to the edge of his seat and didn't move from that position until she had finished explaining everything. As he slid back into his desk chair, William Clarkson took a deep breath.

"Now that is some story Melissa, you don't mind me calling you Melissa, Dr. Speyer, do you?"

"No, of course not, but please tell me what you think."

"I would start by saying that there are many psychic events that take place in our normal lives. Things we sometimes don't even recognize or aren't fully aware of form the basis for these events. That's what I teach in my class, to look into everyday events as more than coincidence or just plain fate. Your story, on the other hand, crosses over the normal type of events one might encounter. I mean, who could ever say what caused those visions? Were the drops that you placed in your eyes, a typical medication prescribed for an infection, the catalyst for such events? Probably not. And could you, all of a sudden, develop a new superpower to see into someone's future, probably not."

William looked to make sure Melissa was still following and continued, "There have been a number of documented cases of people, who under severe stress, will create in their own mind an imaginary psychic experience. Often times, these occur in their sleep or when daydreaming. The mind, as you know Melissa, is a very complicated organ, and it can do things we don't fully understand. I recall seeing some very interesting MRI studies of brain cell function. The participants taking part in the study were given suggestions to create various levels of stress while the MRI scanner took instantaneous images. The brain cell activity always increased and the scans proved that the more the person's brain was exposed to stressful events, the more the brain responded with brain cell activity. The MRI's didn't lie Melissa. Of course in your case, there may be other reasons why you started to have these psychic experiences. Tell me, did you recently loose a loved one?"

"Yes, my Mother passed away suddenly a few months ago."

"I see, well this could be a factor. The loss of a loved one, especially a parent is among the most powerful stressors. Any other meaningful events?"

"I'd say, there's my father's situation which is confusing and worrisome. He is not yet retired and out on disability with a work-related injury. He needs rehab and may have to go to a healthcare facility for extended care. And to top it off, my brother is under severe financial difficulties with his fledging business while dreaming of success. This is placing a lot of stress on all of us." Melissa watched William sizing up her situation as the realization began to form in her mind. Just about every vision she had, matched a person in her life who happened to be in a extremely stressful phase." Oh, oh, she thought, is that what happened?

"And how are things going with your practice? Any problems getting new patients or referrals?"

"The problem I have is overdoing the worry and concern I have for some of my patients, especially the ones born premature who need a great deal of intervention like my little Anna and Jason." As soon as she said the name Jason, another tumbler clicked and fell into place, "I think I see what you're getting at. All the visions and images that I experienced were related to stressful events?"

William raised both hands, leaned forward and added, "Frankly, it sounds so believable, now don't you agree?"

Melissa thought for a moment and replied, "I'm afraid I do."

They talked for another hour or so and then Melissa thanked him for his time and for being so understanding. Professor Clarkson cautioned her that she might overcompensate and there may be a short period of depression to follow. He did reassure her that in the end, knowing the probable cause would end up being a great benefit. He also told her that, if she had any other questions or wished to discuss other aspects of her experience, he would be happy to meet with her again. They exchanged business cards, shook hands and William escorted her out.

A few weeks later, Melissa was starting out on her morning beach run when she started to think about those eye drops once again; about all the problems they had caused and all the wasted time. At that moment, she reached into her backpack and found that small vial. She grasped it tightly in her right hand and without warning flung the vial out to the ocean. She watched it fly across the clear blue sky and enter the water with a splash. There was an emotional release within her as if she had rid herself of a great weight. She didn't look back as she increased her speed feeling the cool sand on her bare feet.

Over the next month, Melissa found herself able to forget those eye drops and the futuristic images along with the feelings of great power. While she did miss the unknown excitement, she valued her normal routine and went about her daily activities determined to once again live every day with the same zest for life she had always felt. Daily, she dealt, the best she could, with all sorts of lingering questions and all kinds of ideas about what might have been. One problem in particular, was the nagging guilt she felt over the argument she had had with Dr. Biddle. It bothered her that they had words and that she never went back and apologized to him for the way she behaved. So, one day, while completing a speech and language assessment with a newborn patient in the hospital, she decided to pay him a visit. As she walked into the eye clinic she noticed some of the staff huddled together as if sharing some secret. As she approached the reception area, there was Dr. Biddle's assistant at her desk sobbing into a handkerchief. Melissa stopped and asked,

"Excuse me Cathy, I can see you are upset. What is wrong, why are you crying."

"Didn't you hear? It's about Dr. Biddle. He was killed in a car accident earlier today as he left his home."

"Oh my god, no" Melissa exclaimed! That can't be . . ."

# CRAZY IS,
# AS CRAZY DOES...

*Life is a tragedy when seen in close-up,*
*but a comedy in long shot.*

Charles Chaplin

**"L**et me see if I fully understand your question, you want me to tell you when it was that I first realized I was in-fact crazy? Um, you don't mean insane? I see, crazy, insane, it's all the same? Okay, I can tell from your enthusiastic nodding that that is the question. So, let me see. Well, one answer would be many times. Excuse me? Oh, just the first time, then the answer had to be the first time I thought I was crazy was the very first time the man up the block brought me into his house and touched me where he shouldn't have. I was about nine years old then. Yes, it happened a few times not just once, but the first time for anything is the one you remember, right? No, nothing like that happened, one-day he just moved away. Yes, I think I was very lucky in one-way, and unlucky in another. But wait, before you say anything. Actually, the first time could have been the first time my dad took off his belt, closed the door to my bedroom and taught me that I could never trust him or feel safe in my own home ever. I was even younger than nine the first time that happened.

How do you decide the very first time for anything anyway? Okay, okay, I know you want me to answer. It's just hard to figure out the first time because I always thought I was crazy from the very beginning. Even more crazy than that guy in Edgar Allen Poe's story, "The Tell-Tale Heart." You remember that story right; sure he was really nuts. I mean who wouldn't be what with an evil eye on you and a beating heart and all. Yes, I know it has nothing to do with my situation. Yes, of course I know that. Well, it just seems like we have a lot in common. Oh, except, I didn't really mean to say, a lot. I meant to say, a great deal, at least that's what Mrs. Clark, my fourth grade teacher, always rammed into my head. Yup, I had to write that silly little phrase hundreds of times on the chalkboard and thousands of times on loose leaf paper. You would think that after all those times; I would remember to say, *a great deal.*

Okay, back to your question. Oh, you smiled eh, you would like me to get back to answering your question? I thought so. Maybe it was the time when I was lost at *Great Adventure Park* and couldn't find my mommy. I cried all day, well at least for two hours straight and I thought I would never have a mommy or be found again. What? How old was I? I was five or six at the time. It seemed I wandered away when my mother was busy watching my brother ring the little bell on the red fire engine that went around and around. Why didn't I go on the ride? That's simple, I hate fire truck rides and their dumb little bells. Now, that question was a lot easier than trying to figure out the very first time I realized I was crazy, I'll tell you that much. No, it wasn't because I hated my brother. At least, I didn't hate him back then, no that came a little later. But no, that didn't make me crazy.

Sure you can ask me about that, no I don't mind at all. My nightmares, that's what they said. Yes, I had terrible nightmares back then. Those nightmares kept me up all during the night and caused a big problem in our house. At the time, my mom and dad really freaked out over that, they were at their wits end when it came to my nightmares. School? What about school? That was a problem back then too. Something about me being disruptive. Well, I had a hard time focusing. The only one who could understand what was happening to me was the psychologist I was seeing. Well, at first it wasn't easy, but as I got along it got easier. What do I mean "as I got along?" Oh, I mean as I talked about the things that happened to me, it got easier because she helped me understand why I felt the way I did. Yes, a woman shrink, imagine that? She was great. At first I didn't want no part of a shrink, but they made me. Especially, my mother who cried a lot, oops, I meant to say, *a great deal* back then. You know the one line I hear in my head more than any other? Can you guess? No, not that one. Nope. So you give up? The one line I hear in my head more than any other is, "it's not your fault . . ." It's a great line you know. Years later I watched the movie, *Good Will Hunting* with Matt Damon and Robin Williams and I found out that they used that line too. Yeah, Robin Williams played the psychologist who was helping Matt Damon work out issues and Robin Williams told him about ten times in a row, "It's not your fault, it's not your fault." Don't you think everyone would want to hear that line at some point in their lives? I bet they would, yes I do. You like that line too. I know, it says it all, almost.

Excuse me? You want me to get back to your original question? Okay, no problem. I do recall another incident that may have been the very first time I thought I was crazy. One day, after school a bunch of us were playing around the Long Island Rail Road storage yard in Babylon, and my good friend Billy; now *he* was one crazy kid. What were we doing in a train yard? Good question. I don't know really, it was just there, just a place to go that's all. Anyway we were walking around the train yard, you know like teenagers looking for trouble. And crazy Billy decided to play chicken with one of those big engines and I swear, to this day I think the engineer driving that engine saw Billy and could have blown his whistle or did more to stop or something. But no, he ran down Billy while we all watched him trip on the tracks trying at the last minute to get out of the way of that five ton engine. I still twitch when I think about that day and yup, that may have been the very first time I thought I was crazy. I mean Billy was sliced like white bread and when his head rolled to a stop at my feet his eyes were wide open as if he was more scared than we were. What did you say? Oh, yes you're right, it was hard on us all and it was the kind of thing that plain freaked me out for a long time after. Why didn't I tell you that when you first asked me? I don't know, it didn't occur to me, I guess. Yes, I went back to talk some more with the lady psychologist. Actually, I got to miss her anyway. She made me feel better about many things and she taught me about myself too. And there was a lot to . . . darn, there I go again. I meant to say, there was a *great deal* to work on, for sure.

Oh, I forgot about one experience that may have taken the cake. Yes, I know I'm jumping around. Just try to keep up with me, okay? It was about Sharon Smiley and I was twenty-five years old and in love like there was no tomorrow. Actually, that's just what happened, there was no tomorrow. *Why,* you asked? You know, you're getting pretty impatient. I'll tell you, just keep your shirt on. There was no tomorrow because, at the time Sharon Smiley was the love of my life. We were engaged to be married and she decided to show me that you can't believe in love and you can't trust your very best friend. What happened was, as I was whispering in her ear one night that I loved her, she whispered back that she and my best friend

Tom were having an affair and that she wanted to be with him. Shit man, my best friend.

Hey, you know what bugs me. Not that it makes me crazy in a big way or anything like that. It's just, the way they sneak up on you. What am I referring to? I'm talking about those little tiny screws in eyeglass frames. The way they loosen up by themselves and fall out just at times when you need to be wearing those glasses too. These little guys right here, the most annoying thing, don't you think? No, you don't? Oh, you don't wear glasses, well, that makes sense. Sorry to go off on a tangent, that thought just popped into my mind. No, it's not one of the reasons why I'm crazy. It's just a little nudge, that's all.

Of course, before my best friend Tom stomped around on my heart with combat boots there was an event I will never, never ever forget. I mean, how could I. Um, good question, well I guess I pushed it out of my memory, that is until now. How long ago? It was nearly eight years before I met Sharon. I used to love motorcycles; did you know I was crazy about motorcycles? Okay, you're right, did you know I loved motorcycles? No, not anymore, I haven't been on one since my brother . . . well here's the way it went. I had just bought this used chopper. It had chrome everywhere and sounded so powerful with every rev of the engine. One day, after I finished washing the bike and polishing every bit of chrome—it had a lot of . . . oops. Why do I keep doing that? It had a *great deal* of chrome, did I mention that already? I think I did. Sorry, it's just that whenever I talk about what happened with my new chopper that day I get very nervous. Thanks, yes, I'll take my time. I was riding that chopper down the street that warm summer day, back and forth, back and forth making a ruckus and enjoying the feeling of riding that two-wheeled beast. Of course, like always, my kid brother asked me if he could try it? Listen, I was only seventeen, but my brother Frankie, he was just fourteen and he kept at it over and over again. Frankie kept asking me to give him a ride. Wait, no begging me. And the begging I couldn't stand. So, I said all right already, hop on and mind you we didn't wear helmets back then. I gunned the engine and we tore down the road in front of our house squealing the tires and whooping it up. Except, just then, right in front of us, little Susie from a few houses away decided she wanted to see the motorcycle up close. So, after I turned that bike around and headed back up to our house with my brother hollering at the top of his lungs, little Susie walked calmly out onto the street right in front of us. And I had to turn away or I would have run her right down. And I couldn't run little Susie over, right? The bike slipped out from under me and as I tumbled off in one direction, it went sliding along and my brother went flying in another direction. I landed on Mr. Jones' lawn, my brother landed smack into a car parked on the street. I got up and dragged myself over to the small group that gathered around him and what I saw made me gag. My brother's body was bent and twisted lying in a pool of fire engine red blood and he was as limp as could be. Can you imagine this? Can you imagine killing your little brother on your brand new Chopper just because he begged? I mean . . . Thanks, thanks for the tissue. Yes, it's a very powerful story. I know, I know—it's what everyone says. Except, I do. I really do. And I hate him for begging me, ever since that sad day.

So, does it surprise you now? Can you understand why it is that I am completely out of my mind? Let me ask you something, don't you think all these things that happened to me over the years are cumulative, they have to add up to make me crazy, right? Why are you shaking your head? You don't agree? Oh, you want me to tell you the thing that happened with my health? I understand, but I really don't like telling anyone about that. Why? It still hurts that's why. Excuse me, no, I don't think I would feel better if I talked about it. No, not even to you. I can talk about other things that happened, other things that made me crazy. I really wish you would stop asking me. How old was I? Thirty-five, I was just fucking thirty-five. I know I shouldn't use foul language, but you made me angry. All right, I won't curse anymore, I'm sorry. What was that? You think what happened is interesting? I don't care if you find it interesting or amazing or anything. What makes you think other people would? I think it's a boring story. So what? Who cares about what happened to me? Yes, I was proud of what I had accomplished, damn right. You know very well who I was working for, Morgan Stanley. Yes, I was Vice President of Acquisitions. Of course I spent a lo . . . no, a *great deal* of time overseas. Yes, London. Yes, Tokyo. Yes, I was all over. No, I didn't study finance, well at least not at first. Believe it or not, I went to Queens College and studied Mechanical Engineering. Well, after that motorcycle thing and my brother dying my mom and dad split up for good. Yes, it was a difficult time for everyone. The school guidance counselor helped me with the applications and the woman psychologist wrote a very nice letter about me. Yes, I caught a big break. Well, I told you I liked her and yes she always helped me.

Your questions are interesting, I have to tell you that. Well, I hated engineering that's all, but I needed a job. So, I started my banking career working at the Bowery Savings Bank in a training program as a Customer Service Representative. Really, it was only a glorified teller's job, but it was a start. Did you ever hear about the Bowery Savings Bank? No, well it was a big part of New York City back then, when the City was in deep financial trouble. No, believe it or not, the Bowery sort of went belly up, and another bank bought it up. Yeah, I think it was the Dime Savings Bank that took them over and then, there was no more Bowery Savings Bank. It seems I was good at handling people and I received many glowing reports and commendations. Listen, lean over here, I want to tell you something. Just between you and me, banking is boring. It was just a job, that's all. Soon after, I saw an ad for Morgan Stanley looking for young executives. It didn't seem very interesting either, except they offered a management-training program, which included the opportunity to go to graduate school. I jumped on that and found my way into NYU's Stern School of Business. Getting in wasn't easy, but someone higher up at the bank had some pull and one thing lead to another and so, I was admitted. They liked me at Morgan Stanley. No, I can't tell you why? But, I worked very hard and stayed late into the night to get things done. Yes, maybe that was why? I was rewarded with some promotions, more responsibility and a bigger paycheck. Don't forget the high blood pressure and the dizzy spells? I got them too. Eventually, I found my way into the vice president position. They paid me very well and the fat yearly bonuses I received allowed me to buy my own place right down in Tribeca. Are you familiar with that area of the City? No, nothing, never mind. When I moved in, I paid a student designer from the New York Fashion Institute to fix it up and she made the place look spectacular. We spent some time deciding things, but I gave her carte blanche and I swear, it was right out of a magazine spread. She worked at it and turned it to the place of her dreams and mine too. Except, I wasn't there much to enjoy it. No, the travel—remember?

Around that time I met my wife, I mean my future wife. She was this gorgeous looking beauty who could have been a model, really. She worked out at the New York Sports and Racket club more that I did. Every morning, at five forty-five sharp we would bump into each other as we moved through the circuit from one exercise machine to another. For me it was love at first lust. God, what a body. Later, I learned she had a pretty good mind to go with that body too. She worked on Wall Street on the trading floor. Hey, you won't believe this. She was a Wharton grad. Do you know how few women graduate Wharton and end up on the trading floor of a Wall Street firm? That's right, not very many. Well, we hit it off big time. And two years later we were married. She moved into my condo and things went along just fine. I used to say that the first half of my life was shit and that I was looking forward to the second half of my life with Ariana. No, of course not. No, I don't say that anymore. Pretty name though, right? I had a truly beautiful woman as a wife who just happened to have the most beautiful name. I loved to say her name, Ariana. Ariana. There's poetry in that name, don't you think?

Yes, I know it sounds like I grew to have a great life. Actually, I did. Did you know I owned a Porsche? Yeah, a gorgeous black beauty, I mean I loved that car. No, not at all, money was never an issue. I had saved most of my earnings and the bonuses at Morgan Stanley were very generous . . . Excuse me, what? You know about the bonuses, of course. Besides that black beauty, I had a summer place out in the Hamptons and a sleek twenty-nine foot powerboat that I kept out East. Well, the way I describe it is, I was a million miles away from that horrible street I grew up on. Yes, you can ask me about children. Did we want to have children? Well, yes and no. We loved our life and kept saying next year, next year, but then, I ran out of time.

Is that about the point when my troubles started? Is that what you asked? Umm, that makes me laugh. My troubles? Ha, Ha, Ha. How about, that's when my entire fucking world fell apart! I know, but you got me started now and I'm feeling angry again. Humph, well of course I was angry, no, not was. I'm still pretty fucking angry, you can hear how angry I am right? Damn right. Except, as you can tell, being angry never got me anywhere, nowhere at all. How did it start? What, my problem? Yeah, well it was everything, I'll tell you that much. Look, I had a pressure cooker of a job along with more responsibility that any one person should have. I had an office of twenty-five people under me all needing help like little birds in a nest. Except, I needed them to just fly off and handle things on their own.

We had financial goals to meet and I had to make it work. It was very aggravating; you can appreciate that, right? I had long trips overseas to scout prospective business properties, assess them, and set a price tag on what the properties were worth along with an analysis of the company's balance sheet. Ultimately, I had to make a final recommendation to buy or to pass. Yes, very stressful that's for sure. One time I was literally running through an airport to make a connection to a flight home and out I went. Why stop, I'm about to tell you the exciting part? Oh, you're only asking me what "out I went" means? So, there are some things you don't know, eh? Well, that's good to put in the old memory banks. What it means is, I simply passed out while I was rushing, right across one of the seating areas in the terminal. Scared a bunch of travelers to death too. Except, one of them was a doctor and he may have saved my life. Of course, why he bothered to do that I'll never know.

It was my blood pressure that made me pass out at Gate 17. Off the charts they told me. It was that episode with my high blood pressure that got me on-board the health train. What's the health train? Oh, you never heard that expression before? The health train pulls into your station whenever you see a doctor or have a health issue that requires you to get checked out. Yeah, you get on-board and sometimes the health train is an express making only one or two stops, and other times it's a goddamn local. "All aboard, making stops to healthcare along the way, all aboard." You understand now? I thought you would. Well, as luck would have it, my particular health train was a local and it made every stop possible. Passing out and finding out you have high blood pressure makes them want you to have every medical test known to man and when the results start coming in, they want you to see every health expert there is. It's exhausting and very worrisome.

One of the first things they tell you is, "quit your job, before all that stress it causes makes your high blood pressure the least of your problems." What did I do? You want to know what I did? I'm sorry to laugh, yes it can be irritating I know. It's just that when you asked me to talk about this, I told you I didn't want to. And somehow, you got me started. Well, now I don't want to stop. I don't know about you, but I find that very funny. You don't? Well, I think it's hilarious.

Yes, I was still married at the time. Why wouldn't I be? Oh, you heard something about my marriage. Yes, well, that was a little later. Look, would you mind if I had a little water? Yeah, I guess it's making me thirsty, very dry throat too. Thanks. Now, where was I? So, you were listening after all? Yes, I know you are interested in the details. You told me that before, remember? So, after all the medical tests and after all the experts confer, they bring you into their suite of offices and you sit there while they tell you exactly what they think they found. You want me to explain what? How can they exactly tell you what they think they found? Sounds like a paradox, doesn't it? Well, it's what they do in medicine. Haven't you ever been sick? No? So, you've never been on the health train then, eh? I see. Well, let me explain that first. Let me know if I'm boring you? I'm not? But, I didn't start yet. Oh, you want me to explain, good! This might take a few minutes, here goes.

When you go to see a doctor because you are sick, most of the time they have no real idea what's wrong with you. I mean, how could they? So, they examine you and then, maybe, they send you for tests, and maybe, they take blood and urine and other stuff, if it needs to be tested, too. They send that stuff to the lab. Then they read all the reports that have come in, read about your symptoms, look over your medical history, and even your family's medical history. Sometimes, they'll send you for additional tests, which they refer to as studies. Then, when you have waited a couple of more days, while they read over the literature and talk with other experts, they call you in to their fancy offices and tell you exactly what they think is wrong with you. You see, that's just it, they don't really know. It's a guess. They call this guess a differential diagnosis. They'll give you prescriptions for medicines and wait to see if you respond. If you do, they guessed right. If you don't respond to the medicines, they'll order more tests, read more literature and confer with other experts. And then, they'll guess again. And that's how it goes. Sometimes they do know right away especially when it's cancer and the lab reports back on biopsies. The laboratory science part can be very accurate at times. You might get the news that you're terminal. Other times, if they guess you need surgery, they'll send you for a consultation with a surgeon who will make the decision for your doctor. And other times, when the guesses don't work and they are stuck, they have a category for that too. It's called, idiopathic which means, they don't have a clue. You're laughing? Yeah, I know it does sound funny. But, hey, that's medicine.

Well sorry, I did get a little ahead of myself. Where was I, ahh yes, I was telling you what happened after I passed out at the airport. Did I mention the doctor who was waiting for a flight? Yes, oh, I did. Sorry, don't mean to repeat myself. That doctor was a heart specialist and he recognized the signs leading to my fainting and he had some medications that helped prevent a stroke or worse and once I came around, he had me go to the hospital with the paramedics and his quick action no doubt, saved my life like I said. Except, that wasn't the end of it at all. They did a series of tests to rule out heart disease and they did some MRI work-ups on my brain to see if there was any evidence of a mini-stroke. Remember, they're just guessing. I mean, no one ruled out anything and no one knew anything either. At this time I was discharged with a plan to follow up with a cardiologist and a neurologist. They stuck me a bunch of times to find out my blood chemistry, along with a thallium stress test and a fast track CT scan to look into my arteries for blood clots and other fun stuff. Then, after they looked over those results, they wanted me to go for the studies.

These were more serious types of tests of my circulatory system and my respiratory system. No, at the time they didn't give me any reasons why they were looking at my heart and my lungs. They just made all the arrangements and told me where to go. I think they enjoy frightening people, you know that?

The entire experience was exhausting and it took a toll on my wife and I. Yes, quite a toll indeed. What happened after all the tests? Come on, didn't you listen to my explanation? After all that, I walked into their fancy office with my gorgeous wife holding on to me. We sat down and heard their differential diagnosis. By the way, have you followed all this so far? Yes, you think so. Good, because from here on in, it really takes off. They start out by explaining from the very beginning all the things they looked at and studied, as if by doing this it will make it easier to understand. Except, instead of gaining a better understanding of what they are saying, you end up being dulled by their long explanations. And then, you hear it, well, sort of. As they say, "We're really sorry to tell you this, but you have a serious heart condition. It's an atrial septal defect and falls into the larger category of congenital heart disease. No, medicines can't help. No, no operation either. We are hopeful," they tell you half looking at you and half looking through you. "We are hopeful that you can have a heart transplant; we have you on the waiting list. Meanwhile, our nurse will go over a list of precautions with you. And she'll review the medications we'll be prescribing to prevent infections. Of course, we'll call you as soon as we hear anything. Are there any questions?"

You know, I have to tell you and honestly, I hadn't thought of it until right now, but hearing those lines alone may have been the one thing that did make me crazy after all. I know what you mean, but no it doesn't make you feel any better at the time. At the time, you only want to hear the magic words. Don't worry everything is fine; you just have to take these pills to lower your blood pressure that's all. Except, you know what? No? Well, here's the bottom line. It's not fine at all.

Excuse me? What's your question? Oh, you're asking me what caused that heart defect? Well, I can tell you everything because I know everything there is to know about it. That's right, the Internet. You can learn almost anything on the web these days. You use it too? Yes, I can understand why you would. So, I found out that an atrial septal defect is a birth defect that could be the result of a viral infection during pregnancy. Yeah, it seemed my mother had the responsibility for this one. My luck, eh. I found out that the defect they were referring to is an abnormal opening between the two upper chambers of the heart. That's funny, I asked the exact same question. It seemed the opening grew larger as I did, except, I didn't know it was growing. Say, do you really want to hear about this? I mean, it can be boring listening to someone rattle on about their illness? You want to know? Are you sure? You think it's relevant? When I think about it, I feel it's relevant too. You see, having heart disease changes everything. Small defects can repair themselves, and others can be fixed with heart surgery, but they told me that my defect was too large and if I didn't get the heart transplant I would probably die within one year. Imagine that? One year? Oh, and get this. With a defect like the one they told me about, the heart is under serious strain and the disease could lead to high blood pressure, another complication. And to top it all off, they tell you that people with heart defects are often at an increased risk for heart infections, which may be life threatening. Now that's to laugh at right, one year to live and I have to worry about heart infections that *might be* life threatening, ha, ha, ha. You smiled, you see the humor in that, eh?

Terrifying? You think that kind of experience is terrifying? Yes, I can understand that feeling. And I'll tell you something else too. There truly is worse. Why? You don't think so? You wonder what could be worse than finding out your dying and there's nothing they can do about it? Ha, ha, ha, now I enjoyed that thought. You're telling me it would make you go batty to hear that. Yes, I suppose it could. But tell me, would you like to hear how it could be worse? Your nodding very enthusiastically again, I guess you are interested after all, eh? Well, I'll tell you this. When you get unexpected news like that, there are many ways to react to it. Some people might just go along with it and follow their program of medication, a strict diet, and patient waiting. Other people might turn inward and find spiritual strength and go around mending all the wrongs that they have done putting their affairs in order as the end approaches. Still others might fight with all their energy and all their heart, at least what heart they have left. What would you do if you had a little talk like that with your doctor? You don't know? Yeah, of course, I mean who would know? Who goes around thinking about the answer to that question anyway, right? Well, I'll tell you what I did if you want to hear about it? Listen, before I get going again. Do you want to call it quits for the night and pick it up again in the morning? I mean it doesn't much matter to me at this stage. Whatever you'd like is all right with me. So, you want me to continue? Sure, no problem. Do you think I can get a little more water? Oh, thanks.

Did I tell you I was on top of the world when I got that medical report? Yeah? I mean I really was. Had it all. And remember, the top of the world was after I lived half of my life at the bottom of the world. Just like the characters in Gorky's play, *The Lower Depths*. Except my hell was real, just like I had told you. Did you ever read any of Maxim Gorky's work? Some say he was brilliant. No, not French, a Russian author from the late 1800s best known for his plays. You should take some time and read up on him, a very interesting author. So as I was saying, when I got the bad news, at first, I wanted to grin and bare it, as they say. Suck it up and follow their medical regimens and wait. Waiting was hard. Did I tell you about that?

About how hard it is to wait? Yeah, you got that feeling from me? Good. So, I waited and my beautiful wife Ariana waited too. Until, one morning when I woke up and looked in the mirror and decided that frankly, I didn't want to live like this any more. I didn't want to wait anymore. I don't know, really? Perhaps it had to do with the idea of that waiting list? I've never been a patient person you know. And imagine waiting for someone else's heart? How could I really?

I took a long walk one day over at the Bayard Cutting Arboretum down in Oakdale and it came to me what I should do? Well no, it wasn't an easy thing to figure out. But, as I sat there for a while at the edge of the Connetquot River watching the ducks floating around with no particular place to go, I could see my future and it was not good. No my conclusion wasn't a logical one. No, I didn't apply any great formula or anything like that. I just figured I would be better off that's all. That's a funny question, but no I really did not consult my wife. And no, I didn't ask anyone for an opinion. I just figured the best thing I could do was go out on my terms, that's all. What were my terms? Well, the way I saw it, I wanted to be the one to decide things for myself. Yeah, it was quite a revelation, at the time anyway.

The first thing I did was contact my lawyer and we had a long meeting about everything I wanted to do. Yeah, come to think of it, he was very surprised and then again, he wasn't. I think of everyone, he knew me the best. Yes, better than my wife. The first thing I did was resign my position at the bank. My terms remember? Then, I had a buddy from graduate school and I gave him my Porsche. Hell, he really liked my car so, why not? And my boat went to the old guy down at the dock who took care of it for me. Surprised the hell out of him, I'll tell you that much. Then, I had a special dinner with my beautiful wife and explained what it was I was doing. No, actually she was okay with it. Ariana simply told me that she loved me deeply and that she would not get in the way of anything I wanted to do. She just figured that I had every right to act anyway I wanted. She looked at me with tears in her eyes and wished everything was different, but she knew I was dealing with the greatest pain of all. And she simply let me go. Now, that woman loved me for sure. Can you appreciate that kind of love? You're not sure? Well, hopefully some day you'll be able too.

I packed up all my fancy suits, all my tailored shirts, my knit sweaters and everything in between and I gave them to the homeless shelter. They said thanks quite a few times. I wrote out some checks to some friends and to some of my family members too. I emptied my bank accounts. Then, there was the condo and I asked Ariana for a special favor. And she told me what she had said all along, that I could do whatever I wanted. So, I called that young student designer and gave her the keys and the deed to that beautiful place. You should have seen the smile on her face. It was the place of her dreams, remember? The rest, my house out in the Hamptons, all my retirement funds and my considerable stock portfolio, I gave to my wife Ariana, to my love. And then, there was nothing left.

You look surprised? Yes, of course it was a very difficult time. The idea that I was dying weighed on everyone's mind, but for me going out on my terms was the saving grace. Yes, thinking about suicide was not easy. But then again, what alternative did I have? Why? What would you do? You don't think you'd end your life? Well, like I said before, there are many ways to react. And I'll tell you this much, you can't predict what you would do either. No, something happens inside your head when you get the kind of news I received. No I didn't know what I would end up doing. There were many ideas floating around my head though. Like what, you ask? Like going off a bridge, or stepping in front of a speeding train, or just letting the car run in the garage. I was at the thinking stage. Yeah, well you want it to be right. No mistakes of judgment or miscalculations, that's for sure.

What happened to my wife Ariana? She left the state and traveled out to California to be with her sister. She told me I could stay out at the house in the Hamptons for as long as I wanted to. She was planning on selling it anyway. At that point, we said our goodbyes and parted loving each other. So you don't think you could do that? I suppose most people would cling to each other, but not me. No, I didn't want to suffer in front of her and I didn't want her to endure that kind of pain. It was better this way, for both of us. Can you see my point? Maybe? I guess that's good enough for me.

So, I finally decided on a way. Yeah, it was an important decision all right. I decided to simply use a gun. To take a great walk along the beach in Sagaponack and find a deserted area. No, my summerhouse was not in Sagaponack, the house was in Southampton not too far away. I just liked the name, Sagaponack. So I figured, after my walk, I would just sit for a while until that gun found it's way up to head. No, that's the funny thing. I didn't have a gun. Never owned one. Why was that funny? Oh, you don't get it? Well, I had to buy a gun before I could go find that empty piece of beach and you know what happens when you buy a gun in New York State these days? That's right, once you fill in the permit request; you have to wait up to six months for a permit to purchase a handgun. You knew that? Very good, and by the way, I am very impressed with how much you know. For a young man like yourself, it's very notable. Anyway, I knew I couldn't wait six months, I mean damn, if I wasn't going to wait for a heart, I certainly wasn't going to wait for a gun either. So, I went to this small gun shop and got to talking with the owner and he must have felt pretty sorry for me because he offered to sell me a gun privately. He said I could have it in fourteen days. Nice of him, right? So, even after I finally decided how to end it all, I had to wait a little bit longer. Yes, there is plenty of irony there.

Sure, you can ask a question. No, that would be okay. What about the psychologist that talked with me when I was younger? Oh, well, she was a child psychologist. And even though she was terrific, what could she do for me at this stage? We talked a little and yes, she referred me to somebody. A man this time and no, I didn't think much of that one. He tried, but I had my mind made-up. Look, here's the thing. I can tell you this now, because we talked quite a bit and you know me very well. More than most, wouldn't you say? So the thing is, I have been through so much and frankly; no one could possibly help me through all this anyway. You can understand that, right?

So, I waited the fourteen days for my gun to come in and it was a thoughtful, but lonely two weeks. I took many practice walks out in Sagaponack and I even found just the right spot on the beach. Here's a funny thought. I took so many walks, that after a while I started to bring lunch. You laughed? Funny right? Yes, but did you know there's the best deli in the whole world right there in Sagaponack and not far from the beach either. It's just a ways north of the beach on what they call the Sagg Main Road, right next to the post office. Of course I'll tell you the name, it's called Sagaponack Deli and they prepare some great sandwiches there. That delicatessen is a well-known institution for the folks who live in the Hamptons. On the thirteenth day I had a bit of a feast. From their special's board, I ordered Sandwich Number Three, which is fresh ham, provolone cheese, lettuce & tomato on a crusty French bagette with the tastiest basil cream dressing. I had that gigantic sandwich, a side of their pasta salad along with several glasses of Pinot Grigio sitting there near the dunes, at the Sagaponack Beach watching the waves crash in. Just thinking about how good that sandwich tasted makes me hungry as heck. You should go there someday and try it, really. What was that? Maybe you will someday? Good. Yes, it is interesting the details that I can recall. I guess the last days were important to remember.

When the fourteenth day was up, I went back to the gun shop and picked up my new handgun along with a small box of shells. The man at the store spent a few minutes with me and that handgun. He showed me how it worked, where the safety was and how to load the bullets. Was I nervous? Actually, no, and that surprised me somewhat, I was as calm as could be about that. And then later, when I was home sitting at my kitchen table looking deeply at that handgun, I got this call on my cell phone. It was strange because most of the time I kept the phone off, not that I was expecting any calls or anything like that. And come to think of it, that call might really be the real first time I knew I was crazy. It was my wife, Ariana, calling with the most stressful and excited tone you can imagine. She told me that the doctor's office had been trying to reach me for days. It seemed they had some important lifesaving news for me. At first, I figured my heart had come in. You remember, the waiting list? I was on the heart transplant waiting list? Yes that's right, the reason why I wanted to end it to begin with, I couldn't stand the idea of waiting.

Except, the call wasn't about a heart transplant at all, nope and that took me aback, because why else would the doctor's office be trying to reach me anyway? Well, I'll tell you why. They were trying to contact me about a gigantic error. It seems that somewhere along the line, and I found this to be incredibly difficult to believe, I'm sure you will too. But it did happen. Somewhere along the line, my file and another patient's file had gotten all mixed up. Yup, our names were similar and the computer record keeping they use these days just sent the wrong information into my medical records at the hospital. And get this, I wasn't dying; it was just a big computer mix-up. And after all that I ended up doing to prepare for the end too. You know, giving everything away in so many special ways. I know how far fetched it sounds, but hey there are all sorts of medical mistakes all the time. I've heard stories, who hasn't. There was the case of a surgeon amputating the wrong leg, and another removing the wrong breast. Or incorrect positive results on lab work. Yeah, there are all sorts of serious medical errors.

At the time, there were a thousand or so thoughts in my mind and I couldn't keep up with them, all but one anyway. Can you think of what that one thought might have been? No, but that was a good one. Any other guesses? No, okay so I'll tell you, it was what if I didn't have to wait for the gun? Fourteen days is a *great deal* of time—and hey, Mrs. Clark would have been real proud of me that time, right. Yes, a *great deal* of time. So, I made an appointment with that doctor and took the train into New York City to see him. He was friendly and all. And he did his best to apologize for all the trouble they caused. That's when it happened, when something inside my head snapped. Yup, just when he said, "all the trouble they caused." I took out that shiny handgun, pointed it at the bright white lab coat of his, watched the grin fall off his face and emptied it into his body. All the trouble they caused indeed!

So listen, I hope I didn't upset you with that? Oh, you knew about that already, of course, it is public record and all. And I guess you'd say that hearing those words, *all the trouble they caused* was the single first time I realized I was in fact crazy. Anyway, that's what my lawyer told the jury during the murder trial. My lawyer is a very bright fellow and he prepared a great defense for me. Yes that's right, he had me make an insanity plea. He told them, "crazy is as crazy does." And in the end they sentenced me to this wonderful mental institution for the criminally insane.

And I guess that wraps it up then, did you get what you came for? You still think it'll make a good movie? Yes, you do? I see it has all the ingredients people like? Really? It's just hard for me to believe my story would be up there on the big silver screen. I mean, go figure? What was that? You don't think I ever really told you the first time though? I know, I know, but really when you think about it, you could pick anyone of those things I told you about. My lawyer told the jury all of them too. And do you know what that jury told the judge? Come closer now, because you're going to want to hear this. They told him, "Not guilty by reason of insanity." I did have reasons, didn't I? Ha, ha, ha. Now that's funny.

# LITTLE
# SECRETS

*"What would life be, if we had
no courage to attempt anything?"*

Vincent Van Gogh

The police medi-vac helicopter ascended at a sharp angle near exit 37, the Mineola exit of the Long Island Expressway rushing James Draper to the trauma unit of North Shore University Hospital in Manhasset. Watching that bird take off left Sergeant Roy Jones with a mouthful of sand and a wish that he had looked away in time. He turned to continue his investigation of the accident scene spitting out the grit and dusting the sand off his Police Jacket. He was the lead investigator of the Nassau County Police Department's Accident Investigation Unit and as he surveyed the scene, Sergeant Jones realized once again that he would never adjust to the horror of sudden death. He could see officer Malone directing the backed up traffic slowly through the area into the one barely passable lane. There was debris everywhere and the truck that flipped on its side was still billowing dark smoke as the volunteer firemen continued to pour foam over the engine. The truck driver's body lay off on the shoulder covered by a white sheet. The accident scene was littered by emergency vehicles and assorted workers all carefully doing their job.

Sergeant Jones pushed the measuring wheel along the rubber slick cutting across the road to the third vehicle involved in the crash. He deduced that the driver of the second vehicle, while trying desperately to avoid the truck was bumped into and pushed along sideways. The driver apparently trying to stop the chain reaction, slammed on the brakes causing the wheels to lock as the car swerved out of control tumbling over and over knocking into the third vehicle. Judging by the length of the skid, Sergeant Jones figured the car was traveling at roughly seventy miles per hour. The second vehicle was a Ford Expedition, now upside down and heading the wrong way. The female driver of that vehicle lay on the shoulder along with her young daughter both covered with white sheets. Sergeant Jones shook his head at the idea of this tragedy and the loss of so many lives. "Three dead . . . one critical, and for what?" he wondered, as he looked over at the third vehicle, a silver gray import. It was a four door Lexus 350L, but with all it's scrapes, broken glass and twisted metal it was hard to see it's original beauty.

Sergeant Jones walked over to the young officer who was making notes and gathering the personal effects from the Lexus.

"Hey Andy, how you doing?" Jones asked in his best commanding voice.

"About as well as can be expected," the young officer replied. "Except, what am I supposed to do with these Sarge?" he asked holding the items out in front of him.

Jones took one look at the items he was holding and shook his head. "Wow what beautiful roses."

"Yeah, and there's a greeting card in a bag too. Must have been somebody's birthday or something, eh?"

"I guess? Hey, any name on the greeting card or is there a gift card attached to the roses?

I'd like to confirm the name for the guy they took away in the chopper."

"A name? I don't know, let me take a look." The officer opened the white bag with the words Plaza Stationary and Cards across it and slid the card out. He glanced at the cover and then opened it up. "It is a birthday card Sarge and it looks brand new, and nope, no writing inside." He reached over to the flowers and turned them over a few times. "And there's no gift card attached to the bouquet either."

"Um, that's too bad. I guess he didn't have time to fill it out. Listen, put it all in a bag for me okay, I'll be heading over to the hospital soon. Maybe that guy will come out of it and we can get some answers to what happened here anyway."

"Sure, no problem. There's a book here too, a cell phone, one of those personal computer gizmos and what looks like some work folders along with assorted tax forms. You think the guy's an accountant?"

"Maybe so, who knows? Say Andy, will you gather it all up for me?"

"Sure Sarge, no problem."

"I see the ME is working on his assessment, I'll catch up with you in a bit."

"Okay Sarge."


As Roy Jones walked over to the ME, he knew this was the part he hated the most, looking at the dead bodies while the medical examiner tried to piece together the facts. Even after nearly twenty years on the job, looking at the faces of dead people made his stomach queasy.

"Hey Doc, whatcha got for me?"

"Hi Roy. Well to start with, blunt force impact to this young girl's cranium," Dr. Foster explained his findings without emotion as if he was describing what he did over the weekend. "And there's bruising evident on her face, shoulders and arms. I'd say she was not wearing a seatbelt and was tossed around inside the interior of that Ford SUV." He looked up at Sergeant

Jones for a moment and when no questions were asked, he moved to the next victim. He uncovered the sheet and gently rotated the woman's head to the front. "Now I'm guessing here, but this woman is probably the young girl's mother because she looks about the right age and there is a strong resemblance, wouldn't you say? The mother has several severe lacerations on the left side of her face and forehead. I would guess she hit her head on the door glass and was also smacked hard by the air bag when it deployed. The air bag bloodied her nose and cut up her lip. I'll know better when I get her back to the lab, but I would think the force of that vehicle rolling over in the crash snapped her head back and forth violently causing her neck to break." He stood up waiting for Jones to finish his notes and pointed to the male driver. "And the truck driver over there had his head crushed, I think that happened when the truck flipped on its side. Not a pretty sight, I'll tell you that much."

Sergeant Jones closed his notebook, faced away from the bodies for a breath of fresh air and suggested, "Can you forward the autopsy reports to me as soon as you get them completed? I think the families will have a good amount of questions for us from the looks of this scene."

"Sure, no problem Roy. I'm almost finished here anyway. What happened to the driver of the Lexus?"

"The copter took him to North Shore Hospital. That's where I'm heading once I clear the wrecker to impound these vehicles. I want to see if that guy's conscious. Maybe, he's our witness to all this?"

"Keep me posted if you learn anything Roy."

"Sure doc."

Inside the medi-vac helicopter, the paramedics monitored James Draper carefully on his way to the Emergency Services Department of North Shore University Hospital. An experienced team, they recognized how close he was to the end and they did everything they could to stabilize him. His condition was reported-in as extremely critical and as the helicopter approached the landing zone at the hospital, James Draper lapsed into unconsciousness. He was rushed into the Trauma Unit and the medical experts went to work. The paramedics yelled out his vitals along with the details of his injuries as they gave report to the hospital team taking over. Within ten minutes, they had Mr. Draper intubated and on a respirator to assist his breathing. An intravenous drip of saline kept him hydrated and provided a port for other medications. A request was put in for a neurology work up and for a series of CT scans to determine how severe his head injuries were. One of the fellows was talking to the critical care nurse as he entered data into Mr. Draper's chart while she monitored the patient's pulse and heart rate. Over at the nursing station, one of the nurses was speaking to a social worker looking for assistance to locate and notify the next of kin. They had James Draper's wallet and were looking at his driver's license and other forms of identification.

Sergeant Roy Jones parked the Investigation Unit's Trailblazer in the Emergency Services parking area and walked the short distance to the entrance. He checked in at the desk and was told that Mr. Draper was in the rear trauma room and that Doctor Booker was the Attending in charge. Roy Jones looked at the Unit Clerk and asked,

"Have you seen any family around for Mr. Draper?"

"No, I haven't. I don't think the staff knows whom to contact. I'm sure it will be soon though, they've been working on it."

"Shall I page Doctor Booker for you Sergeant Jones?"

"Yes, if you don't mind. It would help our investigation if I could speak with Mr. Draper. Thanks."

Ten minutes later, a short slightly balding physician with a round Santa Claus face wearing wire-framed glasses approached Jones.

"Excuse me, Sergeant Jones?"

"Yes I'm Jones, are you Doctor Booker?"

"In the flesh as they say. You're investigating the LIE accident in Mineola?"

"Yes doc, there were three fatalities."

"Come on over here, we can talk."

"So tell me doc, is Draper conscious?"

"No he isn't and as a matter of fact, he's slipped into a deep coma. He's stable, but we're assisting his breathing and giving him I.V. fluids. His condition is fragile at best and we need to get him into radiology for a CT work up. They should be taking him up in a few minutes. I'm very worried about internal bleeding, he took some big bumps to his skull."

As Sergeant Jones listened to the doctor's explanation, he noticed in the background two very distraught women talking to the unit clerk. One of the women began sobbing helplessly into a handkerchief while the other did most of the talking. The Unit Clerk appeared empathetic and then she had her arm outstretched, pointing over to their direction. Sergeant Jones figured they must be Draper's relatives.

"Excuse me Doc, you better prepare yourself. It looks like Mr. Draper's family has arrived."

Sergeant Jones backed away and watched the two women introduce themselves to Dr. Booker. They were clearly upset and confused. He heard the one woman explain she was Mrs. Draper and the second woman was her sister. Um, that's odd, Jones thought; the one who was sobbing was the sister. He watched closely as Dr. Booker described Mr. Draper's condition and prognosis. Both women listened intently and both were visibly upset by the situation. Jones heard the wife ask,

"Can we see him doctor?"

While Dr. Booker replied, "I'm sorry, they just brought him up to Radiology for tests. You'll have to wait until he returns or is admitted to the hospital. I can tell you his condition is critical, and he hasn't regained consciousness since the accident."

Sergeant Jones let the sound of their conversation sink into the background of his mind as the doctor provided the details of Draper's condition. He let his senses take over as he watched the two women listening to Dr. Booker explain what must be both shocking and disturbing information. He watched Mrs. Draper keenly, wondering what she might have been thinking. Perhaps, her husband had left in the morning for his office expecting an ordinary day and got just the opposite. He could envision the couple at the door of their home as James Draper picked up his car keys from the hall table ready to leave. They would most likely have embraced, he would have wished her a good day and she would have reminded him, as she always did, "now you drive carefully sweetheart." It was a routine that hundreds, even thousands of couples would repeat every morning. Except, this day was different for the Draper's and for everyone else that came in contact with them.

As Jones looked at these two women, he realized that their looks were better than average. He figured from his experience that Draper's wife was in her late thirties and the sister, younger maybe just thirty or so. Jones noticed that while Mrs. Draper wore a wedding ring, the sister did not. They both had brown hair although the sister's hair had blond highlights making her appear younger. Mrs. Draper however, had a little better look about her. Not too sexy or overdone, just a little like the girl next door. At one time, maybe in their college days, they both could have been very athletic. Except now, they both could lose a little weight he decided. His thinking was interrupted by Dr. Booker who must have run out of things to say.

"Listen, let me introduce you both to Sergeant Jones over here, he's investigating the accident."

Jones stood up out of respect and watched Booker do the old hand-off. He realized he was very good at it too.

"Hello Mrs. Draper, I'm sorry about the situation here."

"Hello Sergeant." Mrs. Draper started," as she extended her hand. "Can you tell us anything about the accident?"

Jones gently shook her hand and noticed a very soft, warm feel to her hand before releasing his grip. "Well Ma'am, I can't tell you much, because officially we're still conducting our investigation. Actually, that's why I'm here. I was hoping to talk with your husband. You see, three vehicles were involved in the accident and your husband is the only one who survived."

"Oh, God," the sister exclaimed as she cried once again into her handkerchief.

"Sorry about my sister Sergeant Jones, she is the emotional one in the family."

"Well, everyone handles these sorts of things differently. But as far as the accident, I can tell you Mrs. Draper, that the accident occurred at a high rate of speed and that in addition to your husband's car, there was a truck and an SUV involved."

"What happens to my husband's car? Do we have to take care of anything?"

"No Mrs. Draper, all three vehicles will be transported to the police impound yard where a safety check will be conducted. You don't have to do anything. But, I do have some of your husband's personal items one of the officers collected from the car at the accident scene. If you would like me to, I'll go to my car and bring them in?" Jones took out his notebook, flipped a few pages and read off the items. "There's his cell phone, one of those palm type personal computers, some work folders and a book." He noticed she didn't seem to care much about that stuff. And then he remembered about the flowers. "Oh, and there is a bouquet of flowers and a card. I thought you would want them."

"Thank you Sergeant, that's very thoughtful of you to bring them here."

Sergeant Jones smiled and added, "Well, it just goes to show you, his heart was in the right place."

While Jones went out to his Trailblazer to retrieve the personal items, Mrs. Draper tried to comfort her sister. It was obvious that of these two, Joan Draper was the stronger sibling.

It had always been like that. Joan's sister, Martha, was always upset about something. It was like that in grade school, junior high, high school and even college. Joan thought it had more to do with the babying their parents provided than anything else. Normally, she didn't pay any attention to it, but at times like these, Joan thought, I could use a little support from her, instead of me comforting her.

Sergeant Jones handed the shopping bag of items over to Mrs. Draper and handed her the bouquet of roses too. "And by the way, under better circumstances, I would have wished you a happy birthday." Mrs. Draper took the flowers and developed an odd expression on her face after hearing those words. "I'm sorry Mrs. Draper," Jones added sensing he had said something wrong. "I just thought with the roses and the birthday card, they were for you. I'm really sorry."

"What birthday, Sergeant? My birthday was back in the spring, months ago."

Feeling very embarrassed, Jones nervously stumbled over his words, "Well, we found these items in your husband's car and I guess, the officer at the scene must have planted an idea in my head as we talked. We just figured the birthday card and the bouquet of roses were for your birthday. I'm truly sorry, Mrs. Draper, we didn't mean any harm."

"That's okay Sergeant Jones, it's an honest mistake. I know you didn't mean anything. Don't you give it a second thought." As she said those words her brain went into high gear. You bet she would be giving it a second thought. Here she was in the hospital while her husband lay in a coma upstairs somewhere getting pictures taken of his swollen head and she was here talking to a cop with her heart pounding and her mind racing a hundred miles an hour. After all, if the roses and the birthday card weren't for her, who the hell were they for anyway? And what was my husband up to? Damn him.

Jones took a couple of steps to leave and turned back, "Listen Mrs. Draper, here's my business card. I would appreciate it if you would call me if you find out anything that has to do with the accident."

"Of course Sergeant, and thank you once again for your kindness."

"You're welcome Ma'am, and if you have any concerns at all, you just give me a call."

Joan Draper took his card, smiled and assured him, "Of course, thank you for everything Sergeant, you have been most kind."

As he turned again to walk away, Roy Jones sensed something wasn't exactly right with that exchange. What could she be thinking, he wondered?

Joan grabbed the shopping bag and sat down beginning to feel the exhaustion set in. She looked over at her sister and asked in a calm collected voice, "So, what do you think of all that Martha?"

"What? What do you mean? You sound like something is wrong."

"You bet there's something wrong. Come on Sis, look at these beautiful roses here. Jim had to have had something going on."

"You don't know that Joan, why do you always think there's something bad? Maybe he bought the flowers for you after all and the card was just for someone at the office? Could be, right?"

"Oh Martha, really? Why would he be buying a dozen long stem roses surrounded by baby's breath and wrapped in such a sweet red color? Something was going on? I don't know what? But, I'm beginning to smell a rat."

Just then, Dr. Booker approached them with his head down and Joan Draper realized this was not a good sign. "Hi again Mrs. Draper, how are you getting along? Okay?"

"Well Dr. Booker, I guess as good as could be expected. Considering the circumstances that is."

"Yes, these are always difficult situations. I wanted to give you an update."

Mrs. Draper sat up with hopeful anticipation. "Has my husband's condition changed doctor?"

The expression on Dr. Booker's face went blank as he explained, "Changed? No, except we have more information. While there are no signs of internal bleeding, the CT scans have revealed some swelling on the left side of your husband's brain."

"And what exactly does that mean?"

"Well Mrs. Draper, the fact that there is no internal bleeding is a positive sign. Unfortunately, brain swelling is very serious and creates a touch and go situation. The neurologist I conferred with is suggesting we watch him very closely. No surgery at this point, but we can't rule it out in the near future if his condition doesn't improve or if the swelling increases."

"What causes the brain to swell if there is no internal bleeding doctor Booker?"

"After a head injury, sometimes fluid will build up in the brain tissue causing the brain to swell. This is referred to as intracranial pressure and if the pressure continues to rise, the brain becomes compressed against the skull. The compression can cause brain damage, which is very serious and I'm afraid to say, life-threatening. If the pressure continues to increase, he may need emergency surgery to relieve the pressure. We admitted him to Intensive Care so we can keep a watchful eye on him and monitor his condition. You can visit with him briefly."

"Thank you doctor, yes, I would like to see him."

"Listen Mrs. Draper, he's still unconscious and be prepared, his breathing is being assisted by a respirator and we have a number of I.V. lines running. Frankly, he's not the picture of health right now."

"I understand, thanks again Doctor Booker."

Joan and her sister found their way up to the hospital's intensive care unit. They peaked inside the room and found

Jim just as Doctor Booker had explained. A flexible plastic hose connected the tube in his throat to the pulsating ventilator that was off to the side. His chest rose slightly in sync to each whooshing sound of the ventilator as it forced air into his lungs. There were several leads running from his chest to a beeping monitor held above the bed. A white bandage surrounded his head while his eyes were shut tight and his facial features were a bit bloated. The nurse caring for him noticed them peering through the ICU's glass enclosure, waved and went out to speak with them.

"Hello, my name is Patty and I'm taking care of Mr. Draper, may I help you?"

"Hello Patty, I'm Joan Draper, Jim's wife and this is my sister Martha. Dr. Booker told us we could visit with Jim, would that be all right?"

"Yes of course, but not too long okay? His condition hasn't changed, but we're watching him carefully."

Joan Draper and her sister joined hands tightly and stepped inside the room. Neither had ever seen a person in a coma. Martha wanted to ask a question, "Excuse me nurse."

"Yes, can I help you with something?"

"I was wondering, can he hear us if we speak to him?"

"Well that's a good question. Research has shown it depends on the severity of the coma, and how much damage the patient has suffered. Some patients will awake from a coma and explain in detail the conversations they said they could hear. And other patients will simply say they heard nothing. I'm not sure myself, but I always tell the patient's loved one's, if you want to say something go ahead. Just be loving and positive that's all."

"Is he in pain?" Joan asked wondering about that.

"No Mrs. Draper, your husband's in no pain. The doctor ordered pain medication as he would have for anyone who was in a car accident. Even though he's not awake to tell us what he feels, the medication is a precaution."

Joan reached out and touched his hand and pulled it away reflexively. Then she placed her hand over his again and mentioned, "His hand is very cold, I wasn't expecting that."

"Yes, that's a common reaction that visitors have. You both okay now?"

Joan and Martha looked questioningly at each other and nodded affirmative. Patty motioned outside and explained, "I'm just going to be right outside making a few notes in his chart. Call me if you need anything."

"Sure." Martha said.

"Okay, we will." Joan added.

They stood there in a strange silence. Joan decided to speak to her husband. She took a slight look around as if to make sure no one was watching. "Okay Jim, so what were you up to today and where were you going before the accident?"

Martha did a double take not expecting that at all. Then they were both looking back at Jim as if waiting for the truth. Joan squeezed his hand and tried again,

"I'm here Jim, waiting for you to wake up. Whenever you're ready, you can just open your eyes."

Martha decided to add, "Hello Jim, it's me Martha. Can you hear my voice Jim?" And there was nothing, no twitch, no blink, no hand squeeze. And then there was sadness, as if the reality of Jim's condition sank in. They just stood there a few more quiet minutes until Patty the nurse entered to check his blood pressure and pulse once again.

Joan asked, "Patty, can I leave my cell phone number with you in case there's a change?"

"Yes, we would like to have a number to reach you. Just write it down here and I'll add it to the chart"

While Joan Draper jotted down her cell phone number, she added, "We're going to be going home now, you'll contact us if we're needed?"

"Of course Mrs. Draper and we'll take good care of him. Rest assured. And here's the unit phone number, anytime you feel the need to check on things, just call."

Joan took the notepaper and placed it in her bag. She reached her hand out as Patty did the same. "Thank you so much Patty."

"You're welcome Mrs. Draper."

The ride home in the car was very quiet except for the ongoing conversation that took place in Joan's mind. It started once they were on the Long Island Expressway driving home to Huntington. When she saw the green exit sign, Exit 37, Mineola, one half mile, she felt her heart throb for this was the location of the accident that changed their lives forever. What? She wanted to know. What was Jim doing this far west on the LIE in the middle of the afternoon on a workday? Where in the world was he heading and why? Her thoughts wandered to all sorts of places, but mostly she settled on the answer that he was seeing someone. *What else could it have been?* She wondered. And how do I go about finding out? Then she remembered the cell phone and the personal computer the Police Sergeant told her they had found in the car. Those personal computers have all sorts of information stored, and the cell phone might show phone numbers. *Yes,* she figured, *it was a starting point.* Martha must have tired from the quiet because she asked Joan a question.

"Tell me Joan about what you said before, when you asked Jim, . . . so what were you up to today and where were you going before the accident?"

"What Martha, what do you want to know?"

"Just what did you mean by that? And didn't you know where he was going?"

"No Martha, that's just the point. I didn't know about it, where he was going or why?"

"Did Jim always tell you where he was going?"

"Well Martha, we did have a good relationship, if that's what you're getting at?"

"I'm not getting at anything Joan," she said defensively. "I'm just thinking that's all."

"About what?" Joan asked sounding annoyed.

"Well you got me thinking, do I always know where my husband goes? Does anybody? And does everyone have little secrets that we just keep to ourselves?"

When Joan heard Martha ask those questions there was a great pause in her mind. Then, a minute later as she looked over at Martha who was staring straight ahead as if in a trance, Joan saw the tears running down her sister's cheek.

"What is it now Martha?" She asked with a snap. "Are you thinking maybe your husband is stepping out on you?"

Martha laughed out loud as if mocking the idea and then added, "No Joan, Robert would never. He's too in love with his family."

"Oh sure, your husband is the only one in the whole world who would never do that, right!" She dotted that *right* with enough sarcasm that it made Joan angry.

"Damn you Sis, there you go again. Always thinking that you know everything when you don't. Not at all."

"Then why the tears, what is it this time?"

"Because it was me." Martha responded with a calm confident voice.

"You what?" Joan asked feeling confused doing double takes of the road and her sister.

"It was me that cheated."

More surprised than ever, Joan rushed her questions not knowing if she fully heard that statement or comprehended it either. "You what?" Did I hear you right Sis? You? You cheated on your husband?" She said excitedly.

"Yes, I did. It was about five years ago."

"With who?"

"I think you mean with whom? And does it matter?"

Joan chuckled some as she added, "You shouldn't reveal that sort of thing while I'm trying to concentrate on my driving, Ill tell you that much. You'll get us both killed for sure."

"Oh stop being so dramatic Joan. It was only for a short time, six months and then it was over."

"Well it is a big deal Sis. And tell me, was he married or single?"

"He was married too. We were both experiencing feelings of emptiness wondering what life was all about. I think we both were going through a mid-life crisis or something? Anyway, he told me he was drawn to me and when he approached me, I couldn't resist him. He was so handsome and sexy."

"Jesus Sis, what's with you and that kind of talk."

"Well you asked."

"I know, I know but I didn't know about the details. Jeez."

"Well, the whole point in me telling you this now is, it's just, you never know about people . . . that's all."

"That's all? You know Martha, I have a million questions to ask."

"Like what?"

"Like did your Robert ever find out?"

"No, he never did and, he never will. You remember that Sis!"

"How did you keep it a secret all these years?"

"I guess I just put all of those feelings in a little box and buried them somewhere in the back of my mind. That is until you started talking about Jim being somewhere he wasn't supposed to be."

"How did the two of you meet?"

"Oh Sis, are you ever going to stop?"

"Yes, but not until you answer my questions. So where?"

"Remember when I went back to school, to finish my degree? It was in my Sociology class, when I was five years younger and thirty pounds lighter."

"Now that's funny . . . sociology class, ha, ha, ha."

"Stop teasing Sis. He was working on his degree too and one night we went out for some coffee and got to know each other. Then, it was a drink and then we cut class and had dinner and well, you can guess the rest."

Joan turned the car into Martha's driveway and mentioned, "That was the fastest trip home from anywhere. Wow."

"Now you remember, don't mention this to anyone, promise?"

"Of course Sis, not a word. My lips are sealed." And then she laughed.

Not seeing anything funny in that Martha insisted, "Joan, now you promise."

"Okay, okay, I promise. Not a word."

"Listen Joan, are you okay? And how are you doing with what's going on with Jim?"

"To tell you the truth, for a while I forgot all about that. But I guess, I'm as okay as I can be, at least for now. I just need to take a couple of Advils and get some sleep. Tomorrow, hopefully, will be a better day."

Martha opened the car door, gathered her things and bid her Sister a good night. And, as she stood outside about to swing the car door shut, she bent down, poked her head into the car and asked one more time,

"Now I don't have to worry about what I told you, do I Joan?"

"Of course not, I already promised. Come on, it's in the vault and safe with me. Now get going and let me get home."

Joan watched Martha walk up the red brick path to her home. And as her sister used her keys to open the front door, Joan started to pull away for the short drive home. Soon after, she found her way into her bed, exhausted, she closed the lights and fell fast asleep.

Sometime in the middle of the night, Joan's brain woke up long before she wanted to. It started with a nightmare watching her husband's coffin being lowered into a gravesite, except there was an arm sticking out holding a bouquet of red roses. That picture made her bolt upright and she found herself breathing hard. Going back to sleep was another matter, her brain just wouldn't let her. She got up and made some tea sitting in her sunroom in the darkness of the early morning feeling her own dark thoughts begin to surround her. *What would she do if Jim did die? Or if he remained in a coma?*

Her thoughts flashed to those conversations they had about their healthcare wishes just in case something like that happened. Those conversations followed the well-known Terri Schivo case back in 2005 and they had resolved, at the time, to create the legal documents everyone was talking about. She recalled Jim saying, if he was ever in a coma or brain dead, he wanted no extraordinary care no respirator, no feeding tube, nothing that would keep him artificially alive. He wanted to die with dignity, not have his picture all over the media. They made a point of filling in their Healthcare Proxy forms and appointed each other as their respectful healthcare agents, just in case. Then Joan recalled that in the hospital's ICU, she saw the respirator breathing for Jim and she knew she would have to find those legal papers and talk with Jim's doctors about his wishes if it came to that. She swallowed hard at the reality of those thoughts.

She sipped her tea feeling more alone than ever. She closed her eyes and had a sudden vision of Jim with those beautiful red roses in one hand and the birthday card in the other standing in front of some woman she didn't recognize. *Little secrets indeed,* she thought. And that made her blood boil over with anger about being betrayed. She looked out at the backyard and could see the rays of the morning sun begin to signal the dawn of a new day. Joan recalled the PDA and the cell phone the Police Sergeant had given her and she decided to go to work to uncover some of those little secrets she feared. She opened the bag and the very first thing she noticed was a beige slightly torn worn-out jacket of a hardcover book. She reached in and looked with disbelief at the book's cover. She spoke the title out loud, "*The Pursuit of Happiness* by David G. Meyers," Now what? She wondered, wasn't Jim happy with our life either?" She opened the book and found some of the pages dog-eared. She flipped through those pages and read the sections with even more questions. What was he searching for? She wanted to know.

Joan opened the bag and this time she reached for the Palm Pilot PDA. She opened the folder and using the wand she pressed on the address book symbol. She moved the curser down slowly past all the familiar names. Then she saw one listing under the heading "new" and as she opened that folder she saw a group of names she didn't recognize. What do we have here, eh Jim? Who are these people? And why are they in this listing? There were three female names and one male name, but only two phone numbers. One number was next to the man's name, Steven Stills and the other was next to the name Karen Raills. Under Karen Raills was the name Michelle Michaels and under Michelle's name was Sharon Williams. Both phone numbers had two-one-two area codes and she realized that meant the City. Then she asked herself, Could that be the reason he was heading west? She went to the cabinet and came back with a pad and pencil. She wrote the names down just as they appeared including the two phone numbers. Next, she opened the bag and reached for the cell phone. She turned it on and waited as it powered up staring at the display going through its sequence. The phone chirped and there was a display indicating phone mail. She clicked okay and watched the readout indicate dialing for phone mail. She put the phone to her ear and heard the phone mail voice indicate, "You have three new messages, enter your password and then press pound." Joan shuddered, "What password? Shit, I don't know Jim's password. Darn it." She said tossing the phone onto the couch.

She sat there a few more minutes trying her best to sort through all that had happened without going off the deep end. And then there were the sad thoughts. If Jim dies, she would be all alone. And if that happened she was afraid she would end up hating the idea that they never had children. My god, why did we do that? She asked herself more than once. Joan thought again about Jim's Palm Pilot and wondered what might show up in his calendar? Those things have very detailed information in them, she realized wondering if Jim used it that way. So she picked it up and using the wand, she went probing for the calendar and after a few presses and clicks of the curser, the display showed the current month. She clicked on Tuesday, and up came a list of Jim's appointments for that day. She looked at each entry and could easily tell by Jim's notes which entries were work related. One entry jumped out at her, it was the one o'clock meeting and it only had the initials KR, 57th & 5th. Joan's mind flashed to New York City as she pictured the corner. As she did, she realized it was the entrance to Manhattan's Central Park. Now, what would Jim be doing meeting a woman at Central Park? Joan wondered out loud. Or was he meeting her at the Plaza Hotel, which is also at 57th & 5th? The obvious answer to that question brought a cold chill to her body and an empty feeling in her heart. She reached for the pad and made a note about the meeting date, time and the location. Then she meticulously started to work backwards in Jim's Palm Pilot's calendar. Each day that had entries Joan wrote them down on her pad. She could begin to see a pattern and the frequency to Jim's trips to New York City. She sat back in the soft cushiony chair, closed her eyes and felt the pain that comes with betrayal. In her mind, Joan kept asking herself, *Why Jim? Why? Didn't I provide you with everything you needed? Why did you need to be with someone else?*

Finding herself staring at the cell phone, the idea occurred to her that maybe there would also be phone numbers in Jim's cell phone to go along with the names from his Palm Pilot. Yes, that's it, she thought excitedly reaching again for the phone. You don't need a password to access the phone book. She pressed menu and selected recently dialed calls and up they came. At first glance, many of the names and numbers she knew. There were several calls to his office number, a few to his best friend, Victor, a call to the health club, and then as she concentrated more on the listings she could see some names and numbers she didn't know. She grabbed the pad and jotted down another two-one-two number, it had no name but the word private was next to it. "Umph, another little secret Jim?" Joan also noticed a number that looked the same as the listing in his Palm Pilot. And when she compared numbers she realized there was more than one call to Karen Raills. Actually she counted five directly dialed calls in the last week. Well sugar, she thought. You're right up there as prime suspect number one. And what little secrets do you have, eh dear? And why would you be interested in my husband? She also made a written note to contact Victor. Perhaps Jim confided in him? After all, she realized they had known each other ever since high school and that was nearly twenty-five years ago.

As Joan sat there quietly, she became aware of the ticking from the wall clock. As she glanced up, she was very surprised to find that the time had passed by so quickly. It was now 7:30 in the morning. She decided to phone the ICU and ask about Jim's condition. She picked up the phone and dialed the number the nurse had given her. There was one ring, and then another, and another. After a half dozen rings, a voice announced, "Medical ICU, Mindi speaking."

"Hi Mindi, this is Mrs. Draper calling. My husband is Jim Draper."

"Hello Mrs. Draper. Can I help you with something?"

"I'm just calling to check on my husband. Has his condition changed?"

"I'm not his nurse, let me see if I can find out who is? Would you like to hold?"

"Yes, of course I would." When she said that, she thought maybe she snapped at her a little. But, what do they expect from families? These are very stressful conditions. She heard the phone being picked up and to her surprise it was a male voice.

"Hello Mrs. Draper. You're calling in regard to your husband?"

She wanted to yell back, no you idiot I was thinking wouldn't it be fun to hear your charming voice at 7:30 in the morning. But she didn't, she just calmly replied,

"Yesterday, his nurse Patty told me I could call anytime for an update. She could feel her facial muscles tense up as she asked, "Why? Is there something wrong? Has his condition become worse?"

"No Mrs. Draper, his condition is about the same. Except, there is a small increase in his intracranial pressure and I beeped the Intensivist to alert him."

"Intensivist?" Joan asked, "What is an Intensivist?"

"That would be Doctor Bushing and his medical specialty is in intensive care medicine. There's nothing he doesn't know about. Mrs. Draper, your husband is in the best hands, I'll tell you that much."

"I see," she responded feeling more confident. "It's just a nervous time, that's all."

"Of course, the male voice replied. Would you like me to have Doctor Bushing call you when he's checked on Mr. Draper?"

"Yes, I would. My cell number is in the chart."

"Okay, I'm sure it won't be too long. Try not to worry."

"Well, that's not too easy right now. But thanks for helping."

"You're welcome Mrs. Draper. Bye now."

Nearly three hours later, Joan Draper was driving back to the hospital with more questions than she had answers. Dr. Bushing did finally call her back, but since he hadn't finished morning rounds with his patients, he didn't offer any more information than she already had. *How much watching can they do, really?* She asked herself, *I'd like a little less watching and more doing if you ask me.* Victor, Jim's best friend had reacted badly to the news of the accident indicating through a dreary voice, that he would see her at the hospital. She had tried to tell him, that with Jim unconscious there wasn't much he could do. He didn't want to hear about that though, Victor just told Joan, "I'll be there as soon as I can clear it at work." Then there was Martha's surprise revelation about her affair, which Joan was totally unprepared for. Go figure, she thought to herself. I guess you never know about people even those you are close to. And that brought her thoughts full circle back to her own husband and the lingering questions.

She lifted up her cell phone and adjusted the hands free headset knowing it was time to begin calling the people on Jim's phone lists. And that was starting with her number one suspect, Karen R. She glanced at her phone list and dialed the number on her cell doing her best not to run off the road. There were two rings and the call was answered by phone mail, "You have reached Karen Raills, senior social worker at New York Hospital. Please leave your name, number and a brief message and I'll call you back as soon as possible. Thank you." Nervously, Joan hit the disconnect button not completely sure what to do. If she were to leave a message, what would she say anyway? Joan wondered, senior social worker? New York Hospital? What is that all about? She also realized the voice quality had a certain sultry quality making her think that this Karen R must be a very sexy woman. In her mind she pictured a half dressed woman laying across a pillow covered bed looking as sexy as Brittany Spears beckoning to her husband Jim come closer, closer.

She shook that image out of her mind, looked at her phone list and dialed the number listed next to Steven Stills. She held her breath as the phone rang. A woman answered,

"Doctor's office, may I help you?"

Trying to not act as surprised as she was, Joan asked, "Ah yes, I'm trying to reach Steven Stills, is he there?"

"I'm sorry, Doctor Stills is seeing patients now. May I ask who is calling?"

Obviously, Joan had not prepared an answer to that question and fumbled through her response, "Well, I'm calling for my husband. His name is James Draper."

"I'm sorry Mrs. Draper, I don't know the name. Did your husband ask you to call?"

"Oh, ahh, not really. I think he's a patient of doctor stills."

"A patient? I don't think so, Doctor Stills is a pediatric specialist, he doesn't see adult patients."

Not sure how to respond, Joan decided to jump off. "I'm sorry to bother you, I must have the wrong information."

"No problem, you have a nice day."

As Joan heard the phone disconnect, she thought, nice day? So, far things are not off to a very good start and I'm afraid things will be getting a lot worse before they get better.

Joan's thoughts about things getting worse were very prophetic. At the hospital, the Intensivist did his morning examination of James Draper. What he found surprised him; he had measured another increase in the brain swelling of his patient. His review of the chart showed the brain swelling had actually been steadily growing. While the increases have been slow and at first glance one might think Mr. Draper's condition had stabilized, he began to recognize that the opposite was true. He closed the chart, picked up the phone and paged the neurosurgeon; it was time to begin the plan for emergency surgery. The time for watching was over they needed to take action to try and save this man's life.

While Joan turned off the expressway and worked her way over to turn right onto Community Drive, the cell phone she had slipped into her bag earlier started to ring. At first she didn't recognize the ring tone, then it dawned on her that the ring tone belonged to Jim's phone. As she reached into her bag for the cell phone, she smiled knowing it was clever of her to have brought along Jim's phone in case some of those little secrets decided to call. She flipped open the phone and answered the call, "Hello?" There was a moment of silence on the other end and Joan asked, "Is someone there?"

"Excuse me," a woman responded sounding uncertain. "I was trying to reach Jim, did I get a wrong number?"

"No, this is Jim's phone and I'm his wife. Can I help you?" The woman disconnected the call leaving Joan flabbergasted. *Who was that and didn't she sound just like Karen R or did she?* She asked herself. It was frustrating her because instead of getting answers, there were more questions.

As Joan pulled into the Hospital's parking garage, her own phone cell rang. It was the nurse from the Intensive Care Unit.

"Hello, Mrs. Draper?"

"Yes, this is she, who is calling?"

"This is Patty from the ICU, Doctor Bushing asked me to contact you."

"Is anything wrong? My husband didn't . . ." She stopped mid sentence as if unable to complete the thought she was so afraid of hearing.

"No Mrs. Draper, but he is being prepped in the operating room."

"Oh, my God, what is happening?" Joan asked clinging to hope.

"It's the brain swelling, Doctor Bushing spoke with the neurosurgeon and they decided to take action. Mrs. Draper can you come to the hospital? There are some papers you need to sign."

"I'm already here and just parking the car. Where should I go?"

"Just come up to the ICU, I'll be waiting for you."

Joan pulled into the first parking spot she could find, turned off the engine, closed her eyes and said a short prayer.

While she wasn't overly religious, she did attend church services with Jim weekly. And at this moment, she felt she needed her faith to be strong. Joan took a deep breath and left the car feeling a new urgency. After all, it was never the kind of news you wanted to hear. What could be worse than brain surgery? She thought to herself as she rode the elevator to the ground floor. She rushed across the street to the main entrance and found her way up to the Intensive Care Unit. Patty noticed her walk up to the nursing station and waved her to the side. They went into a small room and Patty paged the surgical fellow. Then Patty turned to Joan and explained,

"Mrs. Draper, we need you to sign the surgical consent form. Dr. Bushing's fellow, Dr. Jacobson will explain everything to you."

"I also brought these papers," Joan said as she handed them over to the nurse. "These are the Health Care Proxy form and the Do Not Resuscitate form. My husband had very strong feelings about these things you know."

Patty looked at the Proxy form responding, "Okay, we'll read them over and add them to his chart. I see you are his health care proxy?"

"Yes, that's correct."

As she said that, the door to the small conference opened and in walked a very tired looking young man in green operating room scrubs. Patty introduced him and sat back quietly as Dr. Jacobson explained in detail, the risks and benefits of the brain surgery. By the time he was finished saying all the risks that were associated with the procedure, Joan had forgotten what the benefits were. When he was all finished, he placed the consent forms down on the table handed her a pen and pointed out where to sign. It was all going a little too fast for Joan, but as she signed the form she tried her best to stop her hand from shaking. The fellow left with a copy of the consent and Patty made a couple of suggestions to Joan.

"Listen Mrs. Draper, I know this is very hard, but it's going to be several hours. If you plan on staying, there's a small chapel down on the first floor if you feel like spending some time in prayer. Also, the coffee shop near the lobby is open."

Joan glanced at her watch and realizing she had no where else to go right now, she told Patty, "Yes, that's a good idea. Thank you. But, how will you get in touch with me?'

"Figure after the operation, he'll be coming right back here. You can go to the surgical waiting area and sign out a beeper. If we need to reach you, we'll just signal the beeper. It works as long as you stay at the hospital."

"Surgical Beepers eh? What will they be thinking of next?"

Joan took the elevator down to the first floor and went directly to the coffee shop. She didn't have any breakfast and figured a cup of coffee and a muffin wouldn't be a bad idea right now. She sat at a small table along the glass wall and stared aimlessly at the people walking by in the main corridor. Funny, she thought, how many overweight health care workers there are. You would think they, of all people, would know the importance of keeping their weight down. Go figure. And then she saw this familiar figure approach and as she watched him go by she thought to herself, wait that was Victor, Jim's best friend. Where is he going? She jumped out of the seat and caught up with him down the corridor.

"Hey Victor, not so fast. There's no hurry right now."

"Oh, hello Joan," he said relieved to find a friendly face.

He took her in his arms and held her close. "So, how is he doing Joan," he asked letting her go.

"Well, there's quite a bit to explain, come on and have some coffee with me and I'll fill you in."

They walked back to the coffee shop and after he picked up a cup of coffee, Joan told Victor that Jim was in the operating room. She explained about the brain-swelling problem and how that was caused by the head trauma he suffered in the accident. Joan gave him the details of the new information and reminded him of everything else. Victor still couldn't believe the unfortunate turn of events that Jim experienced since he had seen him last. Recognizing the need for conversation, Victor looked over at Joan and told her.

"I guess you never know when or what will happen whenever you leave the comforts of your home, isn't that right?"

"No Victor, I guess not. Thanks so much for coming down here. I know you're busy at the office."

"It's the least I can do for my buddy, Joan. And if there's anything else you need, just let me know. Okay?"

Joan reflected a moment on how to word her response knowing that the most important things are always the hardest to say. "You know Victor, I do have some questions I have been meaning to ask you, but they don't have anything to do with Jim's condition. Well, at least I don't think so."

"I'm sorry Joan, I'm not getting what you're trying to say?" What's going on?"

"I'll explain, but just give me a few minutes before you respond. This is not easy for me at all."

"What Joan, what is bothering you?"

Joan decided to let go of all her anxiety and to just take her time. "Well Victor, it all started after the accident. A number of things surfaced and it made me wonder about Jim's state of mind before the accident. Were you aware of anything that Jim would want to keep from me?"

"Joan, I really don't know what you are referring to?"

"Come on Victor, I know Jim was up to something and I had hoped under the circumstances you would be straight with me. For example, why would Jim be reading a book about happiness and keep that sort of thing from me?"

Victor was startled by that question and decided to ask, "Joan, you of all people should know if Jim was happy or not? But I can tell you, that for the last year he was questioning everything; his work, his goals, where he was going and where he was coming from, he wondered about his whole life. We laughed, because over a beer or two we got to figuring he was a classic case of a man having a mid-life crisis."

Joan listened to all of this and all she could muster was, "Really?" But then her mind got its second wind and she asked the very big question. "Victor answer me this, considering all he questioned, do you think he was seeing another woman?"

Victor raised his eyebrows at that question, looked his best friend's wife in the eyes and asked, "You mean romantically?"

"Yes, romantically, sexually, all the above."

"Joan, just because a man gets to thinking about everything, it doesn't mean he's out there fooling around. I mean the bars of the world make a fortune with all the confused men everywhere sipping their drinks wondering if they have gotten enough out of life. What makes you think he was involved with another woman?"

"It's a little silly, actually. But when he had that car accident, the police sergeant investigating the accident came around to see Jim hoping he could ask some questions about the accident. And he had brought with him several personal items that were found in Jim's car. Among these items were a bouquet of red roses and an unsigned birthday card. Of course, since there were no names written anywhere they gave them to me thinking it was my birthday. But as you know, it's not my birthday and it made me wonder what little secrets Jim was keeping from me?" When she said those words her thoughts flashed to her sister Martha, and how true it was that you never know about people and their secrets. But she kept that part to herself as she had promised and continued in a very serious pitch. "The flowers and the card added to the mystery and I started looking at his calendar on his Palm Pilot and his cell phone call log and I found some names and phone numbers I never heard about. And several of the names belong to women."

It was Victor's turn this time as he looked at her with keen interest and asked, "Really?" With that, the two of them leaned back into their chairs as if they both needed to take a break from the heavy conversation.

Victor broke the silence when he reached across the table and took Joan's hand in his. He was a sweet man and was never afraid to show his affection or his sensitivity. Holding her hand he tried his best to explain, "Joan, Jim never told me anything about another woman. Roses, cards and phone numbers? These things I don't know about. If he was involved with someone, he kept it to himself . . . I can tell you that for sure." Joan looked into his eyes feeling in her heart of hearts that Victor was telling the truth. If Jim was seeing someone, it wasn't something he talked about. Joan reflected on those thoughts and sat feeling glum. Victor sensed her sadness and added, "You know Joan, when it comes to secrets, it's not what we keep to ourselves, it's what the people in our lives let us tell them. Have you thought of it that way Joan?" Joan clasped her hands under her chin took a deep breath in, reflected for a moment and responded.

"It's just that I thought we had a good relationship, all these years and I never held anything back from him." Joan looked over at Victor as he nodded slightly in agreement, closed her eyes and realized she was no closer to any of the answers than she was earlier. Yes, she had more information, but none of it led her anywhere in particular. Feeling frustrated, she decided to move up to the surgical waiting area. "Victor, I'm going to sit in the surgical waiting area to wait for news about Jim's operation. Would you like to join me?"

"Sure Joan, that is if you really want company?"

"Yes Victor, I don't want to be alone right now. Thanks."

They left the coffee shop and headed over to the elevator banks. And just then, the beeper she placed in her pocket started to vibrate. "Victor, the beeper went off, the surgery must be over. Come on let's hurry. Just as they arrived in the surgical waiting area, Joan's name was called by the volunteer in the salmon colored smock sitting at the desk. She felt her right hand go to her chest as if she could hold onto her heart and went to the desk, "Hi, you called for the Draper family? I'm Mrs. Draper."

"Well Mrs. Draper, the surgeon called to say the operation is over and he would be here in a few minutes to speak with you."

"Okay, thanks for letting me know."

Joan went back to a seat next to Victor and explained in a whisper as if everyone in the room was listening in, "It was the surgeon to say he would be up in a few minutes to speak with me."

And Victor whispered back, "And I guess that's good news, don't you think?"

"Good news?" Joan asked in a questioning voice. "Let's just wait and see."

And they didn't have long to wait because in came this scholarly looking man in green operating room scrubs and the volunteer at the desk was pointing right at Joan.

The surgeon walked over and asked, "Mrs. Draper?"

And Joan nodded, "Yes, that's me."

"Well, I'm Dr. Klein the neurosurgeon. I wanted to talk with you about your husband's condition, there's a consultation room off the hallway; it'll give us some privacy. Please, this way. Joan was looking for an indication, any indication that things went well and Jim would be his old self in no time. Except, judging by Dr. Klein's reserved manner and unhappy look, Joan figured the pit in her stomach had it right. This would not be good. She started to follow the doctor to the consultation room as Victor signaled her he would be waiting. Joan motioned to him to come along with a pleading desperate expression that made him stand and follow them. They sat in a very small conference room as Dr. Klein closed the door behind them. The surgeon sat across from them with no hint of a smile, you could cut the heavy air in the room with a knife.

Mrs. Draper introduced Victor as a close family friend and the doctor only nodded an acknowledgement.

Then, he started, "Mrs. Draper, I'm afraid I don't have good news for you. We rushed your husband to the operating room because the brain swelling had increased to very alarming levels. I'm not sure what they had told you, but it works this way. When a person experiences head trauma, fluid gathers in the tissue causing the brain to swell. While the skull is designed to protect the brain from injury, when the brain swells the skull actually can be very harmful. There is not much space between the brain and the skull and if the brain is pushed against the skull it cuts off the oxygen and normal blood flow destroying brain cells and if this continues to happen it can lead to brain death."

When Joan heard the last part of doctor Klein's explanation the tears started to rain. She reached for a tissue from the box that was a part of the room's decor and did her best to control her emotions. Victor placed his arm around her shoulder to comfort and brace her.

"I'm sorry Mrs. Draper, I know this is difficult. In your husband's case, we thought we had time to relieve the pressure, but as in many of these accident cases, we don't always know what we will find. There was more damage than we were aware of."

"Is he dead?" She asked that question feeling as if someone had cut her heart out of her chest.

"No, he's not dead, but this is where it gets complicated. When a person lapses into a coma we know through neurological indicators that there is still brain activity. However, when a person's brain stops this activity, the patient is described as brain dead even though the heart is beating and the person is still breathing."

"Are you telling me that Jim is brain dead?"

"Yes, I'm afraid that is the case."

She squeezed Victor's hand tight in reaction and continued, "And he's still breathing and his heart is still beating?"

"Yes, Mrs. Draper."

"So, what happens? Is there a chance he can recover?"

"Generally, no. Once parts of the brain dies, they can't be rejuvenated or repaired."

"I see, so what happens next?"

"Well, that's up to you and to Jim if he signed any of the advanced directives. There's no rush to do anything. He's in intensive care and being cared for. We can arrange for you to speak with one of the social workers who specialize in these types of cases."

"Yes doctor, I would like that. Can it wait for tomorrow, I'd like some time to think things through and to speak with my family to try and gain a better sense of what should be done?"

"Of course, I'll speak to the nurse and have them contact you in the morning." Doctor Klein stood, indicated how sorry he was and left the room.

Joan just sat there feeling so empty, nothing had ever prepared her for this experience or for the way she felt. In a few minutes she tried to stand, and victor needed to steady her until she gained her balance. She fell into his arms with an emotional outburst, "Oh Victor, my Jim's gone."

He couldn't find any words never mind the right ones, so he just held her tight.

Well, as it turned out, the doctor was right and Joan didn't need to do anything in a hurry. The hospital's social worker had considerable experience handling these types of cases and was invaluable to Joan and her family. Everyone was supportive and comforted Joan as she tried her best to deal with Jim's fate. The most surprising thing of all was the phone call from Karen Raills who asked to meet with Joan. Considering all that happened, Joan dreaded that meeting figuring she would finally learn what Jim was up to and she decided after all, she really didn't want to know about his cheating if that's what he was doing.

When Karen Raills entered the house, Joan nearly gasped at her beauty. As she showed Karen to the living room, she figured that she didn't stand a chance. Karen surprised her even more with her explanations. First, she apologized for hanging up on her earlier in the week when she had called Jim's cell phone. Karen told her when she heard her name she panicked. But not for the reason Joan was thinking, she panicked because she had promised Jim to keep his secret until he was ready to share it with his wife. It turns out that Jim was truly searching for some meaning in his life. After all, Jim felt he had everything and there were so many people who didn't, but he was unsure of what to do or where to turn. Then one day, Jim read an article on bone marrow transplants and how it was a miracle cure for so many people dying of cancers. So he looked into it quietly at first, figuring that when he passed the screening process and knew he could donate his bone marrow, then he would share the joy with Joan. When she heard that, she sighed and tears slid down her cheeks. Jim had learned that there are several bone morrow registries; one of them was right in New York City. And all you had to do to start the process was sign some papers and be willing to go through the screening. Jim had decided to go ahead and arranged for the screening and testing stages at New York Hospital. Jim also learned that not everyone can be a donor and there's not always a bone marrow match, since there has to be so many points to the chromosomes. Usually, siblings have the best chance of being a match, followed by the parents and other family members. People outside the family can donate, but the quality of the match is not always perfect.

After Jim had the bone marrow extracted a few weeks went by and he learned through the New York Bone Marrow Registry that there was one close match to a patient. It was not a complete match, but so close that there was great hope for the transplant's success. The patient was a ten-year-old girl named Caitlin who was dying from Leukemia and the bone marrow transplant was her last hope. As if being sick like that wasn't enough for any little girl, Caitlin had also lost her dad in the 9-11 World Trade Center attack. Karen explained that

Caitlin had no siblings and her mother and other members of the family were not good donor candidates. Jim's bone marrow on the other hand, by some chance, matched Caitlin so closely that it seemed like it was meant to be.

Joan finally got the answers she was looking for, well, at least most of them. For it was on the day of the accident, that Jim was actually on his way into New York City to meet Caitlin and to visit with her and her mom. Not at the hospital, but at Central Park, one of Caitlin's favorite places. Karen Raills was the social worker on the case, she had made all the arrangements, and she had told Jim that the day they were to meet was Caitlin's birthday. It seems the birthday card and the roses were for her. Karen shared with Joan all the signed consents and the paperwork that Jim had taken care of. She also showed her a photograph of young Caitlin and the encouraging letter from her doctor, Steven Stills.

Then she asked, "Do you think you would still consider going ahead with the donation?

And Joan was dumbfounded and said, "That's not possible, Jim is brain dead now.

Karen told her that it is possible for a person who is brain dead to donate bone marrow. Joan stood, walked over to the living room window, took a few minutes thinking about the request, turned to Karen and replied,

"Sure, I think if it was something my husband wanted to do, then let's see it through. In a way, it gives some meaning to all of this sadness. Just tell me what I need to do.

A few months later, Joan Draper drove down the small path to the family plot in Huntington Cemetery. She left her car and found her way to the gravestone marked, *James Draper . . . a loving caring man*. It was a habit she turned into a weekly event. She usually spoke directly to him, more as a comfort to herself than anything else. On this visit, she had some good news to tell him about. She told Jim that the bone marrow transplant had worked and how Caitlin was now cancer free. She wiped the tears from her cheek, bent down and placed a bouquet of red roses next to the gravestone. She whispered to him, "no more little secrets between us now Jim."

# JEEPERS, CREATURES...

*When I was younger, I could remember anything,*
*whether it had happened or not.*

Mark Twain

Angelina was told more than once not to go out, she heard it hundreds of times. Except she always figured she had nine lives and couldn't remember ever spending even one of them. After all, the world outside the apartment was so exciting and she felt so alive finding her way around. Getting out was another matter and not so easy even for one as smart as she. As Angelina watched the door open, she had to time her escape through the apartment's heavy metal door just as it was released and closing. And she had to be quick about it or else. A few times she even lost some of her pure white hairs, but not this time as she slipped out feeling the wind of the closing door brush her fluffy tail. Angelina knew that gaining her freedom was well worth the risk wondering what treat she might hunt down. She stayed close to the banister as she slinkered down the three flights of stairs to the basement exit. This exit was the least traveled and led directly down to the first alley. Angelina knew where she was heading; she had visited that particular spot many times before. Her tongue wisped at the corners of her mouth as she recalled how tasty that last meal was. And maybe, she thought, she would find her luck had changed once again. After all, what was she doing in this poor neighborhood? It was a question she always wanted to have answered. She was a Pure White Angora and her lineage descended from the Egyptians. She just figured with a heritage like that, she should be living in a wealthy area, not this dreadfully poor one.

Angelina found her way to the basement exit and as usual the door was propped open with an old red brick. Once outside, Angelina rushed the last steps to the cement floor; she paused and looked up at all the windows circling the square courtyard. She saw the usual items stretched across the courtyard of assorted shapes and colors fluttering in the breeze. Her head slowly turned from one side to the other wondering how many other felines trapped within the building would love to have her spot, her freedom? Angelina decided to continue her exploration taking several steps to the center of the courtyard. She looked left at the alleyway leading to the main street in front of the apartment complex. There, at the foot of the stairs, were the building's metal garbage cans lined up and overflowing. At times, Angelina would give chase to a pigeon or two pecking at the bags or a small rat working its way around. This time out, Angelina decided to search the old coal bin long abandoned and littered.

As she entered the darkness of the coal bin, she picked up an unusual scent and froze. She could see the evening sunlight glistening through the cracks in the boards that covered the window at the far end of the long cement bin. Then a moving shadow caught her eye and she immediately squatted down low to the ground as her fur rose along her back. Something was very different in the semi-darkness, and Angelina started to wonder if maybe this time her adventure was a mistake.

The strange unpleasant scent was getting stronger and yet as much as she wanted to run, she knew that any movement might give away her position. A slight rustle of a discarded newspaper made her eyes dart right. Then she realized she should have run, because at that very moment the jaws grabbed onto her and she could feel the sharpness of its teeth sink into her flesh. She tried to escape, but the weight of her attacker pinned her down. Angelina felt her paws twitch several times and then numbness slowly enveloped her entire body. She felt herself being dragged away unable to move any muscle and yet feeling excruciating pain. Angelina closed her eyes giving in to her fears.

After school the next day, J. J. was excited to continue the fight. He rushed his homework, as any eleven-year-old boy would, wanting to call for his friend Manuel. He yelled to his Mom that he would be home later for supper, grabbed his light saber and ran out the apartment door. J. J.'s family lived on the top floor of the old apartment building, the sixth floor. He bounded down the stairs nearly knocking over Mrs. Black as he rounded the landing on the third floor.

"Sorry Mrs. Black," he exclaimed half serious and half laughing at the expression on her face.

She turned and quickly asked him, "J. J., if you see Angelina around let me know, she went off on another one of her adventures. I'm worried for her."

"Sure Mrs. Black," J. J. yelled back not missing a step.

Reaching the first floor, he rushed up to Manuel's apartment and knowing the bell hadn't worked in years, he knocked excitedly on the heavy medal door. Within a minute, Manuel's Mother opened the door as she was yelling in Spanish for Manuel to finish his homework.

"Hello Mrs. Diaz," J. J. said as he entered the apartment smelling the aromas of fried tortillas simmering on the stove.

He loved her cooking and always enjoyed eating supper with Manuel's family.

"Hey J. J.," Manuel yelled from the kitchen. I just need five minutes to finish these math problems, have a seat and I'll be ready soon. Say hi to Grandpa, he's watching baseball on TV."

J. J. always got a kick out of Manuel's grandfather. He was a crotchety old man sour to the idea of leaving his beloved Mexico and wasting away in this town called Astoria. There is an Astoria in the State of Oregon, but this Astoria is part of Queens, one of the five boroughs that make up New York City. J. J. loved to hear Grandpa's stories, loved to listen to the tales he would tell about life in Mexico.

"How are you today little one?" Grandpa asked.

"As good as usual." J. J. answered looking thoughtfully at the old man's worn out leathery face.

"And you Grandpa, are you enjoying the baseball game? Who's winning?"

"Baltimore's taking it to the Yanks, and figuring how much these Yankee players make every minute they are playing, they should be ashamed. Like this fellow Giambi here, what good is he and why do the Yanks pay him so much money? I like it when they lose, it reminds me that you can't buy everything. I'll tell you what they need. They need a Martinez or a Pena to get them going. Ballplayers from Mexico would make a difference you know. And what are you and Manuel up to today little one?"

"We're going to meet up with our friends and play."

"Have fun and stay out of trouble."

As Grandpa said that he turned and gazed over at J. J. with a kindhearted smile and a gentle feeling. It made J. J. smile back as the crack of the bat brought their attention back to the game. An easy pop-up by Giambi retired the sides and Grandpa just sat there shaking his head.

J. J. wasn't the biggest kid around, at four feet five, if he was seventy-five pounds soaking wet that was a lot. Except, he was smart as a whip and quick-witted too. Getting good grades was J. J.'s idea of a way out of the neighborhood and a way out of his situation at home. The initials J. J. were short for John Junior. And he hated the name John Junior for it reminded him of the sad fact that he was the son of an Italian drunk. He preferred another name and a different father, but was stuck with both.

True to his word, Manuel came walking out of the kitchen five minutes later with his usual ear-to-ear grin. Unlike his grandpa, Manuel was one happy kid loving his life in America. And why wouldn't he with all the opportunity that was within reach. Manuel's father worked with J. J.'s dad at the Coca-Cola bottling plant around the block on Thirty-sixth Street. Ending up as a factory worker wasn't Manuel's idea of a happy future, but for now having a father with a regular paycheck, even a small one, brought some stability to this Mexican family. Actually, Manuel knew from talking with other Mexican kids at school, that these days, having a father with a job, made him one of the fortunate ones.

Manuel and J. J. left the apartment ready to join up with their friends. The three attached apartment buildings in the complex were much like the others in the neighborhood. Faced with old cement and worn out reddish-brown bricks, the buildings and their small apartments were well over sixty years old. J. J., Manuel and their friends were a symbol of the neighborhood's diversity. J. J. was the Italian representative and Manuel was the boy from Mexico. In the next building lived Jippy from Germany and Frenchie from France. In the third building lived Johnny Jam from Canada. The one boy in their group who lived around the corner was Ruben. Ruben and his family were from the Philippines and Ruben's Father owned the Royal Yo-Yo Company. A huge bonus for the group of kids at Christmas time, for they all received the newest and the best of the Company's yo-yo collections. There was only one girl in the neighborhood their age, her name was Darlene and she lived across the street in another complex of apartments. Darlene wasn't part of their little gang either and she was only allowed to enter their cellar clubhouse if she offered to play spin-the-bottle. Which wasn't very often.

One by one the group met up in the alleyway, each carrying their light sabers and preparing for battle. Jippy wore the black headgear of Darth Vadar and breathed deeply as his deep voice quieted down the group.

"We must protect the Death Star at all costs. For the one they call Luke Skywalker will do his best to destroy her."

"Too late, you ugly excuse for a dark villain, we're already upon you." And with that, the boys turned on their light sabers and the iridescent green glows lit the dim light of the courtyard. One of the boys hummed the theme to Star Wars out loud for effect. They crossed their swords and fought each other off until one group decided to flee. They only did that to add to the fun by creating a chase. Into the alley past the garbage cans they ran, rattling their lids with their toy swords. Then, they went up the stairs and onto the sidewalk paralleling Steinway Street. The chase continued over to and down the stairs of the middle alleyway of the second apartment building heading to the courtyard with assorted whoops and hollers. J. J. who played Luke Skywalker ran into the courtyard quickly hiding next to the wall. As all the boys ran out from the alley through the courtyard, he let his light saber touch the shoulder of the last soldier in line. As the soldier turned to see who had tapped his shoulder, J. J. sliced his saber across his belly telling Frenchie,

"You're dead, you're dead, now wait for everyone at the cellar hideout."

"I don't want to be dead," Frenchie pleaded.

"Well, you are dead and you have to go over to the cellar." J. J. added.

"All right" Frenchie told him as he turned and walked away with his head down. And J. J. ran to catch up with the group knowing that Luke Skywalker had outsmarted them again.

Frenchie walked over to the cellar using the back alley path. The courtyards were centered in the middle between each building with a stairway at the front and another stairway at the end of each alleyway. In the front, the stairway led to Steinway Street and in the rear, the other stairway led to the back alley of the apartment buildings. The back alley was a concrete path stretching from the first building to the last ending in the back wall of a sandwich shop. The concrete path was littered with small items of trash long neglected and left for someone else to clean up. Behind the apartments were a number of smaller houses some with small lawns as backyards, but all with fences in-between. Some of the fences were simple chicken wire and some were made of wood boards. A few of the yards had tree branches hanging over the fences and large unclipped shrubbery added to the separation and cluttered the area. As Frenchie walked down the stairs and through the alleyway toward the cellar entrance, he noticed a trail of blood leading from the old coal bin across the courtyard and into the darkness of the cellar. Hey, he snickered and thought. Did someone really get killed in our fight? Well to his way of thinking, it didn't matter what it was that made that trail of blood, Frenchie wasn't going anywhere, certainly not inside that dark cellar alone.

Soon after, Johnny Jam showed up and Frenchie asked him, "You dead too?"

"Yeah, they got me and Ruben at the same time. He should be along in a minute."

Frenchie pointed to the blood trail and asked Johnny Jam, "What do you make of that?"

"Wow, where did that come from, is it real blood?" he asked bending down to get a better look.

"Hell as I know," responded Frenchie, "but it looks real enough don't you think?"

About that time, the rest of the gang showed up and everyone was amazed at the sight of the blood trail.

Jippy asked in a hesitating voice, "So, who wants to go into the clubhouse"

There were echoes of not me's and I don't think so's.

And then Ruben walked to the entrance and said, "I'll go in, I'm not afraid."

So, they all hunched up and stayed close behind Ruben as he walked into the dim light of the cellar. Manuel feeling devilish decided on a prank, he clapped his hands as loud as he could and yelled, "BOO!" Making everyone jump and scream at the same time, as if they didn't feel nervous enough. They all wanted to kill him after that silly scare. Then they reached the first ceiling light and J. J. pulled the cord and heard the click of the light switch as it turned on. Instinctively, they all looked around at their feet half looking for the blood trail and the other half looking for the unknown. To their surprise, there was nothing there. No blood trail or anything their young imaginations may have thought up.

Jippy broke the nervous silence, "If there's no blood trail here, maybe it went in the other direction toward the storage bins?"

Johnny Jam asked, "What do you mean, it went in the other direction? What? What went in the other direction?"

And Jippy answered back feeling nervous, "I have no clue, except we saw the blood trail go into the cellar and it's not down this end, right?"

J. J. joined in suggesting, "Hey, let's get a flashlight and go check it out?"

"What are you nuts?" Frenchie wanted to know.

"Nuts? No, but I'm no chicken either."

Ruben added, "Maybe it's a headless chicken running around." And to add to the effect, Ruben pulled his shirt over his head walking in jerky movements making believe he was headless.

Manuel gave Ruben a shove and added, "I don't know about you guys, but it's close to suppertime. I have to get going. How about we meet up here after school tomorrow with as many flashlights as we can get our hands on?"

"Okay, I'm game," J. J. said.

Frenchie added, "Me too."

The rest of the gang chimed in in-agreement and they all left the cellar for the evening knowing tomorrow would bring a great adventure.

Later that evening as the darkness fell onto Steinway Street, old man Samuel Johnson ambled down the stairs into the alleyway of the third building. He carried two large plastic garbage bags over his shoulders. One half-filled with the empty cans and bottles he had gathered from the building's garbage cans and the other filled with all of his worldly possessions. Samuel Johnson was a homeless man who mostly kept to himself wandering the streets during the day and finding a cozy alley to sleep in during the night. The cans and bottles he collected daily brought him some welcomed food money. Samuel used to work as a short-order cook and grille man at the Airport Diner over on Astoria Boulevard, just a stone's throw from LaGuardia Airport. One day last year, after being dressed down by his boss for breaking the egg yokes of a patron's over-easy breakfast order, he yanked off his apron and took to walking the streets never returning to his job or his normal life.

As Samuel adjusted the position of the two garbage bags on his shoulders, he walked past the center courtyard and up the back stairs. There in the corner were the large cardboard sections he had left stacked against the fence. As he opened them up to create a miniature shed, he noticed a pile of small sticks, a few bird feathers and bits of a shredded tee shirt in his spot. He kicked at the pile scattering them about. He crawled inside the cardboard shed removing from one bag a discarded blanket he used as a bed. He curled up taking a large yawn as if he had worked the fields all day.

In the middle of the night, he half-awoke feeling a bothersome cramp in his right leg. Samuel stretched his legs outside the shed trying for relief from the cramp. That's just when he felt something brush up against his leg and he reflexively kicked at it feeling his foot push against some heavy object. He rattled the bag of cans to scare away whatever was outside his shed. He spoke out doing his best to feel brave, "Listen you mutt or whatever, you better be getting along now or else." Samuel shook the bag of cans again as he heard a loud hiss. Wondering what kind of a dog would make a hissing sound like that, he peered through the cardboard opening noticing the shadowy shape of a large creature back away. Samuel shuddered in amazement, wondering if his imagination was getting the best of him. Was he seeing things, or did that big dog have the largest most unusual tail? Then there was silence . . . an un-natural silence.

Later that night, the rays of the full moon cast an eerie brightness to the darkening gray clouds. It was after midnight and it was the time of the nocturnal creatures. Up from the broken drain they came one following the other. They were a family of rats that lived in the building's sewers that were connected to the main sewer lines along Steinway Street. There were many sewer grates along the street and many avenues of escape. In the courtyard of the third building, the five inch drain cover had been broken for months and since no one had noticed it, no one had fixed it either. So every night, up they came all five of them scrounging the area for bits of food. They would find their way to the garbage cans at the foot of the stairs, sniffing the contents of the bags until their keen sense of smell found something worth digging for. The father rat, of course the largest and most experienced of the family, spent many a nights teaching his offsprings how to use their sharp claws to pierce and then rip apart the bags. The mother rat also taught the little ones. Her job was to teach them about safety and how to recognize the sounds of danger as it approached.

They sniffed the bags and at one spot in particular, they ripped open a bag finding the bare remains of a turkey carcass. Alongside the turkey were assorted discarded vegetables and bits of deserts and they all dived in to enjoy the feast. The mother rat, watching her offspring enjoying themselves, picked up a scent in the air that was new to her. She sat up on her hind legs, sniffed the air unsure of what it meant. She lifted her head and darted to one side of the cans and then back to the other. The other members of her family were too distracted by the food treasures they had found to notice her alarming movements. The smell was very close now and the mother rat knew she needed to take action. So, she ran across the lids to the spot where her family feasted and quickly moved back and forth squealing an alarm. One by one, the little ones realized their mother was warning them of danger and they also started to squeal and move about. They jumped to the ground and following their mother they started to race back to the open drain of the courtyard. They didn't see the large shadow waiting in the darkness and as the last little one paused for just a moment to look back at the garbage bags with a fond memory, the father rat shoved him out of the way in time to feel the jaws take hold. The little one raced back to his family as the group scurried away. The mother rat took a second to look back at the father trapped by something very, very different, wondering to herself how she would manage the family alone?

The father rat tried to bite back to force his release, but whatever had pinned him had a heavy coat of armor protecting it. The rat's teeth, as sharp as they were, were no match for the tough armor. Very soon, the father rat felt its limbs go numb and all feeling left its body. At that point, the father rat felt itself lifted into the air as it was carried away into the darkness.

After school the next day, the entire gang, J. J., Manuel, Johnny Jam, Frenchie, Jippy and Ruben all met up in the courtyard outside the cellar's entrance as they had agreed. They were checking their flashlights and pointing the beams of light toward the dried blood trail. The cellar was an amazing labyrinth having numerous walkways leading to assorted rooms. In one direction, the hallway led to a series of rooms containing poorly constructed woodbins that the apartment dwellers used to store their unneeded items. Midway to the woodbins, was the entrance to the buildings main boiler room. And what a contraption it was, large enough to provide the heat for each individual apartment in the building, there were pipes leading everywhere. The boiler, once fed by shovelfuls of crystal black coal, had given way to modernization and was now oil-fired. If you went past the boiler room in the opposite direction, there were a series of large basement rooms. One of the rooms contained the large storage tanks for the heating oil. Another was a workroom where the building's super kept his tools and materials. The agreement the boys had with the apartment building's super was a simple, but clever one. The boys could use one of the cellar's main rooms as a clubhouse, as long as they did no mischief or damage to any of the other rooms or any of the items in the cellar. And it worked, because in addition to causing no damage, they kept an eye out protecting their gang's turf. Well, they weren't really a gang. How could they be an official gang, with the youngest being eleven and the oldest thirteen? They liked to think of themselves as the Steinway Street Gang, but they didn't have colors or an insignia and they never participated in any real street gang fights. They only played together and had make-believe fights pretending to be Star Wars characters.

Except right now, whatever they were about to trail was no make-believe creature, oh no, not at all.

Feeling restless, J. J. decided to get things going,
"Okay, okay, who wants to lead this exploration? How about you Ruben, you were brave yesterday?" he concluded with a bit of sarcasm.

"Oh, I don't know, it seems I'm always the one. How about someone else be the leader?"

The boys were looking from one to the other hoping someone would step forward. This time it was a surprise. "How about me?" Johnny Jam volunteered. And the rest of the gang starred at him in disbelief wondering what in the world had gotten into him? Johnny Jam was the overweight kid in their group. He was the slowest one, and the least likely kid to be picked for the stickball games they played on the weekends. So, who would have expected Johnny Jam to volunteer to track down the trail of blood leading into the cellar's darkness? So, they lined up in a row and unbelieving, one by one, they followed him inside, their flashlight beams nervously moving ahead in all directions crisscrossing each other as if they were unable to hold the lights steady. Johnny Jam followed the blood trail, which veered off to the right, toward the storage bin area. They could hear the rumbling noise of the boiler and each took a quick peek in the opening to the boiler room as they passed the doorway. Once they reached the first ceiling light and clicked it on, they started to make jokes feeling more relaxed and less nervous. As they continued to follow the blood trail and the ceiling light faded on the path their voices lowered to a whisper. Johnny Jam stopped short and they all bunched up nearly knocking into each other.

Frenchie asked first, "Hey, what's that over there?" pointing the beam of his flashlight over the remains of a small animal.

"I don't know for sure J. J." commented, "but it looks like the shape of a pigeon—at least what's left of one."

Jippy looked closely at the remains and said, "Shit man, there's bugs crawling around in there, yuk!"

And the other boys added, "eewhhh . . ."

"Well come on now," Johnny Jam told them. "The blood trail is still here, it leads further back. Let's keep going." And so they started to follow it again and as they took several steps there were small puddles of water on the cement floor.

"Can you see the blood trail?" Ruben asked feeling much less brave than he was the day before.

Johnny Jam replied, "Yeah, it seems like the trail goes under the puddles."

"Hey, check it out," Manuel said pointing to a strange footprint on one side of the puddle. "What could have made that?" They all aimed their lights at the print and crowded around the nearly dry prints for a closer look.

J. J. placed his hand near one of the prints and told the group, "This print is almost as big as my hand, whatever made these footprints must be pretty big for sure."

"Come-on let's keep going," Johnny Jam pleaded starting the group walking again.

Then, as they came to the next ceiling light Johnny Jam pulled the cord and as the switch clicked the light bulb stayed dark.

"Come on Jam," Jippy yelled to him. "Stop kidding and turn the light on."

Trying to make it go on with several repeated clicks, Johnny Jam told them, "I'm not fooling with it, the bulb must be burned out."

And some of the boys spoke out in disappointment making a bit of a racket. Suddenly, there was a sound of a crash coming from one of the storage bins and everyone hushed up quickly pointing their flashlights toward the origin of the sound.

Manuel, noticed something move around the corner and yelled, "There it goes, on the left. It just moved around the wall."

"What did you see?" J. J. asked.

"I don't know exactly, except it was low to the ground and had a long tail."

"Frenchie volunteered, "Maybe it was a monster?"

"Oh great," J. J. added. "A monster in the cellar on Steinway Street."

"Well, I saw something, that's for sure." Manuel added wanting to convince the group.

"Hey you guys, you know something, it really stinks in here?" Jippy commented.

"I thought it was Johnny Jam letting go a big one. Ha, ha, ha." Manuel joked.

J. J. added, "It smells like an old clogged up toilet."

"It wouldn't surprise me if there's more of those rotten animals down here." Jippy added.

Then Ruben asked, "I guess we have to figure out what we're doing? Do we go on or what?"

"What's the *or what part?*" Frenchie asked not liking the sound of that.

"I don't know," started Ruben felling pretty nervous for such a brave kid. "I guess I meant or what like maybe we should be doing something else and get the cops to check out this place, not us."

"The cops?" J. J. echoed. "Yeah, I can just picture that one. But officer, I swear that pigeon was really dead."

Frenchie added, "Hey, Ruben's got a point there. Maybe the cops should be the ones to look into the blood trail."

"I say we continue what we started. I mean, come-on, we don't get many opportunities for an adventure like this one. I say, the hell with the cops, this one's ours. Who's with me?" After he said that little speech, Johnny Jam got more looks of disbelief. Who would have believed it for a minute?

A few of the boys followed Johnny Jam into one of the back room where the storage bins started. Their lights focused clearly on the blood trail that went directly into the room. The bins were stacked two high and most of them had a padlock holding the flimsy plywood doors shut. They stood there in the center of the room moving the flashlight beams around the room. The blood trail ended right at one of the bins. They saw a wood crate on the ground in front of the open bin figuring that's what had made the noise they heard. They moved closer to the bin and bent down low to see what was inside.

"Hey you guys," J.J. yelled to the other group waiting down the cement hall. "Check this out, you won't believe it." As the other boys joined them, they all looked with amazement inside the bin. It was the bloodied partial remains of Angelina just lying there with her eyes wide open as if she was thinking about something important. It was where the blood trail ended, right inside the storage bin with a puddle of blood right under Angelina. And just then, there was a loud hissing sound that startled them all and one by one they ran for their lives getting out of that cellar before any of them could say, "*What in the world was that?*"

Once outside they gathered together on the apartment stoop all chatting nervously about what they had seen and heard, and what they think was down there.

"Holy shit," Johnny Jam started, "I've never been so scared in my life."

"What the hell was that down there?" Frenchie asked sounding terrified.

Ruben thought up something and responded, "You know I heard one time that they found alligators in the City sewers. Maybe that's what we saw and heard in the cellar."

"Yeah, I heard that too. Manuel said excitedly adding, "It makes sense too. Alligators have long tails and maybe that's what I saw and they open their mouths and hiss too." He used his hands to imitate the jaws opening and closing in pantomime fashion making a hissing sound at the same time.

"How do you know alligators make hissing sounds Manuel?" Frenchie asked mocking him as kids often do.

"I saw it on TV, it was a Discovery Channel special about alligators. And you guys better be careful, alligators would eat you up. They are known to attack people you know."

"Damn, do you really think we have an alligator living down there?" Jippy asked hoping they were wrong.

J.J. tried to be the voice of reason, "Oh, I don't think that at all. Alligators like water and there's no water in the cellar."

"Well, there were those puddles and those wet prints," Frenchie added.

"What about the sewers?" Ruben asked.

And J.J. countered, "The puddles were only small amounts of water and there's no connection to the sewers big enough for an alligator or crocodile or whatever."

"What about a snake?" Frenchie asked, "They look like long tails and hiss too."

"Yeah, maybe it was one of those giant ada-con-conda or whatever snakes from the Amazon?" Johnny Jam explained sitting down and looking more frightened than ever.

"I think you mean a giant anaconda, but no, you're all wrong," J. J. volunteered drawing their immediate attention.

"Oh yeah, why is that?" Ruben asked.

"It's easy to tell. Snakes and alligators don't take bites out of their pray, they eat them whole in one big swallow. Remember? We saw the partial remains of a pigeon and the remains of Angelina. I don't think a snake or an alligator would leave their food like that."

"Holy shit, I think you're right about that." Johnny Jam said jumping up again in excitement.

"Well if it's not an alligator or a giant snake, what is it?" Ruben asked wanting an immediate answer.

J.J. thought about it and answered, "I was thinking of a really big rat. They've been known to get as big as dogs you know."

"A rat? How about a bunch of rats? Maybe that's what it was down there?' Jippy added.

"And don't forget," Ruben added sounding very sad. "Somebody has to go tell Mrs. Black about Angelina. She's gonna be brokenhearted about her stupid cat."

"You should tell her J. J." Johnny Jam suggested. "You know her better than any of us. She lives in your building too."

"All right, I'll go tell her, but we also have to figure out what to do next?"

Frenchie asked, "I vote we don't do anything. What do we know about chasing giant rats, snakes and alligators?"

"I vote we set up a trap down there." Ruben suggested feeling particularly brave again. "All we need is bait. We can get some chicken pieces and a big milk box, then we can turn it over to the cops."

"Trap it?" J. J. asked figuring Ruben had lost his mind. "What are you some sort of expert animal poacher?"

"I say we should try that," Frenchie added getting the group excited again. "We've been down there, we know where to put the trap. What's the big deal?" Ruben told them matter-of-factly like he was the leader of this young gang.

"Hey look, no one's stopping you." J. J. responded. "You guys want to go down there again and set a trap for who knows what, go ahead. I just think we should wait until tomorrow, it's Saturday and you'll have more time. Meanwhile, I'm going to go ahead now and talk with Mrs. Black."

After a bit more discussion, the guys agreed to wait until tomorrow morning to go trapping in the cellar and J. J. went knocking on Mrs. Black's door. She opened the door and was surprised to see J. J. standing there. She invited him in as he started to explain about what they had found in the storage bin. And she cried at the loss of her beloved Angelina. She asked J. J. some questions about her condition and wept sadly when J. J. described what he and his friends had seen. She couldn't believe what he was telling her and decided to telephone the authorities because if that could happen to Angelina, then no one's pet was safe.

After J. J. left, she dug out the old phone book and flipped it open to the City Government pages. Her fingers walked down the section and stopped at a listing, New York City

Department of Pest Control. She picked up her phone and dialed the number and listened carefully to the prompts. She selected, reporting a pest problem. The number rang five times and a squeaky voice answered the phone.

"Hello, Pest Control, this is Henry, may I help you?"

"Yes, thank you Henry. My name is Mrs. Black and I live in the Apartments on Steinway Street near Northern Boulevard over in Astoria."

"Hello Mrs. Black, what can I do for you? Is there a pest problem over there?"

"Why yes, Henry, why else would I be calling? It's about my poor little Angelina."

"Who's Angelina," Henry asked.

"Angelina is my most beloved cat in the whole wide world."

"Maybe you called the wrong department Mrs. Black, perhaps you wanted the ASPCA?" Henry told her that beginning to feel bored with the conversation.

"Oh no, I called the right number. You see, Angelina liked to take late evening walks even though I told her many times not to." At this point Henry was holding the phone off his ear mocking her conversation.

"And two days ago, she took a walk and never came back."

"Let me connect you with the animal pound, maybe they have her?"

"Oh no Henry, they don't have my Angelina."

"How do you know that Mrs. Black?"

"Well, the boys from the apartment building were playing in the cellar as boys might do, and they found my little Angelina. At least they found what was left of her."

That got Henry's attention and he asked quickly, "What do you mean, what was left of her?"

"That's what I've been trying to tell you Henry. A big rat or a snake or something must have half eaten her like that. The boys said they heard a loud hissing sound in the cellar too."

She started to cry as she added, "I think you ought to send some expert over here to find that killer before someone else looses a pet or worse."

"Okay Mrs. Black, don't be upset now. I can schedule a visit to look into the matter; it'll just be some time next week. Now, what was that address?"

Early the next morning, a lone Blue Jay was perched on his usual tree limb starring down at the breadcrumbs that were scattered about the ground on the back alley. The breadcrumbs were scattered there by one of the lonely tenants wanting to spread some joy to the neighborhood birds. The Blue Jay wanted to fly right down there and gobble up as many pieces as he could fit into his stomach. Food was rare and whenever he spotted some, the urge to replace the hunger with satisfaction was uncontrollable. Except, something inside that bird kept nagging at him to remain on the tree limb and to be patient. His head lifted high on his neck and he looked downward in all the directions he could for any sign of danger. He spotted a few small sparrows fly down pecking away at the breadcrumbs and he knew if he waited too much longer, there would be nothing left for him. Only, there was something in the air, a strange scent and an uneasy feeling. He was wondering about the rather large, strange looking rock that was along side of the fence. Had it moved? Was it getting closer to the breadcrumbs or was the hunger within making his imagination get the better of him? He knew rocks didn't move on their own and yet, this one seemed like it did. He watched keenly as one of the sparrows pecking at the breadcrumbs moved close to the rock. Without warning the rock grabbed for the little bird trapping it. There was a commotion as the remaining sparrows flew away screeching. The Blue Jay stood still not fully believing what it had witnessed, and yet very glad to have trusted it's own instincts. For the rock started to move, carrying away the little sparrow that within a moment of being taken, had stopped struggling.

Right after breakfast the wall-phone in J. J.'s kitchen started to ring; it was Ruben. He wanted to ask J. J. to join them when they went exploring the cellar again. The guys had wanted J. J. to be a part of it and Ruben had been elected the one to make the phone call. At first J. J. argued the point of safety and tied his best to convince Ruben to skip out on this one. Ruben explained their plan to set the trap. They would tilt the milk crate back and place some chicken pieces in the middle holding the box open with a small stick. A piece of rope would be tied from the chicken to the stick, so if the chicken was moved the stick would be yanked away and the box would slam shut. J. J. was intrigued and put up less of a fight and then he started to make suggestions too.

"A camera," J. J. explained. "Make sure someone brings a camera to take a picture." And we'll have to bring a few weapons, maybe even carve a couple of long wood sticks into spears, in case."

Ruben answered back, "Of course, J. J." And "that's a great idea." And then it was agreed; J. J. and the gang would meet up at ten o'clock in the courtyard near the cellar.

Johnny Jam was the last one to arrive taking gasps of air as he hurried over. He was holding the camera tightly with the strap wrapped around his wrist. He knew his father would kill him if anything happened to that camera. Frenchie was checking the balance of the milk crate on its edge while Jippy was trying his best to tie the string onto the chicken.

"Hey man, this chicken is slippery, anyone got any ideas on how to make it stop sliding?" Jippy pleaded as the chicken slipped from his grasp.

"Here," J. J. told him. "I'll hold the chicken steady while you wrap the string around and tie it off. Yeah, that's it."

"Let's tie this to the top of the box," Johnny Jam told them holding out a small pair of bells. "When the box closes, the bells will signal our trap worked."

"Great idea Jam," J. J. told him. "A signal for the trap, just what we need."

"How are these?" Ruben asked as he and Manuel put the last sharp point on the remaining stick.

"Wow, they look like real spears." Frenchie told them as he picked one up and used it to make several make-believe jabs at the air.

"I guess we're ready," Johnny Jam announced to the group. Let's check our flashlights and get going."

The gang picked up their items and in single file entered the dark cellar seeing the day-light fade behind them. There was an eerie hush amongst them, more from nervousness than reason. They reached the boiler room entrance and shinned their lights inside one at a time as they passed by. Then, they reached the first ceiling light and Johnny Jam clicked it on. There was a collective sigh of relief as the bulb glowed providing some light in the cellars dim hallway. They took more steps and as they did, their hearing became keener. And then they reached the second ceiling light except this time, Johnny Jam took out a light bulb from his pocket.

"Here, J. J. you're the lightest, climb onto my back and while the guys hold you steady, change that light bulb will you?" With that, Johnny Jam got down on all fours under the light.

"Okay, here goes." J. J. said as he climbed up on Johnny Jam's back. He unscrewed the bulb and started to insert the other when from deeper inside the cellar, there was a loud hissing sound.

"Oh, man, hurry up," Johnny Jam pleaded.

"Okay, it's in." J. J. responded climbing off his back.

Johnny Jam regained his footing, reached up and pulled the light chain. As the light filled in the darkness, they all looked around to check if anything was in the hallway. It was empty.

"That was the same sound we heard yesterday," Manuel told them."

"I think you're right," Jippy confirmed.

J. J. asked the question everyone was thinking, "So, what do we do now? Do we go on?"

Ruben looked in the eyes of each friend as he said, "I say let's keep going, I mean we made it this far."

"Yeah, I'm with Ruben," Jippy exclaimed. We've got everything we need with us and I don't want word gettin out that the Steinway Street Gang's scared of noises or anything like that."

"Hey, I hear you," Frenchie added. If we get this thing, we'll be the talk of the town. It'll put the Steinway Street Gang on the map for sure."

So, Johnny Jam looked right at J. J. and asked, "So, that's it then, we go on."

J. J. didn't argue nor did anyone else and off they went. The ragtag Steinway Street Gang on its way to the adventure, or maybe even the scare of a lifetime. Before they knew it, the bright light started to dim in the hallway and they had to rely once again on their flashlights. Jippy was banging his light with his left hand trying to keep the lamp from flickering.

"Damn," he said as he wacked the flashlight again. "Why doesn't this stupid light stay on?"

"Here, let me see that," Ruben told him as he took the flashlight from Jippy. He unscrewed the end to the battery compartment and then, tightened it up once again. As he did that, the light glowed bright once again. Jippy took it back staring in amazement at the result and then rushing ahead to catch up to the others.

As they approached the entrance to the storage bin area, a quiet hush took place. They reflexively sniffed the air looking more for reassurance that the coast was clear than for something amiss. They went about their business of setting the trap and preparing the bait. It wasn't easy to balance the milk crate on its edge with the stick holding it open at just the right angle. Ruben attempted to tie the string to the stick and every time he did, the box would fall closed and snag his hands. It made the other guys laugh and feel at ease. Then finally, J. J. held the box in place while Ruben secured the string and placed the chicken pieces inside the box. Johnny Jam took the bells out of his pants pocket and fastened the string to the top of the box. He lifted the bell and gently shook it from side to side making sure the bells would work They guys stood up and backed away pleased with their accomplishments.

"All we need now is for the creature to show up," J. J. explained. "Except, who's gonna stay to listen for the bells and make sure it's really trapped?"

"Yeah, and who's staying with the camera? You Jam?" Manuel asked seeing the giant hole in their plan.

"You mean someone's gotta stay here?" Johnny Jam asked hoping he wasn't the one.

J. J. looked at Johnny Jam with surprise and added, "Well, you're not gonna hear the bells from your apartment Jam, and how do you think the picture would be taken?"

"I don't know, I didn't think about that part." Johnny Jam explained almost in tears.

Ruben had an idea and suggested, "You know, you don't have to be right here next to the trap. I'm sure we could hear the bells father away, even back at the cellar entrance."

"J. J. liked that idea and suggested, "Why don't we try it? Manuel and I can stay here while you guys go to the entrance. Then, we'll shake the box to make the bells ring and you can yell back if you hear them. How does that sound?"

"What about the picture?" Johnny Jam asked as if his brain stopped working.

"That's easy," J. J. explained. After we hear the bells we can run back here and take the picture. We'll be safe because it'll be inside the trap."

"Yeah, after we stick the creature a hundred times with our spears, you'll have a great shot for the newspapers." Jippy explained, as if he was a bloodthirsty pirate.

So, they did the test with the bells and as J. J. rang them, he could hear Ruben yelling back that they heard them. Manuel and J. J. made sure everything was set and then they backed out carefully and returned to the entrance. When they got back, there was a discussion going on about who would stay to listen for the bell. They worked out a schedule pairing up and changing the watch every two hours. J. J. and Manuel volunteered the first watch. Johnny Jam pleaded with J. J. to take special care of the camera.

"J. J. my Dad will kill me if that camera ends up broken."

"Don't worry Jam, I'll take good care of it."

J. J. and Manuel grabbed some abandoned wood boxes to sit on and waited for the creature to spring the trap. Of course, it never did.

J. J. told Manuel, "My Mom has a saying that fits this situation, "A watched pot never boils." It's not going to work while we're waiting."

"You know J. J., it wouldn't bother me if it never works," responded Manuel as his eyes darted side to side. "What would we do with a rat the size of a dog anyway?"

"I know, I know," J. J. told him. "And you're probably right. Our watch is almost over anyway, Frenchie and Jam should be here in a few minutes to take over."

J. J. was right, because along they came with Jam holding a lunch size brown bag.

"What's in the bag Jam?" Manuel asked.

"A peanut butter and jelly sandwich and some Oreo Cookies." He shrugged his large shoulders and added, "I get hungry you know."

"Okay guys, we're off duty." J. J. told them as he and Manuel started to walk out of the cellar.

Manuel yelled back, "Be careful with the camera Jam, we wouldn't want your father to kill you." And then he laughed as he heard Jam curse him back.

Sometimes two hours can pass by quickly, and then there are the times when even a minute seems to take forever. That's what it was like for Jam and Frenchie, their two hours on the watch took forever. Except finally, they heard Jippy and Ruben approach and they knew their time guarding the trap was over too.

"Hey you guys," Ruben started to ask. "Anything show up?"

"Naaa, nothing at all," Frenchie answered. "It's been boring."

"I wonder if anything's gonna happen anyway?" Jippy asked. "Maybe there's nothing in that cellar after all."

"Well, somethin' ate little Angelina and that pigeon. Remember?"

Just as they were all taking turns guessing, there was a sound from the storage bin. The bells started ringing and it took the guys a few seconds to realize it was the signal.

"Hey, did you hear that?" Jam asked knowing that the bell sound meant the alarm on the trap went off?

"Let's get going," Ruben suggested. "We don't want to miss this part."

So, Ruben, Jam, Frenchie and Jippy grabbed their flashlights and spears and headed down the cellar with their hearts pounding in their chests. Jam had the strap from his father's camera so tightly wrapped around his wrist it almost cut off his circulation. Each time they reached one of the ceiling lights, Jam reached up and pulled the cord turning them on one by one. For some strange reason, the bells kept ringing and this made them even more nervous. When they reached the entrance to the storage bin room, they stood in the doorway and shinned their flashlights toward the ringing bells. There along the wall, in the dark shadows was the milk-box half over some strange creature as it moved from side to side trying to shake off the milk-box and free itself.

The guys were frozen scared stiff not believing what they were witnessing. The creature was more than three feet long and the milk box only covered a little more than it's head. Ruben threw his spear and missed the creature, the box and everything else. Jippy nervously took a few steps toward the creature and reached out with his spear only managing to push at the box slightly. Johnny Jam was trying to undo the strap on his wrist and free up the camera when somehow the milk-box flew off and the creature headed right for the boys hissing that dreadful sound. Jippy tried to get out of the creature's way and almost loosing his balance, he dropped his flashlight. It hit the ground, spun around several times and rolled to a stop with the beam partially blinding the boys. Frenchie was about to turn and run when he bumped into Jam, knocking into him just as he pressed the shutter button and the flash went off a couple of times Jam turned quickly trying to take some other shots as he spotted the creature moving quickly out of the room. There was such a commotion of nervous boys and beams of light. You never saw four boys clear out of a cellar as fast as these fellows did.

Once outside they gathered at the front stoop catching their breath and gathering their thoughts. Ruben started the ball going with the first question.

"Did you get him?" Ruben asked.

"No, I wasn't very good with my spear." Jippy answered.

"Not you, who cares about the spear, I wanted to know if Jam took the picture?"

"I don't know," Jam answered. "Everything happened so quickly and Frenchie here found a way to sabotage what I was doing by knocking into me."

"I didn't mean to bump into you Jam, but that thing was heading right for us."

"What was it anyway?" Jippy asked.

"I don't know," Johnny Jam answered. I didn't get a good look at it."

"Me either," Ruben added. "But, I know it wasn't a snake or an alligator, I'll tell you that much."

"I think we should go tell J. J. and Manuel and bring the film into the store to have it developed. Maybe the pictures will give us the answers we need."

In the late afternoon, as the six of them walked over to the photo store up the street, J. J. and Manuel walked with their mouths wide open not believing a word of what the guys were telling them.

"How could you let it get away?" J. J. wanted to know showing his frustration.

Ruben answered, "It's not like we let it or anything, it's just that the creature was too big for the trap."

"Yeah, and we're lucky it didn't bite any of us or worse." Frenchie added for emphasis.

"Well I'll tell you this much," Jippy started. That creature is still down there and we better think twice before we attempt another capture."

"Oh, don't worry," Frenchie added, "I won't be going down into that cellar for a long. long time."

The man behind the counter took the film from Jam and told him it'll be ready Monday afternoon. So, the kids decided to get their minds off the creature by going over to the park to play on the swings. They needed a break, as brave as they were this was proving too much, even for them.

Monday morning, while the boys were off to school, Mrs. Black was putting away her breakfast dishes when she heard her doorbell ring. She hurried over to the door and looked through the peephole.

"Who is it?" She asked as her voice cracked.

"Hello, my name is Henry Carver and I'm from Pest Control. Is Mrs. Black home?"

"Oh, hello Henry," Mrs. Black responded rushing to open the locks to her door as if she had known Henry Carver for years. Henry stood there in his overalls with a clipboard in his hands.

"I'm so glad you could find the time to look into this thing that happened to my poor little Angelina."

"Yes, Mrs. Black, the City takes pest control very seriously. Where do you think we could find the Super of the building?"

"Oh yes, the Super, but tell me Henry would you like a little tea?"

Henry took out a weathered old handkerchief and wiped his forehead more out of a nervous tick that needing to wipe off any perspiration, "You know Mrs. Black, I would love to sit here and enjoy some tea with you, but duty calls you know."

"Oh yes, duty. I understand fully Henry. Now about the Super, his name is Jose Ramirez and he lives by himself in an apartment downstairs on the first floor. Come-on, I'll take you there."

So, Mrs. Black escorted Henry Carver to the door of the Superintendent and rang the bell. When he did not answer, she tried again and then a third time. After that, Henry knocked hard on the door and as they looked at each other they realized Jose was not home.

"You know, come to think of it Henry, I haven't seen the Super around the building the last day or so. And I usually do see him working on this or that. I wonder if he's away or something? Do you need the Super to do your job?"

"Well, I suppose not, if you can show me where the cellar is, I can probably find my way around."

Mrs. Black escorted Henry Carver down the stairs to the courtyard, along the same route her little Angelina took. He made a couple of trips to his Pest Control truck to gather his equipment. He selected a helmet light, a canister of rat poison, one of his pump sprayers, and several traps. Mrs. Black explained about the ceiling lights and about the storage bin rooms on the right end of the cellar, just past the boiler room. She also mentioned details regarding the location where the boys had found Angelina's remains. Mrs. Black felt a shiver pass through her when she explained that part. Noticing her discomfort, Henry Carver thanked Mrs. Black for her help and lifting the canvas sack containing his gear over his shoulder, he took several large strides into the cellar. He found it pretty typical of most of the cellars in the city, poorly lit with a damp musky smell. Except, this one had another odor too and it made him wonder what he might find at the end of the cellar.

As he walked, Henry focused the beam of light from his helmet along the edges of the hall looking for droppings or other evidence or rodents. Soon enough, he came across the first ceiling light nearly passing it by with his attention focused on what the light beam was revealing on the ground. Henry stopped, turned back around and reached up to pull the light cord. The lamp glowed extending it's light in both sides of the hall. Henry took a good look in both directions and up ahead he thought he spotted the remains of an animal. He kept his light beam shinning on that spot as he moved quickly ahead. Henry reached the animal remains and squatted low to get a better look. It was the remains of a pigeon half pulled apart by something with very sharp teeth. By the look of the path behind it, Henry guessed it was dragged here and abandoned. What would do such a thing? He wondered. Rats don't behave like that; neither do any of the snakes he had come across in his day. Then he heard the hiss for the first time, it was a way off but as he concentrated on listening to that distinctive eerie sound, Henry realized he never heard any animal make a sound like that. That's when he swallowed hard.

He took a few more steps into the cellar, this time a bit more cautiously. To the left was the opening for the boiler room and Henry gazed around the room as he entered it. The burner was fired and running at the time causing the room to be both noisy from the pump pushing the hot water through the system and hot with the massive burner igniting the oil in it's fire-head. He glanced around the back of the burner and as the two walls formed the corner, he thought he recognized some droppings. That's where he decided to set his first trap. He was squished down low to reach the corner just as he heard the hissing once again. Henry froze in his tracks. This time the sound was much closer; as a matter of fact he thought it was so close he had no time to retreat. So, he just stayed there as small a shape as he could make his body. He let the beam of light from his helmet shine at the doorway, determined not to move a muscle. Henry figured, whatever was coming down that hallway making that hissing sound might very well just pass him by.

And it almost worked except when Henry Carver's eyes saw that creature for the first time entering the light beam, the words, "What the fuck?" left his lips and drew the attention of the creature. At that moment it turned to enter the boiler room, Henry Carver felt real panic take over for the very first time in his life. He tried to move further behind the boiler for protection, but only ended up trapping himself in a tight squeeze. He couldn't reach his gear bag and couldn't find a way out either. He tried to use his helmet light to locate the creature, but only found empty walls. And then, as quick as that, it was upon him lunging for his leg taking a huge bite making Henry squeal in tremendous pain. The creature would not release his grip and within a couple of minutes, all feeling in Henry's leg was gone. He was no longer able to kick or pull it or move either leg in any way. Soon after, it was the same with his arms and then, as his head sunk low to the ground no part of his body was able to move no matter how much Henry Carver willed it to. And then, he lost consciousness no longer feeling the pain in his leg. The creature tried to drag Henry away, it pulled with its body not letting go of the bite his powerful jaws had on Henry's leg. Then, realizing it was not able to move the large weight before him, it opened his jaws and left the boiler room.

Every hour or so, Mrs. Black looked out her front window seeing Henry Carver's Pest Control truck still parked out on Steinway Street. Then, it was afternoon and with no sign of him, she started to have a dreadful feeling about Henry. She decided to call the police and report him missing. The 911 operator was less than sympathetic no matter how much Mrs. Black argued her point. In the end, the operator agreed to send a patrol car to investigate, but it wouldn't be right away. Mrs. Black added, with some sarcasm, that maybe they should send over some combat troops to take care of whatever was down in that cellar.

After school let out the boys gathered at the front stoop. They were talking about the New York City Pest Control truck parked on the street wondering if it had any connection with the creature in the cellar? Then, when Johnny Jam showed up, they took the short walk to the photo store. They pooled their monies to pay for the developing and immediately tore into the sealed envelop. They were all impatient handing the photographs to each other as their comments showed their disappointment. Most of the images were undeveloped, and those frames that showed something were fuzzy and underexposed with bright spots where the flash went off. There was one picture taken sideways showing the funniest expression on Frenchie's face and boy did they all laugh over that one. And then, there was one photograph that actually showed something and stopped them laughing.

"Wow, look at this one," J. J. said seeing with his own eyes an image showing part of a creature even if it was crooked and somewhat out of focus.

"That thing must be huge if we only have a part of it," Jam added.

"You can't really tell how big it is from the picture, but that's a real strange looking color. It's some kind of a pink and black skin?" Jippy said excitedly.

Ruben asked, "It look more like rows of scales than a skin, doesn't it?"

"Yes, I think there are scales on that thing, nothing like I've ever seen, that's for sure." J. J. said that feeling more worried than ever.

Just then, Mrs. Black came out of the apartment building happy to see them, "Oh boys, am I glad to see you."

"Hello Mrs. Black," they responded almost in unison.

"Boys, I think we have a really bad situation down in the cellar?"

"You're telling us," Manuel said in a troubled tone.

"You see boys, I called the Pest Control Department and this very nice man named Henry Carver came over this morning to investigate what happened to my little Angelina and I haven't seen him since then. That was hours ago and his truck is still here."

"You think he went into the cellar?" Ruben asked hoping the answer would be no.

"Oh yes, he went in there telling me there was nothing he hasn't seen in the cellars of New York City. I watched him go in. I called 911, but they said they can't send the police over in a hurry because a missing Pest Control expert is not an emergency."

"Well, what can we do about it?" Frenchie asked feeling nervous.

"It's up to you boys to go and rescue Mr. Carver, he could be stuck down there somewhere."

Jam stuck out the photo of the creature so she could see it, "But Mrs. Black, we know there's a creature down there see. And we have no weapons or anyway to fight something like this."

"Not so fast Jam," J. J. responded taking the picture from his hand, maybe we do have to go and help that man. If he's stuck or something we can free him up before this creature finds him."

"Yeah, let's do it." Ruben added.

"Count me in." Jippy told the group.
"Me too." Manuel told them.

So, they grouped together and walked down the steps
to the alley leading to the courtyard. As they left, Mrs. Black
felt her heart beat faster knowing how brave those boys were.
There were some last minute rumblings as the Steinway Street
gang tried to figure out a plan, but instead they just walked
right into the cellar talking loudly to make sure that creature
stayed away. To their surprise the ceiling lights were turned on
and glowing brightly as they reached each one. Continuing
along they ran out of things to say, so they just sang a song
at the top of their lungs making as much noise as possible.
Then, when they reached the doorway to the boiler room, they
found the room brighter than usual. There in one corner was
Henry Carver's helmet light still burning strong. It was Jam
that noticed the hunched up figure of a man tucked into the
back of the boiler. As they tried to talk to Henry, they realized
he wasn't speaking.
"Is he dead?" Jam asked almost ready to cry.
"Can't tell, maybe he just passed out." Ruben told him.
"Shit man," Manuel said as he jumped back. "Look at his
leg, there's blood and torn clothing."
J. J. responded, "I bet that thing tried to get him, we better
call for an ambulance. I'll tell you what, how about Manuel
and me will go use the phone and you guys keep making a
racket. I promise we'll be right back, okay?"

No one disagreed, and as the boys kept on their yelling
and noise making, J. J. and Manuel ran to his apartment to
make the call because it was the closest. There was some
commotion as they rushed in yelling, "We need the phone
mom, there's a man down in the cellar." Manuel's mom asked
a question or two and then dialed 911. She reported the
man was unconscious and needed an ambulance. Manuel's

grandfather asked them what was going on and Manuel raced ahead explaining the details about the man in the boiler room and the creature they found down there.

Then, after fifteen minutes or so, in the background, there was the sound of a siren and they all ran out front to see if it was the ambulance. And it was, the driver pulled it up to the curb and as two paramedics emerged carrying their emergency cases and a small collapsible stretcher, Manuel pointed down the steps and J. J. added, "This way, he's down in the cellar." The paramedics followed J. J. and Manuel into the cellar and as they rushed down the hall, they could hear the singing and one of the paramedics sounding annoyed asked.

"This better not be a joke, we're not in the mood for a joke."

"It's no joke," Manuel answered back. "Our friends are making noise to keep the creature away."

"Creature?" The other paramedic asked just as they reached the boiler room opening.

"He's over here," Jam told them happy as heck to see grown-ups for a change.

The boys moved out of the way so the paramedics could reach Henry. They found him unconscious with a very faint pulse. He was unresponsive to sound or touch, but his eyes responded when one shined a light on the ocular nerve. They managed to free Henry from the boiler pipes and placed him on the stretcher. The one paramedic worked on the leg wound cutting away the clothing and cleaning the wound. The other paramedic used his radio to call into central reporting the patient's condition and requesting the police respond. They moved quickly to the courtyard and before they knew it, the boys watched the ambulance doors close and the ambulance pull away. As the red lights of the ambulance faded in one direction, the siren and red lights of a police cruiser appeared from another.

It didn't take long for the boys to explain all that happened since they discovered the creature down in the cellar. At first, the two officers found their story far-fetched and wondered if they had answered to a practical joke. Except, that's when Mrs. Black explained about her poor little Angelina and old man Samuel walked up to tell them about his run in with some creature in the back alley. After a while the information the officers had taken down was being collaborated and with the leg wound on the Pest Control guy, they figured something was down in the cellar after all.

Off to one side, J. J., Manuel and his grandfather were excitedly discussing the photo of the creature. And then Manuel's grandfather told the boys,

"I know this creature. I've seen them before in the foothills of Sonora, Mexico where I used to live."

"What is it Grandpa?" Manuel wanted to know.

"The creature is a very dangerous lizard called a Gila Monster. It is venomous just like certain snakes and believe me, you don't want to be bit by a Gila Monster. The bite releases a powerful painful venom that causes its victim to loose all muscular ability. It was said that once the Gila bit you, it wouldn't let go until you were paralyzed. We always stayed far away from them."

"What's it doing here in Astoria?" asked J. J.

"I'm not sure little one, they are very rare and have been declared an endangered species. It is illegal to collect or sell them, but the black market in Mexico is always interested in making a profit. Who knows?"

Manuel asked his grandfather, "How big are these monsters?"

"Oh, they can grow very large for a lizard. Sometimes up to three or four feet in length. For their size, they can move very fast and have powerful jaws."

"And we were thinking we could capture that thing?" Manuel told J. J. remembering how they tried to actually trap it.

"I know, we sure were lucky. Unfortunately, that Pest Control guy was not as lucky. I sure hope he'll be all right."

Well, as it turned out. Manuel introduced his grandfather to the police and they went over all the details with him about the Gila Monster in the photo. The police must have realized how dangerous this creature was, because they radioed into Central and asked for an animal expert from the Bronx Zoo to come over and give them a hand. There was some disbelief over the radio too, because some jokes and name-calling took place. It was pretty late in the evening by the time everyone and everything was ready to locate the Gila Monster in the cellar. The boys stayed outside this time standing off to one side of the cellar entrance retelling the story of their trapping adventure to some of the adults who gathered in the courtyard to watch. The reputation of the Steinway Street gang was growing by the minute.

About an hour later, the two police officers and the Bronx Zoo expert emerged from the cellar, half carrying and half dragging this large creature with several rope snares securing it. They had located the creature after searching every storage room in the cellar. When they had reached the very last storage area, what they found astonished them. The room was lined with an assortment of cages, some containing exotic lizards, a few odd looking animals and even some snakes. The Gila Monster was hiding in back of one very large cage in what appeared to be a large nest of assorted sticks, rags, and other trash. They shot it with several darts containing tranquilizers. Once they knew it was sleeping harmlessly, they used the snares to secure it. Then, as they searched the storage room area, they found two things they didn't expect. They found the partially decomposed body of a man under one of the bins. And in the nest, to their amazement were six large eggs.

Henry Carver, the City's Pest Control expert who did his best to help Mrs. Black recovered from his injuries. He had been bitten and left paralyzed by the Gila Monster's powerful venom. He described the painful process of feeling the muscles in his limbs go numb and how he could see and hear everything around him, but not being able to move or cry out for help. Toward the end, his breathing slowed as he fell into unconsciousness. He awakened in the hospital having been rescued by the young members of the Steinway Street Gang and the two paramedics who managed to pull him out of the boiler room.

It was many weeks later that the mystery of the animals and the decomposed body was solved. After contacting the Mexican authorities, it turned out that the dead man was Jose Ramirez, the missing Building Superintendent. He was part of an international smuggling ring using the cellar storage room as a holding cell for the animals they smuggled out of Mexico into the Northeast. There were many wealthy clients looking to own these exotic animals as showpieces and they would pay a hefty fee to obtain them. The smuggling ring figured using the low rent building in Astoria would be a great cover. Who would have looked for a Gila Monster or any other exotic animal in Astoria? And yet there was another lingering question that bothered the authorities. They had found a nest and in the nest were six eggs, if they captured the female Gila Monster, where in New York City was the male?

# Also by J. P. Cardone . . .

Established in 1976, the Midwest Book Review publishes several monthly publications for community and academic library systems in California, Wisconsin, and the upper Midwest. To see the review: go to—http://www.midwestbook review.com/mbw/apr_06.htm#shelley

☆☆☆☆☆
"Without Consent"
by J.P. Cardone
Xlibris, Inc.
Available at: www.Xlibris.com
ISBN: 1413401821, $18.69

Dr. Elaine Edwards is beginning her medical career as Director of the Golden Shores Nursing Home. Because of a loving relative, Elaine has a deep understanding of the hardship of "the golden years" and is determined to take Golden Shores to a new level of service. But as she arrives for her first day of work, she is faced with two patient deaths and the murder of a health care worker. Something is amiss, and Dr. Edwards quickly becomes the target of murderous thugs intent on keeping the secrets of Golden Shores from prying eyes. Elaine quickly realizes she is over her head, and enlists the aid of an ex-cop named Henry Monroe whose brother was one of the murder victims:

"Then it hit her. There was one cop who could help. That person was an ex-detective with an interest in this. She forced herself to remember the forms. Seeing the Monroe name, her memory recalled the information on next of kin having a Lower East Side address. Yep, she thought, she would ask Henry Monroe for help."

**WITHOUT CONSENT** is a fast-paced, eminently readable thriller that keeps the reader turning page after page as Elaine journeys from innocent new staff medical director to hunted victim. It seems there is no end to the possible abuses of the pharmaceutical industry, and those in the know have created an entirely new genre of medical mysteries to keep us all on the edge of our seats and wondering about that next prescription we need filled.

J.P. Cardone writes convincingly and well. Elaine is a likable, if somewhat naive, character who is forced to come to terms with the thugs around her. She rises to the occasion admirably and unlocks the key to not only the murders at the nursing home, but uncovers the big picture as well. WITHOUT CONSENT is a timely mystery that hits a sweet spot. J.P. Cardone should be proud of his first effort. He is a clear and effective writer.

Shelley Glodowski
Senior Reviewer